DARK
CHAMPION

FLIRTING WITH MONSTERS

EVA CHASE

BOOK
4

Dark Champion

Book 4 in the Flirting with Monsters series

First Digital Edition, 2020

Copyright © 2020 Eva Chase

Cover design: Yocla Book Cover Design

Ebook ISBN: 978-1-989096-80-2

Paperback ISBN: 978-1-989096-81-9

1

Sorsha

You wouldn't think anything could be worse than the most ancient supernatural beings in existence wanting to murder you before you ended the world. Tough luck—it could.

For starters, you could wake up in a room so dark you couldn't determine a hint of what it held other than dank, stuffy air and a lumpy mattress that was poking your backside, with no idea where you were or how you'd gotten there. Or how many people might be lurking in that darkness preparing to murder you at this very moment. Then you could sit up and discover one of your wrists was chained with a heavy metal cuff to some fixture that refused to budge, making the possibility of lurking murderers even more likely.

And to be clear, by "you," I mean me.

The frame that held the mattress squeaked with my

movement. I tested the cuff with a jerk of my arm. The chain clinked, holding firm—and light washed through the space. A fairly dim light, really, cast by an electric lantern, but the darkness before had been so complete I was left blinking the glare from my eyes.

The room around me appeared to be some kind of underground bunker. Rough rock walls, floor, and ceiling surrounded me. The metal cot had a dappling of rust on the frame and squatted next to a matching metal cabinet that I guessed held some kind of supplies. The whole space couldn't have been more than ten feet both long and wide, and standing in the middle of that space, gripping the lantern, was the most powerful supernatural being I'd had the irritation—and, okay, sometimes enjoyment—of actually meeting.

The wan artificial light turned the angles of Omen's narrow face sharper. His icy blue gaze fixed on me, as piercing as ever. His tawny hair lay flat, slicked back over his head, which meant he had his temper in check for now. I supposed I should be glad his hellhound fangs and claws weren't out.

He didn't look like he was planning on murdering me *quite* yet.

I couldn't take a whole lot of comfort from that fact, though, or even from knowing that up until now this monstrous man had been fighting whole-heartedly on the same side as me. Wherever this room was and however we'd reached it, this dude had dragged me here. The last thing I remembered was him clocking me hard enough to knock me right out.

My temple ached dully where his fist had rammed into it. No doubt I was sporting a pretty spectacular bruise. Thank furtive fiddlesticks I didn't feel any signs of a full-out concussion.

Hey, might as well count my blessings, meager though they were.

Omen hadn't turned me straight over to the Highest, at least. If he had, I'd probably already be dead. As long as I was still alive, I had a slim chance of staying that way.

Why the hell had he brought me to this wretched place?

My mouth, as it so often did, started moving without consulting the rest of me. "What a coincidence, running into you. Come here often?"

Omen's voice came out as little more than a growl. "Sorsha..."

I raised my cuffed wrist, which I could now see was attached to one of the legs of the cot—which was in turn bolted to the stone floor; fat chance of wrenching that up by hand. The metal chain clinked again as I waggled it. "You wanted to dive right in with the kinky stuff, huh? Next time, you could just ask."

We *had* actually hooked up once before, chains not included but with plenty of fire. The hellhound shifter didn't appear to appreciate the reminder. A few tufts of his hair rippled upward. He bared his teeth, which were already looking pointier than they had a moment ago. "Do you *ever* stop joking?"

I leaned back on my hands and gave him a tight smile.

"Nope. It's called a coping mechanism. Look it up, dog-breath."

All right, so insulting one's captor, especially when that captor is a highly dangerous shadowkind, was probably in the *What NOT To Do* column of advice for kidnapping victims. I couldn't claim to be a paragon of wisdom.

But despite my attempt at keeping my spirits up, when Omen took another step toward me, both fear and anger jittered through my nerves. The jolt of adrenaline set off a flare of heat in my chest that tingled all the way up to my skin—and sent fire licking across both the collar of Omen's shirt and my bare forearms.

As Omen slapped at his shirt, I smacked my arms against my sides as quickly as I could to snuff out the flames. They vanished, but they left my skin pink and prickling with a fresher pain.

Omen took one last swipe at the singed fabric around his neck and held the lantern out—to check my arms, I realized. To see how much damage I'd done to myself. He wouldn't have bothered with that if he was sure I'd be kaput within the next few hours anyway, right?

"Look," he said, his tone oddly less growly than before I'd set him on fire, "I'm not happy about this either. But you've just proven exactly why I can't completely ignore the Highest's warnings."

"So you decided to haul me off to some desolate cave?"

"I need time to think and decide what to do without your fan club interfering."

He meant the trio of shadowkind men he'd brought into this realm to help with his mission, who'd ended up more entwined in my life than I'd expected to let anyone get these days, let alone a bunch of monsters. But sweet Snap with his eerie demonic powers, sly Ruse with his incubus passion, and stoic Thorn with the haunted weight of his warrior angel past had made me feel like I was getting the better end of the bargain.

What did they make of all this? We'd barely had time to process Omen's announcement that I was the supposedly fearsome being named Ruby that the Highest had spent decades searching for—and that it'd been their shadowkind lackeys and not vengeful mortal hunters who'd killed my parents and sent my fae guardian on the run with me—before Omen had grabbed me.

My trio had been obsessive about ensuring my safety even when I wasn't doing anything riskier than walking down a street. Left without any idea where their boss had taken me or what might be happening to me there, they'd be frantic.

Unless they decided that if the Highest of the shadowkind were terrified of me, they were better off free of me too.

I wet my lips, my fingers curling into the coarse sheet that covered the mattress. My first urge was to keep snarking at the hellhound shifter, but that hadn't been what had gotten through to him before. The time he'd let down his guard the most—the time he'd let himself indulge in that act of searing intimacy with me after swearing it would never happen—it'd been after I let go of the fight and simply been open and honest with him.

Back then, I'd told him I wasn't scared of him. I'd told him I knew he cared about me. Maybe we knew things now we hadn't back then, but I could summon some of that faith again.

Inhaling slowly, I forced my own temper to settle. "Do you really think I'm some huge threat to all existence?" I asked, holding Omen's gaze. "That I'd destroy all the beings I've been risking my neck trying to save? That I *could* cause mass destruction on the scale the Highest are talking about?"

"I don't know." He considered me. "You warned me before. The fire inside you frightened you. Are *you* sure you couldn't burn the realms down?"

At that question, I couldn't help thinking back to the moments when we'd squabbled and the raging inferno had surged in my chest. Just remembering it called up a waft of that blaze. I didn't like being trapped here—I didn't like being betrayed by someone I'd been starting to care about. Somewhere in the depths of my being, a little prickling voice whispered, *Burn. Burn it all. Burn the fuckers to the ground.*

My lungs constricted. I willed that desire away, but the heady heat lingered, nibbling at the edges of my chest.

Was I totally confident that I could control it? No. Let's be real—just a few minutes ago, I'd scalded myself with that power without meaning to.

Could I say it definitely wasn't as big and bad as the

Highest claimed? I didn't want to think it was. But there'd been moments when I'd been able to picture leveling entire cities. Just how fiercely could those flames fly if I gave them free rein, if I let them build and build—?

The nibbling turned into a scorching gnawing. I dragged in another breath, dampening the inner fire as well as I could.

Omen was still studying me. The taut slant of his mouth suggested he'd been able to read a fair bit of my inner struggle. The fact that I hadn't answered yet was probably answer enough.

"I don't *want* to destroy anything," I said. "Well, other than the Company assholes... and I suppose that former co-conspirator of yours who's apparently supporting them?"

His revelations about my past had been interrupted by a much more current shocker: our plan to demolish the Company of Light, an organization dedicated to ridding all realms of the creatures they considered monsters, had been foiled by a powerful shadowkind Omen had once associated with. He'd believed this sphinx named Tempest was dead, killed centuries ago on the orders of the Highest for the havoc she'd wreaked among mortals.

Why any shadowkind would want to help mortals torment and destroy her own kind was beyond me, and Omen hadn't appeared to have any idea either.

Now, he grimaced at me. "No changing the subject. I'll deal with Tempest when the time comes. The problem you pose is more pressing."

"Why? Can't we just assume I'll get my superpowers under control with a little more practice, like you've always said? I've managed to go twenty-eight years without decimating the entire planet—how urgent can it be?"

"You hadn't really activated your powers until a few weeks ago. In that time, I've watched them grow swiftly. I don't think you'd be able to make much of a case with the Highest based on that argument."

My stomach was starting to sink, but there'd never been a situation where a little spin on an '80s song couldn't brighten at least a little. I raised my eyebrows at him and let a lyric slip out. "I'm starting with the man even nearer. I'm asking, rearrange this day-a-ay."

There came the fangs again. "Do you really think buffoonery is the answer to—"

"Fine, fine. I'm trying to stay in glass-half-full territory. I can be a model of seriousness that'd make even Thorn proud." I put on my best somber expression, definitely channeling the stalwart wingéd. "Why do you care what the Highest want anyway? They hardly bother with this world unless some shadowkind is causing a total catastrophe, right? I'm assuming you didn't *tell* them you've been hanging out with the horrifying human-shadowkind hybrid they've been searching for. Couldn't we get back to crushing the Company, and if my powers start heading in a direr direction, then you can make a decision?"

"It's not that simple," Omen said, and paused, as if he was debating whether he could get away with leaving it at that. I cleared my throat as a prompt to continue, and he glared at me. "The rest isn't your concern."

Oh, yeah? I drew on whatever reserves of calm I still possessed and managed to ask the question in a quiet, earnest tone rather than the acidic one that I'd wanted to toss at him. "Considering what happens here is a matter of life or death for me, I think it's more my concern than it could be anyone else's. If there's something else going on, don't I deserve to know?"

Omen's jaw worked. "It isn't about what you deserve."

"What is it about, then?" When he continued to balk, I peered up at him, wishing I had Ruse's skill for cajoling. "Hell, maybe if you explain it to me, I'll see some loophole you haven't noticed. I'm very good with getting out of tight situations, as you may have observed."

He let out a rough chuckle. "I think this is beyond even your thieving talents, Disaster."

"I've proven you wrong before." I sucked in a breath. "Please. I just want to understand. I thought—I thought we'd gotten to a place where we *did* understand each other pretty well. If you're going to lead me to the slaughter, I'd just like to know why."

Something in my voice must have gotten through to him. Omen turned away with a muttered curse. He paced the width of the room, his hands clenched at his sides, and then turned back to me.

"The Highest didn't just tell me what you are and what they'd like to see happen to you," he said. "They outright ordered me to inform them of where 'Ruby' is as soon as I found that out."

"From what I've seen, you don't generally follow orders just because someone gave them to you," I felt the need to point out.

"Yes, well, this is a special case." He fell silent, and for a moment I thought he might clam up again. But then he spoke, low and terse. "I didn't see the error of my infernal ways soon enough. Before I ended my vicious games with the mortals, the Highest caught wind of them and of my past schemes with Tempest. They would have ended me the way they did her if I hadn't managed to convince them it was worth their while to strike a deal instead."

A chill rippled down my spine. "What kind of deal?"

"I carry out ten tasks of their choosing, and then we're even as long as I keep my nose clean. Until then, they've got a magical choke chain around my neck that they can tug on whenever they please. They made finding Ruby my last task."

"Oh." Even though I was sitting still, my balance wavered on the mattress. "So until you deliver on that..."

"I remain in their grasp," he said grimly.

"And what would happen if they found out you know where I am but didn't turn me over right away?"

"I'd imagine they'd decide I've reneged on our deal and that it's fair play to eviscerate me after all."

I swallowed hard. All he had to do was point the Highest my way, and he'd have his freedom back. I had plenty of experience with the hellhound shifter's pride—I couldn't imagine how much it'd chafed at him having that leash around his neck all this time. By even thinking it over, he was risking his entire continued existence.

It was a miracle he hadn't pointed a blinking neon sign my way the second they'd made their demand.

An unfamiliar emotion rolled over me, suffocatingly heavy. Hopelessness—that was the word for it. I wasn't just backed into a corner but down the bottom of a deep, dark pit without a single avenue out.

"Well," I said, and for once in my life I didn't have any words to follow that with.

"Yes." Omen sounded more resigned than anything. "You're welcome to put your sticky situation skills to that."

I met his eyes again, searching them for some kind of answer there. "Why haven't you thrown me to them already?"

The narrowest of smiles curled his lips. "You've made an impression." He set the lantern down, produced a plastic bag that he tossed onto the mattress beside me, and tipped his head toward the floor beneath the cot. "Something to eat, and there's a bucket if you need to take care of other bodily needs. I'll leave you to it while I contemplate my options."

With that, he vanished into the shadows, leaving me wondering if there were any options at all that didn't end with me flayed and gutted.

2

Snap

The gash on my arm was already closing up, but it still stung beneath the gauze Thorn had wrapped around it. The way I'd gotten that gash stung far more, though. First Omen had lunged at Sorsha, and then he'd attacked the rest of us when we'd started to intervene. During that skirmish, one of his hellhound claws had sliced through the flesh just below my shoulder almost all the way to the bone.

If we hadn't been so shocked by everything we'd just found out and by his sudden hostility, surely between the three of us, we could have stopped him? But I hadn't been prepared to tackle our leader as an enemy. When he'd hit my beloved, my first reaction had been confusion. All those precious seconds I'd lost while I realized I wasn't mistaken, he really *did* intend to carry her away from the rest of us, perhaps to the Highest who wanted her dead...

Our failure clearly weighed heavily on Thorn too. He strode back and forth in the narrow hall of the Everymobile, his expression the grimmest I'd ever seen it, and he wasn't a being who spent much time smiling even on good days.

When Omen had charged off with Sorsha's limp body, we'd chased after him, but in his hellhound form he'd outpaced us in minutes. After he'd vanished into the sparse wilderness where we'd parked outside San Francisco, we'd retreated to regroup, but looking at the gouge marks on the glittery cupboards and the crack now running through the table, I only felt more scattered.

Could Omen really mean to turn Sorsha over to beings who'd kill her? The thought of losing her caused the most stabbing pain of all, so sharp I could barely breathe.

It was hard to imagine him taking that step. While, yes, he'd been annoyed with her now and then, they'd seemed to be getting along well enough in the past couple of weeks. She'd done so much for us. How could he think she'd ever turn around and harm us, let alone all the other beings in both realms?

The little dragon our mortal had looked after appeared to be equally bewildered. Pickle darted here and there through the broken shards of plates and wine glasses that littered the floor, letting out harsh little squeaks at no one in particular. I tried holding out my hand and clucking my tongue at him the way I'd seen

Sorsha do, but he just snorted louder and snapped at the table leg as if it were responsible for her disappearance.

Thorn opened and closed his massive fists at his sides, still pacing. His low voice boomed through the room. "If he's already harmed her—he'll face a reckoning, I can say that much."

The other wingéd among us, an equally massive shadowkind man named Flint who'd joined our party only a few days ago, glanced up where he was sitting across from me at the table. "If he saw something in her that made him feel she was that much of a threat—"

The warrior rounded on him. "You don't know anything about her! *He* would still be in the Company's clutches, enduring their torture, if she hadn't helped us free him. She is the kindest and most compassionate being I've ever had the honor of standing beside. I've never seen her hurt any who didn't deserve as much ten times over."

Flint set his jaw as if it were made of the same stone as his name, apparently deciding it was better not to speak at all. Omen had wanted to keep the full secret of Sorsha's identity secret from the newer shadowkind in our group, so we hadn't shared the entire story with them, but it'd been impossible for them *not* to notice him tearing off with her. I supposed we'd have to tell them some version of the truth, just not all of it.

Ruse swiped his hands over his face, which turned pallid in the time since Omen's betrayal, and looked up at us from where he was leaning against the wall near the driver's seat. "All that is true, and Omen could still be doing whatever the hell he wants with her. How can we stop him? It could already be done."

"He might not have completed that betrayal yet. He knows how valuable she is to his cause, and he wouldn't want to jeopardize that. I *know* he's dedicated to ending the Company's plans." Thorn swung around again, a dark crimson gleam flashing in his near-black eyes. "I might not have anticipated this, but I have known him a long time. If he's still in the mortal realm, I may be able to locate him."

My heart leapt, and I sprang to my feet with that sensation. "What are we waiting for, then? Let's find Sorsha."

The incubus straightened up too, but Thorn shook his head at both of us. "I'll move much faster on my own with no need for explanations, and I'm the only one of us who has any chance of matching him if it comes to a fight. I'll return as soon as I'm able."

"Thorn!" Ruse protested, but the warrior didn't respond. He vanished into the shadows and had raced off beyond the range of my awareness before I'd so much as blinked.

"Big bad angel taking off without the rest of us," Antic muttered in a sing-song voice, crunching broken shards under her feet in time with the rhythm. The imp took a couple of jabs at the kitchen counter, which was about the same height as her head. "I'd give that hellhound what-for."

"Yes, and a few seconds after that, you'd be cinders," Ruse said dryly, but I could tell his heart wasn't in the attempt at humor. He grimaced at the floor. "I should have realized as soon as he started talking about—all of it. I should have... I don't know. Fuck."

He cast about as if looking for something to hold onto, and a glimmer of an idea quivered through my head.

"Did he touch anything?" I asked, glancing around.

Ruse paused and stared at me. "What? Who?"

"Omen. When he was in here."

"I don't see what that matters after—"

I didn't normally interrupt my companions. Normally I listened carefully to whatever they were saying, since all of them had much more experience than I did in either realm and especially this mortal one. But the sting of Omen's violent departure and my wrenching worries for Sorsha sent a surge of determination rushing through me.

I had a purpose here. There was a reason Omen had brought me onto this mission—there were things I could *do*.

"Of course it matters," I cut in with a voice louder and more forceful than felt totally comfortable. A twinge ran through my chest at the stricken expression that crossed the incubus's face, but maybe it was time he listened to *me* for once. Sorsha was mine, and I was hers, and if there was a way to save her, I would find it.

I squared my shoulders and went on. "If Omen touched anything with his bare hands—or any other bare skin—he might have left an impression that could tell me where he was thinking of going. Do you remember whether he touched any spot on the walls or the table or wherever while he was talking to us?"

After he'd grabbed Sorsha, he'd had his hands full with her. The wreckage on the floor had mostly been caused by us colliding with objects around the room as he'd shoved us away. He hadn't transformed into his hellhound shape until he'd been loping across the ground outside, my beloved slung across his back—

An even stronger jolt of hope rushed through me. I motioned vaguely to the others, including the night elf who'd remained huddled in the shadows since Omen's violent frenzy. "Take a moment to think about it. I'll have a better chance outside anyway."

Out in the humid air that had collected under the thick clouds overhead, I hesitated for a moment. The ground was dry and covered with patches of yellowed grass and weeds—and a jumble of faint footprints, the soles of human shoes. Had Omen's hellhound paws left a mark anywhere? He'd run off in this direction...

I hurried between the trees. He'd definitely shifted by the time he'd reached this spot.

There—scratches in the dirt where his claws had scraped the ground. I bent down and flicked my tongue through the air over them, tasting the impressions he'd left behind.

Images even more fragmented than usual flashed through my awareness. The feel of Sorsha's slack weight on his back, the hellish heat coursing over his skin, the effort of his swift strides—and a tangle of resolve and regret. He hadn't been happy about lashing out at us.

That didn't reassure me much. He'd done it anyway, so who knew what other awful things he might do next?

I couldn't pick up any sense that he'd known where he was going. He'd simply wanted to be as far as he could get from us, far from the possibility that we might stop him. What if he hadn't decided yet?

I shoved that thought away and prowled onward, stopping here and there to test other patches of disrupted earth that appeared to be caused by animal rather than human-like feet. The impressions I gleaned tasted mostly the same as that first one. No clear sense of direction other than to keep moving as quickly as he could. He hadn't been heading for a rift yet, as far as I could tell. That was one small relief.

When I pushed myself upright after the tenth or so testing, uncertain whether there was any point in continuing as the trail got vaguer, Ruse stepped through the trees to join me. His hopeful look faded at the sight of me. "Nothing?"

My frustration at that fact prickled through me. "Nothing that would tell us where he's gone. But... I don't think he was heading straight to the Highest. He felt the weight of some responsibility toward them, but he was resisting it."

"I suppose if she's still in this realm and alive, Thorn does have the best shot of tracking the two of them down."

A fierceness that surprised even myself erupted out of me. "He should have given us the chance to help. If he'd waited just a few minutes, I might have been able to tell him something that would narrow down his search." I spun on my heel, unable to stop myself from glaring at the trees. "*Omen* should have given us a chance. We know her better than he does—he should have listened to what we had to say, not followed what the Highest told him. They've never met her at all!"

Ruse raised his eyebrows at my outburst, but when he clapped his hand to my shoulder, the gesture was gentle. "I agree with you, devourer. Unfortunately, I think Omen was also aware that the three of us have become awfully invested in our mortal's happiness. If we'd had more of a chance to rally against him, he might not have gotten past —well, Thorn, anyway."

"Then he should have realized we have good reason for that devotion."

The prickling frustration was expanding, rising through my ribs and up to the base of my throat. Sorsha had saved me not once but twice. She'd woken up a whole world inside me I'd had no idea even existed. I *had* to protect her.

I marched onward, searching for more signs of Omen's passing, but I was reaching the area where he'd outpaced us. I wasn't sure exactly which direction he might have veered in from here. We were getting close to the road, where a whiff of a cloying chemical smell lingered from the occasional cars passing this way.

I pushed past another tree—and found myself faced with a portly mortal man who was strolling along the side of that road. He paused, blinking at me, and the prickling sensation dug into me like the rows of splintery teeth that could spring up within my mouth.

Everything I cared about had gone wrong, and *someone* needed to pay. I could rip his soul to shreds and devour it down—

My body was moving before I'd even finished that thought, propelled by the all-encompassing hunger of my nature. The man's eyes widened, his round cheeks paling.

"Snap!" Ruse hissed, but I was already yanking myself backward. I clenched my jaw before it could extend any farther and propelled myself away from the mortal and the tempting thrum of his life's energy.

I was better than that. I was a monster, and I would bring out my fangs if it helped us—but not just to distract from my frustrations. Savaging that man wouldn't bring Sorsha back.

If only I had a better idea what would.

When the RV came into sight, I stopped with a ragged exhalation. Ruse halted beside me.

"I don't know what to do," I said to him. The urge to rend and tear was still clanging through me. Just for an instant, a small part of me was glad Sorsha wasn't here to see how my control had frayed.

Ruse gave me a crooked smile that looked rather painful. "You've already managed more than I've been able to contribute. Fat lot of good my charm can do for us or Sorsha right now." He sighed. "I think I found a few places in the Everymobile that Omen touched—or rather, slashed or smacked. Do you want to come give them a taste?"

If our leader hadn't been sure of his destination while he'd dashed away out here, I didn't imagine he'd been clearer on it before he'd even made it out of the vehicle. But confirming that would do us more good than murdering random passers-by.

I raised my chin. "All right. And then we find something else to try. We keep trying, no matter how ridiculous it seems, until Sorsha's back with us."

I wouldn't let myself consider yet what I'd do if she was lost to us forever.

3

Sorsha

I f Omen had wanted to keep the location of his hidden bunker a secret from me, he hadn't done a very good job of it. In with the pre-wrapped chicken sandwich and bottle of orange juice in the bag he'd tossed me, I found a rumpled napkin with the logo for the Grand Canyon Visitor Center.

I'd always wanted to take a gander at the Grand Canyon. Of course, I'd have preferred to be looking at it from the rim rather than this incredibly inside view of the rock it was made of. Omen really didn't have the tour-guide instinct.

I had to assume he'd picked this cave as a stash spot because it was nowhere near anyplace mortals generally went in the canyon. I wouldn't be surprised if the door at the other end of the room led out to a nearly sheer several-hundred-foot drop, and the bastard hadn't brought along my grappling hook. No doubt I was about as far from human civilization as you could get in the entire country.

Maybe he'd *wanted* me to see that napkin to dissuade me from attempting to slip my bonds.

After I'd wolfed down the sandwich and chugged the juice—because my chances of survival were hardly going to get better if I starved myself—I examined the cuff around my wrist and the chain that attached me to the cot's frame. I'd melted metal with my fiery powers before. The first time just a pop can, sure, but I'd also wrenched through the bars of cages in one of the Company's facilities.

Even those bars had been significantly thinner than the links on this chain, though. I'd have given it a go anyway, but a twist of uncertainty in my gut held me back.

Fraught emotions always seemed to set my flames veering in unpredictable and sometimes undesirable ways, and I wasn't feeling all that fine and fancy-free at the moment. I'd say there was a not insignificant chance that if I tried to exude enough fire to reduce those rings of steel into a puddle, I'd become a pile of ashes in the process. I didn't have anyone around to toss a bucket of water at me if I turned the mattress or, y'know, *myself* into an inferno.

No, as long as I suspected I wouldn't be able to escape the prison even if I got loose from the chains, I wasn't going to risk it. I might laugh in the face of danger, but only when I was reasonably certain I could dance around it at the same time.

It didn't take long before I started wishing I'd been a little less hasty with my meal. At least eating had been something to do. Being essentially a prison cell, there wasn't a whole lot to occupy myself with other than counting the ripples in the beige rock walls or mulling over exactly how painfully the Highest would have me killed as revenge for evading their grasp for so long.

After a while, I flopped down on the bed and grimaced at the ceiling. At this rate, my actual cause of death would either be boredom or stomach ulcer.

To try to pass the time somewhat constructively, I considered what new arguments I might make to persuade Omen that I wasn't anywhere near a big enough threat for him to worry his houndish head about. I mean, I didn't *want* to blow up both the realms—or even any substantial portion of either of them. I might have fried a few things I hadn't meant to here and there, but I'd always been able to rein those over-zealous flames in before I did serious damage. If I got really concerned about my self-control, I could just not use my powers in the first place, right?

But even as I thought all that, the heat in my chest continued churning so furiously that *I* wasn't totally convinced. Fuck a flipping flounder. Had my parents gone into this hybrid baby-making scheme with any idea just how much hassle they were inflicting on me as a theoretically impossible being?

They'd loved me enough to pull out all the stops to bring me into this world, but I wasn't sure they'd thought the whole plan through all that well. No offense to Mom and Dad, may they rest in peace.

It might have been one very long hour or a dozen short ones when the shadows around the door wavered. Omen formed in pretty much the same spot I'd last seen him, standing next to the lantern. He had another plastic bag that appeared to contain food. Apparently it'd been long enough for me to get hungry again without realizing it, because my stomach gurgled at the sight.

Well, I had to assume he wouldn't be feeding me just to lead me to the slaughter. I held out my free hand, and he threw the bag to me.

He'd ventured farther abroad this time to bring me something more dinner-like: a fast-food hamburger and a carton of fries, as well as a bottle of water. The fries had gotten a little droopy during his journey through the shadows, but I wasn't going to pick a fight about that or the fact that he hadn't brought any ketchup to go with them, as grave an offense as that was.

I popped a fry into my mouth, the salty greasy flavor buoying my spirits a little, and waggled another in his direction. "How did all that brainstorming go? Have you figured out the meaning of life while you're at it? Inside tip: I hear the number forty-two is involved somehow."

The hellhound shifter glowered at me. "You still don't seem to be taking this situation anywhere near as seriously as it warrants."

"Would you rather I was slumped on the bed groaning like I need my appendix out?"

"No. Just—" He cut himself off with a huff, maybe not sure what exactly he would have liked to see.

My life was still in his hands. And until today's events, I had actually been starting to like and even trust this guy. How could I remind him of the woman *he'd* been starting to care about before this whole Ruby problem had exploded in our faces? He needed to see me as a real person and not just a walking disaster.

I lowered the fry and tamped down on my urge to shoot my mouth off, speaking more honestly instead. "I understand I'm in an incredibly serious situation. If I let myself dwell on it too much, I'll end up rocking in the corner like I belong in a mental institution, and I don't think that's going to help either of us. But I definitely don't think it's a laughing matter either." I spread my arms with a clink of the chain. "You've got me at your disposal. What can I tell you to help you make up your mind? Ask away."

Omen gave me a narrow look, as if he suspected me of setting him up for some kind of prank, but he leaned himself against the wall opposite me as if he was settling in for a longer conversation. "Well, since you're offering... Why don't you tell me some more about what it was like growing up with that fae woman who helped your parents? Now that you know the whole story, is there anything that stands out? She must have known the Highest and their minions were after you."

I sucked my lower lip under my teeth, thinking back.

"I don't know what other bits of memory Luna might have glamoured over—but maybe you'll notice if there's a gap I don't realize while I'm talking." He'd been able to break one glamour in my memories already.

"Start talking then."

Lord knew when I'd ever get another invitation like that from him. I drew my legs up on the cot. "Honestly, it was pretty predictable considering I was an essentially mortal kid being raised by a shadowkind. Luna would find us an apartment in one city or another—I'm not totally sure how she even paid for them, but maybe her glamours did the job there too—I'd go to school and all the usual human things, and then every year or so she'd get nervous that the people who'd killed my parents might find us and we'd move to a pretty similar apartment in a different city."

"She never said anything to indicate she was watching to see if you'd show any powers, or that she was worried you might hurt someone?" Omen asked.

I shook my head. "No. I would definitely remember that. Maybe she didn't realize that's what the Highest expected to happen. She was pretty carefree about most things other than avoiding getting murdered."

Even though it'd been twelve years since the Company's hunters had killed her, a pang shot through me at the loss. I could picture so clearly how she used to sashay around the apartment to whatever '80s band she was currently particularly obsessed with, her sparkly hair swishing in its scrunchie-d ponytail, her wings showing in glittery glimpses here and there when she completely let loose. The way she'd always find the perfect joke to make in her melodic voice to reassure me if some asshole kid at school had picked on me. The joy she took in dressing me up in frills and sequins, and her playful grousing when I'd developed enough of my own taste to start chucking those clothes in the back of the closet in favor of darker hues and simpler designs.

I couldn't think of any moment when she'd seriously criticized me, let alone made me feel there might be something terribly wrong with me. Maybe she hadn't been built to fill a parental role, and maybe a fae couldn't produce the same sort of maternal love a human could, but she'd cherished me beyond all reason. She was the only person in my life that I could really remember who'd never been anything but fully devoted to me.

"The time when I guess my powers had the most reason to come out—but didn't—was when I was a kid and this shadowkind jerk thought it'd be fun to work his mind control voodoo on me to use me like a puppet." I'd told Ruse about that incident before, but talking about it out loud made my skin itch. I resisted the urge to hug myself. "Luna told him off and brought me home. She didn't ask anything about how I was feeling. I mean, it must have been pretty obvious how shaken up I was with the way I was crying, but she didn't seem concerned that I might lash out. She just grabbed my favorite ice cream for us to eat right out of the carton and put on my favorite movie, even though it bugged her that I liked something modern rather than her 'classics,' and sat there with her arm around me petting my hair."

In spite of the awfulness of my present, a smile crossed my lips at the memory. Auntie Luna might have learned her cues about human behavior from all that '80s media she'd consumed, but she'd been able to put them to practice pretty damn well.

Omen was watching me intently. "She was important to you."

"Of course she was," I said. "She was my whole world. I didn't exactly have much time to make friends when we were constantly moving... After a while, it seemed like there was so little point in getting to know people better that I stopped putting in an effort. If I wasn't doing the essential stuff, I was hanging out with her. She knew how to make even mundane things like buying groceries or dealing with a scraped knee fun. It was a little lonely sometimes, but she did her best by me. I've managed to pass for reasonably normal, as humans go."

A dry chuckle fell from Omen's mouth. "Only to someone who doesn't know shadowkind enough to pick up on the influence." He paused. "I didn't get any sense of glamoured bits from what you'd said, but I'm not sure I'd pick up on them from general thoughts. And I don't think we have time for you to recite your entire history if there aren't any particular incidents that seem connected to your powers."

"She probably figured it wasn't any big deal, and if I started showing some, she'd deal with it then. She wasn't much of a planner either." I rubbed my mouth, the pang of mourning combining with all the tensions I'd already been feeling in an indigestion stew. Was any of this making Omen more kindly disposed toward me? Maybe I'd be better off reminding him of *his* past—and the responsibilities that came with it—instead.

"It sounds like this Tempest gal is the total opposite of that," I went on, picking at my fries. "How long ago was it you thought the Highest had killed her—several centuries, or something like that? All that time, she's been playing some kind of long game, keeping it all under wraps... Did she ever turn against other shadowkind back when you two hung out together?"

The downward twitch of Omen's lips told me he didn't like the change of subject. "Tempest's main goal was sowing chaos. She mainly did it among the mortals, but she wasn't above ensnaring weaker shadowkind to add to her amusement. I wouldn't have expected a scheme on this scale, but..."

"But?"

He was silent for a moment. "I once watched her spend the better part of a week plucking the claws off little beasts like your dragon so that she could then jab them one by one into a mortal who'd offended her until he resembled a pin cushion. A bloody one. If she's found some way to turn the Company's operations around on mortals in an epic fashion, it's not difficult to imagine her going to even more epic lengths at the rest of our expense to get there."

Ah. So we were dealing with a total psychopath. Not that I'd had much doubt about that after hearing her taunt Omen over the phone, but that little story solidified the impression.

"And you don't think stopping that kind of epic crazy is a little more important than the slim chance that I'm somehow going to explode like a hundred nuclear bombs in the next few days?" I couldn't help saying.

"I think I don't know how slim that chance actually is."

I couldn't argue that point very easily. Time to shift the focus back to him. "Why did you go around with a shadowkind like that anyway? Were *you* that bad back then?" He'd told me that he'd played pranks on mortals—convincing them he was the devil himself had been a favorite—but I hadn't imagined him that sadistic, especially to other creatures of the shadows.

Something in Omen's expression shuttered. "I can't say I was at all considerate of the mortals in my vicinity, but I never harmed any of my own kind purposefully."

"You just stood by while someone else did it."

"If you think I never had arguments with Tempest, or that there was any chance she'd change simply because I said—" He shook his head. "It doesn't matter. I looked the other way too often when it was convenient to my purposes, and I've learned to do better than that. I won't make those same mistakes again. Which is exactly why I'm being much more careful in my associations now."

The pointed look he gave me made me bristle despite my best intentions. "I'm nothing like *her*."

"No, I don't think you are. The problem is, if the Highest are right, you might be even worse."

He straightened up, and then he was vanishing into the shadows without another word. I stared at the spot where he'd stood, but he didn't return.

Had all that talk gotten me anywhere with him, or had I only screwed myself over even more?

4

Sorsha

When I got tired enough that I figured I should try to get some rest, I turned off the electric lantern. I jolted awake sometime later to a room that was as pitch black as my first experience of it. But before Omen even spoke, I could tell from some shift in the air and the prickle of his scorching aura over my skin that I wasn't alone. Probably his arrival was what had jarred my nerves.

"You managed to sleep," he said. The lantern flared on to illuminate his well-built form.

I shoved back the sheet and sat up, rubbing the bleariness from my eyes. I hadn't slept for half as long as it felt as if my body had needed. "It *is* a physical necessity for some of us."

Not that I really wanted him thinking about my mortal side. It might be my shadowkind powers that were causing the biggest issue, but I'd bet he'd be much more inclined to believe that I could control those if it weren't for the weaknesses that came with the human part of me. Although I'd still argue that I didn't have half as many weaknesses as he liked to claim.

His lips had curled with a familiar hint of disdain, but his pale eyes looked only solemn. My pulse hitched. Had he made up his mind about my fate? If so, I didn't think I was going to like the outcome.

The words spilled out of their own accord. "We've come a long way from when we first met, haven't we? I know you're more than an ice-cold bastard. You know I can handle anything you throw at me. We pulled off some pretty amazing missions when we put our heads together."

He raised his hand to stop me before I could keep babbling. His expression hadn't turned any less somber. I closed my eyes, groping for any shred of inner calm I could find. Whatever happened, I was *not* going to die flailing in panic. I had a smidge more dignity than that.

One last mangled '80s song to do Luna proud and offer a final plea? "Hate from the start," I sang at a murmur. "Tell me we can take it all apart..."

"Sorsha." His voice sounded strained. "I don't like that I've had to do any of this."

I could believe that. But he was going to do it anyway. Because why wouldn't he? How could I possibly be worth more to him than finally getting his freedom back after eons under the thumb of these pompous ancients? I was sick of them already, and I hadn't even met them yet.

Delay. Delay, and there was a chance, however miniscule, that I'd figure out another option.

"Can we talk a little more? I can go through some of my strongest memories of Luna in case there's anything she did glamour over, and—"

Omen jerked around abruptly, as if he'd heard a noise beyond the door that I hadn't. His posture tensed. He moved like he was about to spring into the shadows around that door—but at the same moment, an even larger and more muscular figure materialized beside him.

Thorn's brawny bulk made the room feel twice as small, but I'd never been more relieved to see anyone in my life. I'd have leapt to him with a kiss designed to get across every particle of that gratitude if it hadn't been for the damned chain fixing me to the cot.

The wingéd warrior took in my pose and the cuff around my wrist, his expression darkening with horror. He swiveled to face Omen. "What is the matter with you? You've chained her up like an animal!"

"The split-second before you noticed that, weren't you simply pleased I've left her alive?" Omen retorted, his tone now dry. "You know how difficult it is to keep this one anyplace she doesn't want to be."

"You shouldn't have dragged her off to begin with. She isn't going to destroy the realms, and we're not handing her over to the Highest."

The warrior stepped toward me, but Omen sprang in front of him, holding up his hands. "Hold on. It's not as simple as that."

"Of course it is," Thorn bellowed, the reverb of his

shadowkind voice creeping into his words. I caught a dark flicker around his shoulders as if his wings had threatened to burst into sight. "Sorsha is the most compassionate being I've ever known—she'd never harm anyone who hadn't brought it on themselves. She's shown multitudes more dedication to us and our cause than any of our shadowkind brethren."

The hellhound shifter arched his eyebrows. "You have to admit you might be a *tad* biased when it comes to assessing her worthiness. You're not exactly an impartial party after how closely you've been getting to know her."

"Whatever desire I've felt hasn't clouded my mind. She's proven herself time and time again. Get out of my way, hound."

He loomed on Omen threateningly, a good half a foot taller and nearly twice as broad. The hard crystalline ridges that covered his knuckles glinted in the thin light.

My pulse skipped a beat. I'd never heard the wingéd speak to his boss like that before—hell, I'd never heard him talk to Omen with anything less than total respect and deference. The fact that he'd gotten this riled up on my behalf sent a flutter of affection through me, but also a jab of fear.

I'd had multiple occasions to witness Thorn's preferred strategy when people he cared about were threatened. It tended to involve heads wrenched from necks and guts spilling on floors. I would've thought he cared enough about Omen as a colleague that it would at least mostly balance out his determination to help me, but maybe I'd underestimated his devotion. It wouldn't have been the first time.

Omen's natural shadowkind coloring, a dark gray tint lined with glowing magma-line rivulets, broke out over his skin. His hellhound claws formed at the tips of his still —for now—humanoid fingers. He let out a snarl that told me his fangs had come forth too.

"Back down, old friend," he snapped. "This is my responsibility, my call, and I will *not* let you rush or override my decision."

It kind of sounded like he might not have come to a definite decision yet after all. Maybe he would have taken me up on the suggestion to talk more. Maybe he'd only stopped by to ask how I wanted my morning coffee, and I'd started shooting my mouth off before he had the chance.

A hasty remark or two getting me into trouble? It wouldn't be the first time for that either.

Thorn's loyalty was too ingrained for him to push this stand-off straight to a battle without at least trying to reason with the other shadowkind. "What does it matter what the Highest say? They know nothing of who Sorsha is, and we owe them nothing. Only the four of us are aware of what we discovered about her, and Snap and Ruse would never think of sharing that information. If they did, they'd be dealing with a wingéd's rage." The muscles in his arms flexed to impressive effect.

"You don't know what you're talking about," Omen growled, and it struck me how true that was. Thorn clearly had no idea how much Omen *did* owe the Highest or the dire consequences he'd face if he failed to carry out their orders. No wonder the warrior was so furious. He assumed the hellhound shifter had carted me off on the basis of a little hearsay.

Omen didn't appear to be inclined to fill the warrior in on his situation, though. "I'll tell you again," he added through gritted teeth. "Stand *down.*"

I felt the inexplicable need to speak up on my captor's behalf. "Thorn, Omen has to—"

The hellhound shifter wheeled on me, a blaze lighting in his eyes. "Shut up, or I'll sock the mouth right off of you."

"Don't you lay another hand on her," Thorn roared, and shoved Omen away from me. He reached to smash the chain, but Omen spun around and lunged at the warrior.

Hellhound claws seared slashes through Thorn's shoulder. The smoke that shadowkind contained instead of blood billowed up from the wound.

Thorn threw a punch I suspected would have been solid enough to send Omen crashing straight through the door, but the shifter dodged the worst of it, taking only a gash as the warrior's knuckles grazed the side of his arm. He transformed into the massive beast of his hellhound form before my eyes. With a howl, he bounded off one of the walls and crashed into Thorn, his fangs gnashing and his underworldly glow hazing the room with an orange tint.

The warrior stumbled but pummeled Omen in the face at the same time. More smoke flooded the small space from so many more new wounds. It clogged in my throat and stung my eyes.

I scrambled back on the bed just before the fight brought Thorn slamming into the side of the cot. My lungs had constricted. "Stop it!" I hollered at them. "Just take a breath and *talk* about it."

My appeal went unheeded. The way the two powerful shadowkind were going at each other, I wasn't sure if Thorn would even hear me if I revealed Omen's secret—if it would have made a difference at this point anyway.

At this rate, they were going to kill each other. Over me. I valued my life pretty highly, but no part of me wanted to see either of my monstrous lovers end their existence while vying to decide my fate. How much destruction was I going to cause right here without even using my supernatural sparks?

Just thinking that in the midst of the chaos brought a stinging surge of my flames licking up over my chest. As I smacked at them, willing down the fire, Thorn hurled the hellhound against the wall. One of Omen's paws hit the rough stone with a crunch that turned my stomach, but he flung himself back at the warrior with his fangs flashing.

More heat churned up from the bonfire inside me. This wasn't how I wanted this catastrophe to end. *I* was responsible—for myself, for what my powers might do, and for what I allowed to happen here if I stood silent and let these two men tear each other apart.

I'd accomplished a lot of supposedly impossible

things in the past month. Maybe it was time to try one more if that meant I didn't have to watch anyone else die in an attempt to protect me.

"Stop!" I shouted, louder than before, and hopped onto my feet. I stood as tall as I could manage given the length of the chain and waved my free arm frantically. "*Stop!* I'll go. I'll go to the Highest."

The two shadowkind careened past me in their fight without giving any sign of acknowledgment, so I did what might have been the most foolhardy act of my life so far—which if you've been following along, you'll know is saying a lot. I hurled myself right into the middle of that smoky clash of fists and claws.

Of course, thanks to my close friend Chain, I only made it a couple of feet from the bed, but that was enough to propel my arm between the two fighters.

Thorn heaved himself backward with a startled grunt and wild eyes. Omen, for all he'd threatened to rearrange my face a few minutes ago, recoiled in the opposite direction with just as much force. They both stared at me, Omen panting as he shifted back into human form, Thorn checking me over for damage as if he wasn't standing there pouring his life essence into the room.

"I'll go to the Highest," I said again, now that I was sure I had their attention. The words caught in my throat, but I forced myself to keep going anyway. "You don't need to fight about it or make any decisions. I'm deciding. They want me, so I'll go."

Thorn's tan face grayed. "M'lady—they mean to *destroy* you."

"I know." I swallowed thickly. "But they haven't met me yet. I've stolen a lot of things in my life—possibly I can manage to steal a little goodwill too."

When I shifted my gaze to Omen, he looked equally stunned. The fire had gone out of his eyes, and the blue that remained looked more pained than icy. "What are you playing at, Disaster?" he said, but without any of his typical rancor. He sounded almost *worried*.

About my sanity, possibly. I was questioning that too. But I'd made my decision, and I wasn't going to go all wishy-washy now.

"You can tell the Highest where I am and fulfill their orders," I said. "I'm just asking that you also tell them how much good I've done trying to help the shadowkind and how much I want the chance to keep doing that. Tell them I've been trying to *stop* the extermination of your kind, and the last thing I want to do is devastate the realms myself. See if there's any way they'd consider making some kind of deal with me rather than going straight to murder. Please."

He blinked, his expression still frozen in its state of shock.

"Sorsha," Thorn rumbled. "You don't have to do this."

"Yes, I do. Because I like the alternatives even less."

Omen drew himself up straighter abruptly. I didn't know how to read the brooding look he gave me. Then he motioned to the warrior with a jerk of his hand.

"You heard her. She doesn't want to be rescued. Let's go, before you insist on doing it anyway. You can weigh in on where I take things from here—outside, in the fresh air, like comrades."

Thorn shot me an imploring glance that wrenched at my heart. I nodded encouragingly. "It'll be okay," I said, with no idea at all how that could turn out to be true. "Go with him and give him some pointers on how to present my better qualities in a good light."

The warrior grimaced, but at another beckoning gesture from Omen, his bulky form vanished into the shadows. As Omen dove after him without a backward glance, it occurred to me with a lurch of my gut that this might be the last time I'd ever see them before I faced the direst possible fate I'd ever imagined I might meet.

5

Omen

I nudged Thorn down the dark passage beyond the door of my canyon safe house, out to the narrow ledge of yellow-brown rock where the morning sun shone. He went without protest but with tension still ringing through his presence.

We could have talked in the shadows, but the blurred awareness of the outer world made my thoughts feel muddled. And they'd been muddled enough already after Sorsha had made her offer and her plea just now.

I waited at the mouth of the passage long enough for the cool shade to knit the wounds from our fight to the point that I wasn't worried about how much smoky essence I was leaking, and then I emerged into the sunlight.

Thorn followed me into physical form but stayed in the passage. There wasn't really room for him to join me on the ledge, considering it only jutted about a foot from the entrance and a few feet across. Getting to and from this place while carrying Sorsha had required a precarious scramble down the uneven rock face above, which held nothing wide enough to be considered an actual path. No human could have made it here alone without a host of rock-climbing gear.

We were about halfway down the canyon wall. Rocky cliffs stretched out all around us, towering over a valley flecked with green vegetation on either side of its shimmering river. The wind whistled through the crags, dry and fresh with no hint of human occupation.

The grandeur of the landscape before me might have been the closest any place in the mortal world came to matching the sublime if oppressive enormity of the Highest and their vast hollow in the shadow realm. Looking out over it in the flood of warm light from above, it was hard to imagine that Sorsha had volunteered to trade her existence here for the complete and infinite darkness of the death the Highest wished on her. Even harder to imagine that only minutes ago, I'd been wavering on the edge of consigning her to that darkness.

And the first point was exactly why I was now feeling so unsettled about the second.

Thorn had wrapped a strip of cloth around the worst of the slashes my claws had dealt. With another uncomfortable pang, I watched him secure it. I hadn't enjoyed fighting him any more than I'd enjoyed the idea of subjecting Sorsha to the Highest's potentially irrational brutality.

"You can't listen to her," he said, fixing the full depth of his dark eyes on me. "She was only trying to stop us from hurting each other. She doesn't *want* to die. And you know the Highest won't be moved by any overtures on her behalf. If they'd been willing to believe she might not be such a terrible threat, the twenty-five years in which she failed to incinerate the world while they searched for her should have made them rethink their position."

"Agreed." He hadn't even heard how the Highest spoke about her. I had no doubts at all about how quickly they'd dismiss any appeals I made.

Had Sorsha wanted to save both of us from each other, or only to protect Thorn in case I savaged him beyond repair? I hadn't been aiming for that, had only wanted to force him to surrender, but in the heat of battle, one's intentions didn't always carry through. She could have taken the gamble, hoping that he'd best me, free her, and convey her to safety...

But whatever chance she'd seen of escape, she'd decided it was worth less than the chance of losing Thorn. Possibly even of losing me to *his* blows, though darkness only knew why she'd care about that after the way I'd treated her over the past two days.

The past two days? That was the least of it. What about the past *month*?

I'd cut her only the tiny portion of slack my unexpected respect for her had demanded, and I'd reproached myself for every bit of that, thinking it was emotional weakness. But perhaps she'd been right that

day when my frustration had boiled over into passion—
when she'd told me there was more strength in owning
one's emotions than burying them.

Over and over, I'd told myself that I shouldn't allow
myself to be impressed by her or desire her. That no
matter what I saw, her mortal frailty would come through
and screw us over when it mattered most. And here I was
with her words still ringing in my ears, hearing her take a
greater stand and making a greater sacrifice than I'd ever
been willing to do with all the amends I'd tried to make to
my kind.

Who the hell was *I* to judge a woman willing to lay
down her life to spare our pain?

Yes, she'd risked her life plenty of times in her capers
to free captive shadowkind and during our missions.
Somehow I'd managed to dismiss all that as adventure-
seeking rather than generosity. But there was no
adventure to be had in lying down at the mercy of the
most inhumane—and inhuman—of all shadowkind. That
was pure, selfless sacrifice.

I couldn't shake the sense that at least some small part
of it was for *my* benefit. I might be adept at pretending
away my own emotions, but I couldn't deny the
compassion I'd seen cross her eyes when I'd spoken of my
ties to the Highest and the consequences that would
come from defying them.

Did I really think a woman with that much valor and
forgiveness in her would allow herself to cause some
global act of destruction? By the looks of things, she'd

sooner throw herself on my claws than let herself spiral anywhere near that far out of control.

"Omen," Thorn started again, but I stopped him with a gesture.

"Stop fretting. I'm not turning her over to the Highest."

He paused, his stern face so befuddled in that moment it was almost amusing. "But she— You were adamant— What in the worlds were we fighting over if you had no intention—"

"I did intend," I said tersely. "Then she proved how far she'll go just to spare the two of us from pain. It's a little hard to continue believing she could possibly exterminate us all after that, don't you think?"

Thorn scowled. "I don't fully understand why she made that offer either. I would have subdued you and freed her, given enough time..." He glowered at me as if daring me to argue about his combat prowess.

I patted one of his massive arms. "Don't be a grouch about it. You're getting the outcome you wanted, and it didn't even require any near-fatal wounds—for either of us, which I'm especially glad of."

"She should have seen I wouldn't have come all this way or forced the issue with you if her survival hadn't been more important than a few battle wounds."

The furrows on the wingéd's forehead deepened. No doubt he still couldn't understand why I'd considered turning Sorsha over in the first place. What *could* he attribute it to other than the frequent clashes between us? I might have made demands of her that, I'd admit, looked petty in retrospect, but I'd never been anywhere near *that* vindictive toward her—or anyone, in ages.

But explaining my reasoning would mean revealing the leash I'd allowed the Highest to fix around my neck, the way I'd abased myself to save my life, and the thought of doing that sent a far deeper jab of revulsion through me than the possibility that the wingéd might see me as overly callous. It'd been hard enough admitting it to Sorsha. Thorn would have a far clearer understanding of just what my deal had required of me.

Thorn wasn't the type to dwell on minor conflicts anyway, not when he'd had such a huge transgression of his own weighing on him for so long. After a moment, he shook his head. "You're right. If we're agreed to protect her from the Highest's plans, that's all that matters. Then we'd better go—"

The peal of my phone interrupted him. Maybe remembering what had gone down the last time that ringtone had split the air, Thorn cut himself off into an uneasy silence.

I hadn't been expecting a call... just like I hadn't been last time. Tempest didn't enjoy being ignored. As I pulled the phone out of my pocket, I braced myself, anticipating the blank screen and all that would follow.

The thought of hearing her needling voice carrying from the speaker again made me want to hurl the phone into the depths of the canyon. But I knew better than anyone that my former co-conspirator wasn't a problem you could expect to just go away. Even when a horde of immensely powerful beings went to extreme lengths to ensure she was battered out of existence, somehow she was still here, playing out another of her gleefully malicious schemes.

I hit the answer button and held the phone a good foot away from me, remembering how loudly she'd projected her remarks through it two days ago. "For someone who hid her existence from me for the better part of six centuries, you seem awfully eager to chat all of a sudden, Tempest."

Her voice slithered out in a languid tone I knew better than to believe. "I simply wanted to confirm you hadn't met some sudden calamity after we last spoke. Have you become a much slower traveler in your old age?"

"I haven't started traveling yet," I said. "Funny thing —when you drop out of the blue into someone's life, they often have prior affairs they need to take care of first."

"And here I thought meddling with the Company of Light was your largest concern at the moment. I have all the answers you need on that subject."

"Yes, well, for all your sphinxly wisdom, you never did manage to know everything. How many guesses did it take you to get my phone number right, hmm?"

She would have managed to hit on the right one with a guess—plucking the correct answer to anything remotely like a riddle out of thin air was as much a talent of hers as coming up with riddles designed to confound was. It wasn't an exact science, though. I'd be willing to stake my tail that she'd gotten at least ten wrong numbers before she'd heard my voice on the other end of the line.

That suspicion was born out by the irritation that crept into her tone while she dodged that question. "You sound displeased with me. No rejoicing at the chance for us to join forces again? Have you forgotten what a good run of it we had long ago?"

I hadn't at all, and that was the problem. The question sent a slimy sensation down my spine as if she'd trailed decaying seaweed over my back. Sorsha might call me a bastard now, but what a bastard I'd truly been back then—not ice-cold but searingly sadistic, as selfish when it came to indulging my disdain for mortals as that mortal woman had proven herself the opposite moments ago.

And Tempest had gleefully egged on that side of me. She'd stoked my flames and my contempt, and nothing had made her applaud louder than seeing our mortal targets twisted into agony. If she'd been around when the hunters had burst in on the innocent creatures I'd inadvertently led them to, she'd have laughed at their mistake and found some way to amplify it without a second's regret for the deaths of the lesser beasts.

And maybe I'd have done the same if she'd still been standing with me in all her sly, vicious glory.

But I was better than that now, even if she didn't understand. I was better than that... and was there perhaps a better way through this mess than had occurred to me before?

Tempest might hold a different sort of answer. She might even delight in providing it, if I played the game right. I had known her awfully well, and she didn't appear to have changed much.

"It has been a long time," I said, bringing out all the inner cool I'd worked so hard to cultivate. "But of course I haven't forgotten. I know exactly where I'll find you when I have the chance to make my way in your direction. Since you're so enthusiastic for that reunion, I'll see if I can't make it there in a day or so."

"If you're going to dillydally about it, be prepared that you might find yourself stranded on your lonesome for a good while before *I* get around to stopping by," Tempest retorted, but I doubted she'd leave me hanging all that long. If nothing else, she had to be *dying* to brag about this bizarre, immense scheme of hers to someone with the discernment to fully appreciate it.

I smiled thinly. "I'll see you sooner or later, then."

Before she could respond, I hung up. Let her stew over that rather than think she had me wrapped around her finger.

I turned to Thorn. "We're taking a little trip. It'll be useful to have back-up. Assemble whichever of our allies is inclined to stick with us and meet me in Barstow with the RV—that should make a suitable halfway point. I'll see to Sorsha."

Thorn frowned as if he wasn't entirely sure he should trust me with that responsibility. "We're continuing our campaign against the Company as before?"

"Not exactly as before. I need to determine what precisely Tempest is using those mortals for. But you can be sure I intend to see the lot of them crushed—and for *our* mortal to be right there alongside us making that happen. Now get on with it. Or are you still in an insubordinate mood?"

Thorn's jaw tightened at the memory of just how far he'd pushed against my orders less than a half hour ago. His gaze lingered for a moment on the few wounds his fists had dealt that were still seeping trickles of smoke, and then he dipped his head in acknowledgment.

As he stepped into the shadows, I drew in a heavy breath and headed back down the passage to confront my most recent crimes.

When I slipped through the shadows around the door, I found Sorsha sitting in the same spot on the bed, tensed as if she expected the next being to emerge in the room to be arriving to lead her to her death—or perhaps to kill her on the spot. A reasonable enough assumption, considering what I'd put her through.

At the sight of me, her stance went even more rigid, but a familiar determination lit in her eyes. While she'd agreed to willingly surrender herself to the Highest, she hadn't surrendered her spirit. If I'd been coming to haul her off, no doubt she'd have gone with plenty of choice remarks.

The worst shame of it was how much her defiance made me want her—and how much her surrender had crumbled my defenses against admitting that. Even with her hair rumpled and her clothes wrinkled, her face drawn from lack of sleep, she was breathtaking.

And that damned joke about the chain had wormed its way inside my head. For a moment, I couldn't help picturing chaining both her wrists to the bedframe and then working over her body so thoroughly she'd lose both her own breath and all those snarky remarks, until we both reached an even more ecstatic release than the last time.

I wasn't going to kid myself that she'd be quite so forgiving as to go for that proposition, though. And we did have a maniacal, nearly immortal evil genius of a shadowkind to contend with on top of all the problems we'd been up against before.

I stalked over and unlocked the cuff at Sorsha's wrist, doing my best to tune out the heat that coursed over my body when I stood so near her.

She swallowed audibly. "How are we doing this? Are you taking me to a rift?"

"No. I have a better idea. One that, if it works, will ensure the Highest never think about having their minions brutalize you again."

She blinked at me. "What? I thought you figured they might be right to want me dead."

"I changed my mind. Even shadowkind are allowed to do that, you know."

"But—*why*?"

I grasped her forearm, careful to avoid the reddened marks where the cuff had rubbed her wrist, and tugged her onto her feet. "Don't look a gift hound in the mouth, Disaster." And then, because the nickname had brought a tightness of regret into my throat as it'd rolled off my tongue, "You wouldn't have told me to hand you over if protecting shadowkind didn't matter more to you than your own existence. That's enough for me. It just won't be enough for the Highest."

Sorsha stretched, limbering up now that she had her full range of movement. Her gaze stayed wary. "And what do you think will be enough?"

I smiled again, even narrower than before. "We're going to set it up so it appears you've destroyed someone who's foiled them far more than 'Ruby' ever did. Tempest might even agree to help us with the ploy for the extra chaos it'll cause. If you accomplish more on their behalf than even their most loyal subjects ever did before, how can they possibly accuse you of meaning them harm?"

At least, I hoped that was the case. And if it wasn't, well, then I'd have a battle with their minions on my hands. If Sorsha died at the Highest's command, it'd only be over my dead body as well.

6

Sorsha

I'd never been to any sort of reunion—family, class, or otherwise—but I doubted there'd ever been one as joyful as when Omen ushered me across the cracked pavement of an otherwise vacant lot to the waiting RV.

I was still ten feet from the door when it burst open. Snap sprang out first and dashed to me with his usual serpentine grace.

He wrapped his arms around me and tucked my head under his chin with a sigh as if my arrival had put every wrong thing in the world right. I hugged him back just as eagerly. Didn't I wish our problems could be solved that easily.

Pickle scampered after the devourer with excited little squeaks, Thorn chasing behind the little dragon with a worried glance over his shoulder to make sure no mortals were close enough to the parking lot to see. My foster creature twined around my ankles, still chirping away.

Ruse sauntered over to join us at a more languid pace, but his smile beamed with far more affection than his typical smirk. Heedless of the hold Snap had on me, the incubus leaned in to claim a kiss so intent it left every part of me tingling, in part because I knew just how enjoyable it could be to be adored by both these men at the same time.

Thorn made a sound of consternation but looked as though it was more that he wished he'd thought of making the same gesture than that he objected to the incubus's forwardness. He seemed to decide Pickle wasn't causing any real trouble as long as the tiny creature stuck close to my legs and left off that chase. When Ruse released me, the warrior squeezed my shoulder, not quite smiling himself but with a thrum of pleased energy emanating from his brawny frame.

"It's good to have you back where you belong," he said, which from the wingéd was practically a standing ovation.

"Then I expect an even more enthusiastic welcome than that," I informed him. I bobbed up on my toes with the devourer's arms still around me, and a hint of a real smile crossed Thorn's lips. He brought them to mine, giving me a taste of the passion that resided beneath his stoic front.

The other wingéd man who'd joined us more

recently, Flint, hung back but appeared to at least be not upset to see me. Antic bounded around our cluster with actual applause and bursts of gleeful giggling.

"She's back, she's back; the Highest didn't eat her!" she crowed.

Yes, I was rejoicing that fact too, even if I wasn't totally clear on what had won Omen over. Just for that moment, I didn't feel any need to dwell on that. I was back where I belonged, a monstrous human among monstrous shadowkind, and I couldn't imagine wanting any company more. Not even the bitter tang of asphalt baking in the warm autumn air could cut through my relief.

Omen gave Snap a sharp look. "How much do our new recruits know now?"

The imp's chant appeared to have stirred something in my devourer. He lifted his head just enough to fix his moss-green eyes on Omen. I felt his body bristle against me with a trickle of aggressive energy as if he might be about to rise into full devourer form, both wondrous and horrifying.

"Enough to realize how awfully you treated Sorsha. How could you have even *thought* about giving her to them?" His clear, sweet voice came in a more forceful tone than I'd ever heard it take before. "You didn't even talk to her—or us. You *hurt* her." He touched his gentle fingertips to the bruise Omen's blow had left on my temple, careful not to provoke any further pain. His other arm tightened around me as if he thought the hellhound shifter might change his mind and attempt to charge off with me again.

Huh. Apparently it wasn't just the warrior wingéd who was prepared to do battle to keep me safe. I'd never thought of Snap as much of a fighter, but *I* wouldn't have wanted to go up against him at his fiercest.

I glanced over in time to see Omen practically gaping at the devourer, obviously startled by the chiding. His jaw worked, and his face returned to the same tense, unshakeable mask it'd been since he'd hauled me out of the cave. He took in the rest of our companions assembled around me, all of them now watching him in silence. Possibly wondering whether he was going to attempt to take off Snap's head for insubordination.

I shifted my weight, preparing to do some defending of my own if the hellhound laid into the devourer, but I didn't need to. Omen ducked his head, just slightly, and said, "I acted too hastily. It won't happen again."

He was admitting he'd made a mistake? My eyebrows shot up. "It's the end of the world as we know it," I couldn't help saying.

Omen's eyes narrowed as they returned to me, and I tensed all over again. I had the feeling my release wasn't so much a free pass as a conditional reprieve. And Omen hadn't bothered to tell me what the conditions of my remaining free were. Probably he'd be noting every slip *I* made for any excuse to proclaim me a real disaster after all.

"It had better not happen again," Snap said to the hellhound shifter. "If you try, it might be the end of *you*."

I wasn't sure how easily he could make good on the threat, but given that he had Thorn for back-up, it wasn't impossible.

Omen appeared to take it seriously enough. His voice turned curt, a few tufts of his hair rising with his temper. "If I say something, I mean it. She's back, isn't she?"

Snap made a discontented sound as if to say he wasn't excusing the matter that easily, but he let it drop for now.

Omen scanned the lot again. "Did we lose the night elf?"

Ruse waved his hand dismissively. "Gloam felt 'uncomfortable' with the 'hostile energies' and took off."

My heart sank a little. We were just getting started against an even more powerful enemy that we were anticipating, and we were already shedding allies like a cat shed hair.

The incubus folded his arms over his chest. There was something wary in his expression as he considered his boss. "So, where are we taking things from here?" he asked, a little too purposefully casual to be casual at all. "Off to tackle your good friend who's mixed herself up with the Company?"

"Tempest is not my 'friend'," Omen muttered, and drew himself up a little straighter. He wasn't the tallest of our bunch by a longshot, but the power and authority he exuded simply standing there gave him a stature that couldn't be ignored. "But I do know her well, and I think we may be able to use her to our own ends—both to dismantle the Company and to convince the Highest they can lay off on Sorsha. But first we need to get over there."

Thorn frowned. "Over where?"

"From what she's said, I assume she's set up shop in Versailles. She always used to talk about this dream of convincing some royal figure to build a palace so lavish it outdid all others. She finds mortal extravagance both incredibly amusing and appealing. I thought the Sun King's tastes in that area aligned awfully close to hers—if I'd known she was still alive, I'd have recognized her influence in it immediately."

Omen squinted past the warrior toward the Everymobile. "Do you think you and your wingéd brethren could handle heaving Darlene through the nearest rift—and bringing her out one of the Paris-area openings?"

"I might even be able to manage it on my own," Thorn said without hesitation. "I'm not sure how well the mortal vehicle will adapt to the journey, though."

I'd never heard of any shadowkind taking a mortal-side object that large through the shadow realm before. I'd never been taken into the shadow realm before myself. A chill rippled over my skin despite Snap's embrace. "Are we sure that *I'll* adapt to the journey?"

Omen gave me another of those unreadable looks he kept a collection of. "I'd imagine you're shadowkind enough to survive the trip, but I wasn't planning on making an experiment of it just yet. There may be something about your hybrid energies that would alert the Highest if you ventured into their realm. I was thinking you'd fly over the traditional way, with the incubus to smooth over matters of tickets and passports, and we'll meet up on that side. That way we'll have our living space and transport wherever we have to go rather than starting over from scratch."

That made sense. Before the unicorn shifter and centaur who owned the Everymobile had lent it to us, we'd been going through vehicles like a squirrel went through nuts. Although generally those nuts didn't get blown up. It was awfully handy having a place to crash— if you needed to sleep, like I did—and to hold meetings in and so on that could be on the road at the same time.

And I wasn't in any hurry to make my first foray, however brief, into the world of shadows.

"I approve of that plan," I said, and nudged Ruse. "Can you hook us up with first-class seats?"

He grinned. "Hooking up *is* my specialty."

Even though that sounded delightful all around, Thorn's frown had deepened. "Perhaps I should also accompany Sorsha, to ensure..." He trailed off with unusual reluctance.

"I'll be fine," I said, and hugged Snap to me once more before easing away from him, since I knew the devourer was even more likely to worry about letting me out of his sight. "They'll need you to toss the Everymobile through the rift. It's not as if the Company of Light will be searching every airplane to Paris for me. Omen's friend isn't going to expect his people to be traveling the human way."

"Again," Omen started. "She isn't—"

I waved him off. "I know, I know, she's not your friend. Po-tay-to, po-tah-to." But Thorn didn't appear to be at all reassured. I cocked my head. "Is something else bothering you? You know I look after myself pretty well."

Who would have thought his frown could get even deeper? For a second, he looked adorably awkward—at least, as adorable as a musclebound giant of a man *could* look. "It's no matter, m'lady," he said, starting to turn away.

Oh, no, he wasn't getting away with that non-answer. Thankfully, I'd been around Thorn enough to know exactly how to break through his stoicism. I marched over to him and tucked my hand around his elbow. "A word with you in private, my good sir?"

Even though I was teasing him a little, he couldn't resist the formal politeness of the request. "As the lady wishes," he said, and for once strode off with me to the edge of the parking lot without glancing at Omen to confirm the boss was all right with the delay. Interesting. Maybe their skirmish back in my prison room had left more fault lines in our alliance than I'd realized. I didn't think that was necessarily a good thing.

When we were far enough from the others that they wouldn't overhear us, I turned to Thorn. "All right. What's the matter? And don't tell me nothing—I can tell something's eating at you."

He grimaced and looked at the ground. "It doesn't need to concern you."

"Sure it doesn't, but I'm concerned anyway. And I'm

not letting it go until you spill the beans, so you might as well speed things along by getting right to that part."

He gave me a glower that was as fond as it was exasperated. Then any trace of humor in his face faded. "In the canyon. You forced an end to our fight—you gave yourself up."

"Well, seeing as it was either that or watching you two tear each other to pieces..."

His jaw clenched. "I would have managed to get you free. I struck out at the one I swore to serve to ensure it. But you... you were willing to stay caged? To let the Highest do with you what they will?"

Ah. I could see how that idea might not sit well with him.

I rested my hand on his arm. "I didn't *like* the idea of facing the Highest. I just liked the idea of you or Omen— or both of you—dying instead because neither of you would back down even less. They're not going to stop looking for me, and I've made myself a hell of a lot more visible in the last few weeks, so chances are I'm going to have to face them eventually anyway. But if no one else's lives are on the line, I'll make sure that 'eventually' is as far away as possible."

"I *would* fight to the death if it meant saving you from some awful fate," Thorn began, and I gripped his forearm harder.

"Think about how you feel when you picture the Highest sending their minions to kill me. I felt at least that awful watching you and Omen bashing each other around. If you're allowed to save me, I'm allowed to save you too, remember?"

He opened his mouth and then closed it again. "I see," he said finally. "When you put it that way... It was not giving up. It was simply a different maneuver in your own battle."

"That's one way of putting it." I shot him a smile. "You should know I'm not in the habit of giving up."

"That was precisely why the possibility was so disconcerting."

"Well, you don't have to worry about it. Now I'm totally focused on kicking some sphinx butt the old-fashioned way. Come on. You've got an RV to schlep all the way through another dimension."

When we returned to the others, Snap tugged me to him for a lingering kiss. "If you *should* need anyone else to come with you on the plane..."

I could just imagine how many stares his heavenly beauty would draw. "I think we'll be lower profile if it's just the two of us. But I'll aim to be back with you as soon as humanly possible. And I promise when we don't have murdering psychos to deal with anymore, we'll take all kinds of plane rides until you're bored with them."

He beamed at me and stole one more kiss. Then he shot Ruse a stern look, as if to say the incubus had better take good care of me, before following the others onto the RV.

Only Ruse and Omen remained. The hellhound shifter considered me so intently the hairs rose on my arms under his scrutiny.

"I promise not to crash the plane," I said tartly.

The corner of his mouth twitched upward. "Do hold to that promise, Disaster. And be careful in general. We don't know what minions the Highest might still have on the prowl. If you can manage not to cause any kind of spectacle, that would probably be for the best."

Was he worried I might get myself caught before he could wriggle his way out of his deal? Well, I wouldn't like the outcome of that either. "I'll do my best to remain unchained."

His lips twitched in the other direction at that remark. For a second, I thought he was going to add something, but then he shook his head with a jerk and stalked onto the Everymobile without another word in farewell.

* * *

Ruse went all out on the plane ride. As far as I could tell, he'd decided it was his job to pamper me into forgetting the dingy digs I'd been stuck in for the two days prior.

Along with charming a sales rep at the L.A. airport into giving us a couple of snazzy first-class seats, he somehow managed to get us served an extra posh—as airplane food went—three-course meal complete with fine wine.

"Would you prefer caviar or filet mignon?" he asked me while he held the attendant in his thrall.

I blinked at him. "Is that a joke?"

"There are very few things I won't joke about, but one of those is good food."

Well, if he was offering... "I'll take a slab of beef over fish eggs any day, thank you."

After we'd eaten, he insisted that I pick the movie we watched together on the little screens, and didn't make a peep of complaint when I went with a slapstick comedy with about as much nuance as a steamroller. He massaged my shoulders and my feet until I got dozy. Then he tucked me in with a cashmere blanket on my reclined seat. I'd swear I heard him crooning some operatic French lullaby as I drifted off to sleep.

I woke up with the crackle of an announcement that the plane was about to begin its descent and opened my eyes to find the incubus gazing down at me with an almost fraught expression. It was only there for an instant, and then he was jerking his gaze away before returning his attention to me with a more typical sly smile and possibly the faintest of blushes coloring his pale cheeks. "Rise and shine, Miss Blaze."

Ruse had told me he loved me for the first time less than an hour before our last mission. It'd obviously been difficult for him to reveal that emotion, even though I'd returned the sentiment. We hadn't had time to settle into any kind of new normal afterward—maybe he was feeling a bit awkward about that still.

I squirmed upright with the swing of the seat back and reached over to grab his hand. "You've been awfully sweet the whole flight. Trying to give Snap a run for his money now that he's honing in on *your* usual territory?"

Something flickered through the incubus's expression and vanished just as quickly. He shrugged, a familiar twinkle lighting in his warm hazel eyes. "It's the least I can do."

"Well, your efforts have not gone unnoticed... nor will they go unrewarded." I winked at him and walked my fingers along his jaw to draw him into a kiss, wishing I could slip them right under his cap to grasp his horns the way he liked without exposing them for all the regular mortals around us to see.

With the seatbelt lights already on, I couldn't make that reward a membership to the mile-high club, but maybe that wasn't what Ruse would have wanted most anyway. At least one woman he'd cared about in the past had shown *she* only cared about how well he could get her off in bed. Instead, I rested my head against his shoulder, nestling closer when he put his arm around me.

It was hard to feel all that sour about the bounty on my head when this whole mess had also brought the most fascinating, thrilling, and delectable men I could have imagined into my life.

Once we'd departed the plane, a few texts with Omen directed us to a quiet spot off the road between Paris and Versailles where he and the others had parked the Everymobile to wait for us. As we got out of the cab across the road from the RV, I couldn't stop a startled laugh from spilling from my lips.

"What in sweet Satan's name happened here?"

Maybe to someone who'd never seen it before, the Everymobile in its current state wouldn't have looked that odd. But the trip through the shadow realm had definitely made an impact.

In its current tour bus form, bright purple polka dots spotted the lower edge of the vehicle's otherwise dark walls with their sweeping yellow—made-up—logo. A crooked antenna I'd never seen before protruded at an angle over the windshield. And toward the rear end, a propeller I couldn't figure out the function of was spinning wildly as if in a brisk wind, although the cool evening air around us barely moved.

The door opened, and Omen beckoned. "Stop gawking and get your asses on here."

I reeled my jaw back in, but I stayed where I was. "What did you do to Darlene?" I said, intending to rankle him by using the name he'd given the vehicle despite it not really being his.

He let out a short huff of breath. "The transition through the shadow realm may have had a few side effects. She still runs just fine. Are you coming or did you fly all this way just to park yourselves here?"

I rolled my eyes at him with a teasing smile. "Excuse me for asking."

We tramped on board. In the dining area, Snap promptly pulled me onto his lap where he was sitting on the sofa-bench and planted a possessive kiss on my mouth. The engine started up with a sputter and... a sound like distant bells ringing?

"Keep any commentary to yourself," Omen grumbled from behind the wheel.

"All I have to say is, you definitely can't blame *this* vehicular mishap on me." I made a flourish with my hand toward the road ahead. "Next stop, Versailles!"

7

Sorsha

I'd prowled around quite a few opulent mansions in my time, mostly to separate shadowkind collectors from their cages of lesser beasties, but none of those sights had prepared me for the Palace of Versailles. "Palace" was definitely the word for it, to the power of one million.

Staring up at the three stories of sprawling, ornately carved and gilded walls, my jaw went slack for a few seconds before I managed to recall it and myself.

"I see what you mean about extravagance," I said to Omen as we crossed the vast, shadowy courtyard, keeping my voice low. There wouldn't have been visitors here this late in the evening anyway, and from the signs we'd passed on our way in, the sphinx had contrived some way to shut down the estate to visitors, but I couldn't quite shake my well-trained thieving instincts. We were guessing that she'd ensured an absence of security guards as well, but we hadn't confirmed that yet.

Omen matched my subdued tone. "If Tempest is anything, she's a hedonist. The trouble for most other beings, mortal or otherwise, is the things she tends to take pleasure from do the opposite for everyone else involved."

"A hedonistic sadist with no concern for consent. I can't wait to meet her."

The hellhound shifter gave me a sharp look, as if I hadn't laid on the sarcasm doubly thick. Or maybe because of the sarcasm. "I know restraint isn't your strong suit, but if you could manage to let me handle most of the negotiations, it'll work out better for all of us. She'll ask you some direct questions, so obviously answer those, but... don't give away more than you need to."

"Funnily enough, I do have some experience dealing with dangerous shadowkind." I poked him in the arm.

He bared his teeth at me, but, shocker of all shockers, it looked more like a grin than a grimace. The closest thing to a good-humored smile I'd gotten from him since he'd dragged me off and chained me up. Maybe I'd earned myself a few more points in the Keep Sorsha Alive column without realizing it.

"Considering that your main approach to 'dealing' with me is to provoke my temper in every possible way, I'm going to suggest you take a different tactic here," he said.

"Where would be the fun in that?"

"We're not here for *fun*, Disaster."

"I know, I know. I figure after you've literally had me

in chains, I should be allowed to tug on yours a little to even the score."

As soon as the words fell from my lips—because, I admit it, I really did have a bit of a problem of shooting my mouth off without quite as much forethought as might be wise—a flicker of panic shot through my chest. Had I gone too far, reminding him of the actual if magical chains the Highest had him in? I hadn't meant to imply anything about the bonds that obviously rankled him more than anything in his existence, but that was the problem with not thinking before you spoke.

Omen merely rolled his eyes skyward with a wordless sound of exasperation, so I guessed I wasn't ending up back in my own chains over that affront.

Just as we reached the door, it swung open. Thorn peered at us from the other side. He and Flint had joined us for this meeting so we'd have extra muscle along in case talking didn't pan out so well, and Snap was lurking too, having refused to hang back. With my thieving past, I couldn't help envying the shadowkind ability to slip right around doors and unlock them from the inside as need be.

The hall we stepped into took my breath away all over again. In the thin light that streaked through the immense arched windows from the security lamps outside, gold glittered all across the molded walls and ceiling. Between the gleaming mouldings, richly colored paintings covered nearly every surface. Dozens of crystal chandeliers as tall as I was dangled at intervals.

If I'd been here on burglar business, right about now

I'd have been thinking I should have brought a bigger bag. Possibly an entire trailer.

As Omen and I headed down the hall, Thorn vanished back into the shadows. Our feet whispered across the polished floor.

The looming grandeur made vigilance feel even more necessary. My voice dropped another octave. "Where in this place do you think we'll find Tempest? Or is she going to find us?"

"Oh, no, she'll enjoy having us come to her." Omen tipped his head to the right as we rounded a corner. "Chances are she'll have claimed the queen's bedroom as her own."

Where else? I might have appreciated the shadowkind woman's aplomb if she hadn't allied herself with an army of murderous mortals.

Omen couldn't have been here with her before, but he'd probably been in other bedrooms with her if he could make that statement so confidently. A question prickled up through me that I tried to suppress... but why? It might be useful to know to help me follow the conversation ahead.

"So, you've made it very clear that you're no longer friends with Tempest. Were you ever *more* than friendly?"

Omen's mouth flattened. "If you're asking if we ever fucked, then yes, a handful of times when we couldn't find more exciting activities to pass the time with. It wasn't any kind of love affair. It meant nothing more than momentary physical satisfaction to either of us."

Was that all our passionate tumble into bed had meant to him too? I didn't know if I wanted it to have meant more. The encounter had certainly been off the scales in the physical satisfaction department. And now I was remembering the sear of his kiss and the literal flames that had flowed between us, which wasn't exactly helping my focus, so maybe I shouldn't have brought up the subject after all.

"Well, it's good that you should know your way around her in a bedroom," I said in a breezy tone, and Omen shot me a look so scorching it made me want to feel his kiss again for real.

Whoa there, hormones. I had three other monstrous lovers who weren't watching my every move for signs that I was going to incinerate all life in both realms. No need to be greedy. Or stupid.

We walked through a few more of the ornate rooms that smelled faintly of jasmine. Omen slowed coming up on the next doorway.

A voice rang out from the room beyond in the same sharp, droll tone I'd heard rising up from Omen's phone at the start of this recent mess, the effect amplified when it only had to travel through air. "Here you are at last, Omen. Come on then. Don't tell me you've gone shy."

"Only perhaps a little more cautious," he said, sauntering in.

I followed him into a room so full of splendor it took everything I had in me not to start gaping again.

Two lamps lit the space, catching on the masses of gold that coated the walls and ceiling. There was enough of it around us to buy one of those collectors' mansions back home, gilded across delicate filigree-etched borders and painted in with the pinks, blues, and greens of intricate floral patterns. Between two more crystal chandeliers, a massive gold canopy rippling with sculpted leaves protruded from the wall, flowery curtains falling from its edges to frame an immense bed. The jasmine smell had thickened, adding to the opulent atmosphere.

If this was how royalty lived, sign me up to start a dynasty of my own.

Somehow, the figure lounging on the silk covers of the bed managed to top her surroundings in extravagance. Tempest would have been a difficult figure to miss even without any special trappings: she had to be at least six feet tall and built like an Amazon, both muscular and buxom. Her bronze-brown hair gleamed as brilliantly as the gold around her, twisted into waving locks that lifted and swayed around her face as if they had minds of their own. Like some kind of Medusa— Omen had said she liked to take on different roles.

True to the lion-ish aspects of her nature, her shining eyes held cat-slit pupils, and there was something feline about her prominent cheekbones and flared nose as well. Definitely not a face you'd easily forget. The fabric draped across her voluptuous figure had the cut of a bathrobe, but hardly the kind you'd pick up at Target— this was a bathrobe fit for a queen, scarlet and violet satin strung through with gold embroidery.

Over that magnificent bathrobe, she'd draped so many golden bangles heavy with emeralds and sapphires that I wasn't sure she *could* sit up straight under it all even if she'd wanted to. Good luck walking under all that weight of riches. Although she looked perfectly happy sprawled as she was.

What made the biggest impression, though, and not one I could poke fun at even in passing, was the sense of power that wafted off of her like the wind off a stormy ocean, chilly and razor-edged. Omen might have cultivated his ice-cold bastardom to a T, but the energy that thrummed off him still held his natural heat. Tempest was a bastard down to her bones.

Annoyingly, in the midst of the awe and uneasiness I was already trying my best to tamp down, a jab of jealousy pricked at me too. The hellhound shifter had been so close to this woman, even if he disdained to call her so much as a friend now, even if he said their "fucking" hadn't mattered at all. She knew him in ways I likely never would, considering he now saw me as only slightly better than a ticking time bomb.

Yeah, I really shouldn't have ever asked him about their past liaisons.

I shoved the jealousy aside along with the rest and held myself steady. We came to a stop a few feet from the gilded barrier that ran through the room in an attempt to keep tourists away from the most valuable furniture.

Tempest's gaze slid over Omen to rest on me. "Well," she said in the same tone, which managed to sound like she was making both a threat and a joke, "what have we here?"

"Just a lowly mortal," I replied, attempting to match

that tone. That seemed safe enough to say before we knew exactly how and how much we might be able to work her into our plans.

"Hmm." Her cat-like eyes flicked toward the shadows along the edges of the room. "Let's see your whole troop, Omen. All the indomitable beings who worked so hard to disrupt my plans."

Of course she'd be able to sense the shadowkind who'd stayed in the darkness. Omen had expected that. He made a casual gesture, and our three companions materialized around us.

Omen had said it'd been a force of wingéd who'd attempted to destroy Tempest on the Highest's orders. If the sphinx could identify Thorn and Flint as beings of the same kind, considering she had pretty direct experience with their kin, she showed no sign that their presence bothered her at all. She cocked her head, the locks of her hair continuing their sinuous dance around her face. "This isn't all of them. You had an incubus."

"He's attending to other business tonight," Omen said, which was sort of true. Ruse had offered to stay back and ensure that Antic didn't follow us to insist on contributing her impish version of "help." "Not much my talents can offer against a sphinx," he'd said in a flippant way that had felt a little forced to me.

The hellhound shifter made a point of looking around the room, his stance casual but poised. "You've hardly brought all your allies to this parley. Of course, it appears you've gotten yourself a whole host of them, more than perhaps could fit in this palace. All of them mortals, oddly enough. What grand scheme have you concocted this time, Tempest?"

"Oh, you know me. To some extent I simply play it by ear." The sphinx gave a smile that didn't quite manage to be demure and trailed her fingers across the bed covers. "It's provided immense amusement having a horde of mortals at my beck and call, hating shadowkind with all their being while in service of one."

"They're *hurting* shadowkind," Snap spoke up with some of the new boldness he'd shown since I'd returned. He should know more about that hurt than anyone here other than Omen—they'd both spent time in the Company of Light's cages, tormented by their experiments.

Tempest lifted one shoulder in the most languid of shrugs. "Fewer incompetent beings to irritate me. The Company of Light would hardly be effective if I never let them indulge their basest desires, would they?"

"Effective at *what*?" Omen demanded, commanding but not angry. Not one tuft of his tawny hair had risen yet, as provocative as his former conspirator was obviously trying to be. I couldn't suppress a twinge of affection that didn't have much place in this moment.

He'd used to run wild with this woman, yes, and it wasn't hard to see how tempting she could have made the prospect. He'd been savage and cruel and selfish. And somehow while she'd stayed exactly the same or perhaps gotten even worse, he'd shaped himself into something so much better than that. A leader who could be compassionate as well as harsh, who saw what people were capable of and gave them a chance even when he was skeptical.

Call him a monster all you wanted, but he was a hell of a lot more than that too. And he'd reached that point through lifetimes of effort and determination.

No wonder he'd gotten pissed off at my many attempts to poke holes in his carefully constructed cool.

I suspected Tempest would have liked to do the same, but she clearly didn't know him all that well as he was now. She chuckled slyly and gazed at him through her eyelashes. "I expect by now you've managed to uncover their ultimate plan?"

"They're attempting to create some sort of sickness that will spread through the shadowkind and kill us all," Omen replied. "I expect *you* aren't actually out to commit suicide by mass genocide?"

"Oh, I'll ensure I remain above the fray. The hardiest amongst us will be just fine. The mortals and the weaklings, not so much."

If I caught the slight stiffening of Omen's posture, she must have too. "Then what they're working to create," he said, "you really do expect it to infect and kill shadowkind."

"Oh, don't look at me like that, Omen. I'm sure *you* have nothing to worry about. Eliminate most of the feckless beings who venture out here and might cramp my style, wipe out a good chunk of humanity as well and leave the survivors wrenched with guilt over their miscalculation..." She batted her eyelashes. "It should be a smashing time all around."

My stomach had plummeted to my feet. Omen had assumed the Company's stated mission was also a front for some other scheme of Tempest's. Not so much, apparently. This went so far beyond trampling a few lesser creatures on the way to screwing over some mortals that we might as well be in a different solar system.

Chances that she'd be willing to set aside those plans to participate in a ploy where I pretended to defeat her, just to foil the Highest for a brief moment? I'd place them at about a trillion to one.

Thorn shifted on his feet, and I could feel the horror he must be reining in while he let Omen take the lead. Snap couldn't restrain a shiver. He was the youngest of my shadowkind crew—was *his* accumulated power enough to protect him from this menace and her constructed disease?

Did it even matter whether they survived when either way, scores of shadowkind—and humans—were going to die because of the path Tempest was leading the Company down?

"They're almost finished," she boasted as if she had an audience avid with enthusiasm rather than alarm. "Just another leap of inspiration or two, and we'll have it ready. You've been a thorn in my side for the past little while unintentionally... Are you ready to get in on the most epic strike of both our careers?"

My stomach twisted. I glanced at Omen, wondering if he'd play along to humor her for the time being. But his jaw had clenched even tighter, an orange sheen of hellfire glowing over the pale blue of his eyes.

"When did you move from games to outright warfare?" he asked. "This plot is so far below the Tempest I associated with that I can't believe you don't see that."

She sniffed. "I haven't sunk at all. Perhaps the problem is that you all have forgotten what you're meant to be. They call us monsters for a reason, don't they?" She narrowed her eyes at each of my shadowkind companions. "You must have leashed your hound so long you've forgotten what it is to run free, Omen. Where's the vicious fury at the pathetic arrogance of mortals that used to fuel you? And you wingéd, aren't you done sulking over your losses yet? What do you use that spectacular physique for now— squashing cockroaches? Or do you offer leniency even to them?"

"I have bashed open plenty of skulls and rib cages in *defense* of my fellow shadowkind," Thorn rumbled, unable to hold himself back any longer.

"As if they were worth the effort." Tempest gave a tinkling laugh like shattering glass that made me want to punch *her* skull in and turned her attention to Snap. "And a devourer—one of the rarest of all our kind, and yet what are you putting your talents toward other than looking pretty? You ought to be out there rending soul by mortal soul apart to become as great as you're meant to be. You could contain a multitude if these insipid sympathies didn't hold you back."

"Those souls belong to the mortals who contain them," Snap replied, but he'd shivered again at her words.

The color had drained from his face, leaving him wan beneath his golden curls.

That was the moment my tongue got away from me. "You're one to talk, acting like you're some pinnacle of shadowkind when you've spent how many decades now encouraging a bunch of mortals to annihilate your own people. As far as I can tell, *you're* the one who's forgotten what you are."

The sphinx's eyebrows arched. "Brave—and ridiculous—words from the mortal who's currently standing alongside *these* shadowkind. Have you convinced yourself you'll ever be more than a groupie to their evidently deviant tastes?"

The jab rankled me more than it should have. "You have no idea—" I started, and managed to yank my temper back under control before I said something I'd regret. "You know nothing at all. And here I thought a sphinx could at least pretend a little wisdom."

Unfortunately, while I could harness my words, I wasn't quite so good with my powers. I'd barely finished speaking when the revulsion and rage churning inside me lurched with a flare of my inner fire.

The flames shot up from my elbows toward my shoulders. Thorn caught them for me with a clap of his broad hands against my arms before they could set my hair alight.

My mouth went scorchingly dry. Tempest was staring at me now with far more interest than she'd shown anything else in this conversation so far. The sweep of her gaze over me left an uncomfortable prickling in its wake.

She sat up straighter as if to look at me even more closely. I resisted the urge to back away, holding my ground and raising my chin, daring her to comment. But when she did, it wasn't in the mocking tone I'd expected.

"Not so mortal after all." She laughed again, but this time it was more breathless with awe than disdainful. "And here I thought the devourer was your greatest find, Omen. Where on earth did you acquire a phoenix?"

I should have been gratified that she was impressed, but everything about this woman told me she wasn't the sort of being I should want to awe. A phoenix? Just because I caught myself on fire along with whatever else I was aiming at?

Watching me, Tempest's lips curled into a smirk. "You didn't know, did you? Oh, I am glad I'll be around to witness this. When you burn, the whole world will burn with you."

A wave of cold flooded me at that declaration, washing away any lingering fire. My voice came out tart. "Then it's a good thing I'm not planning on burning."

"You keep telling yourself that, darling." The sphinx rose to her feet, her innumerable baubles swaying around her, and peered down at Omen from the bed. "Well? Have you come all this way just to grimace your disapproval at me, or will you remember yourself and join the revelry?"

"It's been a long time," Omen replied in a low voice. "I no longer revel in the same things you do."

"Then we have nothing left to discuss. Stay out of my business, and I'll leave you to the rest of yours. You know what you can expect if you deny that request."

"Tempest," Omen started, but she was already leaping into the shadows. At a jerk of the hellhound's hand, Thorn and Flint threw themselves after her.

My legs had taken on an uncanny resemblance to spaghetti. When they wobbled despite my best efforts, Snap was at my side in an instant, his hand on my back.

"It doesn't matter what she called you," he said. "We know who you are."

Did they? Did *I*?

Omen's hands had clenched at his sides. At the return of our wingéd warriors with no sphinx in sight, he didn't look surprised.

"We failed to detain her," Thorn said with a pained expression. "She traveled so swiftly—"

"Don't apologize. None of us quite anticipated what we'd find here." The hellhound shifter exhaled roughly.

"She's not going to help with the plan to appease the Highest about Sorsha," Snap ventured.

Omen gave a bark of a laugh. "No, I'd say not."

My own fingers curled into fists. I crossed my arms over my chest, burying the sphinx's needling comments *—the whole world will burn with you*—under the immensity of everything else she'd admitted to.

"There's one very obvious answer to that problem," I said. "We always meant to destroy the Company. Now I'll just have to add defeating her to that to-do list—for real."

8

Sorsha

No one had turned on the Everymobile's radio, but it'd decided to start blaring about ten minutes ago, switching back and forth between strident classical music and a talk show where everyone seemed to be yelling in Russian—which was particularly odd considering we were currently in Paris.

Ruse and Antic jabbed at the buttons to no avail. Finally, Thorn strode over to the dash.

"My apologies," he said solemnly to the RV, and slammed his fist into the radio controls. The noise sputtered, but it did die, as just about everything did after a punch from the warrior.

Omen grimaced at the smashed spot we'd have to find some way to explain to the equines when they reclaimed their ride, but he didn't criticize Thorn's tactics. He turned back to the rest of us from his usual post leaning against the kitchen counter. No doubt it really would signal the end of the world if he ever lowered himself—both figuratively and literally—to sitting on the leather sofa-bench with us.

"Our observations across the past few days have made it quite clear that we can't rely on our previous tactics," he said. "Whether based on Tempest's urging or their own initiative, the local Company facilities are under total lockdown. We can't charm or threaten anyone into getting us past the outer defenses if no one ever comes out in the first place."

"Do you really think all the Company workers are living inside those buildings?" Snap asked. He nestled me even closer against him as he spoke, which was quite a feat when he'd already had me practically on his lap. He seemed to have become extra possessive after our confrontation with Tempest a few days ago.

I gave him a peck on his cheek to return the affection, and he beamed at me before continuing. "The facilities we found didn't appear to be made as homes. Won't the Company people get bored spending all their time at work? Won't some of them have families they'll be separated from?"

"I'm sure the answer to both of those questions is yes," Omen said. "They're just willing to sacrifice a few freedoms to make sure they can continue screwing us over."

I drummed my fingers on the table. Days of surveillance and no real action had left me restless, especially with my resolve to defeat Tempest hanging over me. "To be fair, being bored and lonely probably beats getting beheaded or disemboweled. If they think they're in mortal danger, I could see them putting up with a lockdown for quite a while."

Thorn glanced at Omen. "The sphinx knows we'll be investigating in this city. Our prior sources have indicated that the mortal leader of the Company of Light travels across Europe. The map we saw displayed several bases of operations here. Might they be less stringent elsewhere?"

"I don't think Tempest will be cutting any corners. Even the leader himself might be cloistered somewhere until she feels we no longer present much of a threat." The hellhound shifter rubbed his jaw. "She was only able to interrupt our last plan, which came very close to working, because she intervened quickly enough. If we could find another point of access and distract her well enough at the same time—or even attempt to take her down completely before we tackle the mortals... But without that point of access, we have no way of getting at their current operations or potential weaknesses."

"I could put out feelers for another mortal with hacking skills," Ruse suggested. "Someone who's not already working for the Company but who might be able to dig up some data that'll give us a lead. These jackasses can't run their operations without *any* interaction with the world around them."

Omen nodded. "Good idea. Your computer person back in the US contributed quite a lot. Run with that. And while you're tracking an appropriate human down, the rest of us will head underground. Paris has a mass of tunnels and catacombs that sprawl under a significant portion of the city. We'll split up and check the areas near the Company facilities for any alternate means of entrance. It's a long shot, but we might as well try whatever we can."

"I'll test for impressions in case the Company has used those passages themselves," Snap said, brightening at the opportunity to contribute his non-lethal supernatural talent.

"Excellent. In case we run into trouble, let's have someone with plenty of combat experience in each party. Snap, you go with Flint. Thorn, see if you can wrangle the imp into some sort of usefulness. And our disaster"—he rested his icy eyes on my face—"is coming with me."

Because he didn't trust any of the others to keep a close enough eye on me? I bit back half a dozen snarky remarks I'd like to have tossed at him. After seeing the echoes of his history in our conversation with Tempest the other night, I'd made a point of not hassling him quite so much, and I'd been succeeding at that pretty well, if I did say so myself. Why ruin my winning streak just to get a tiny dig in?

"It's a date," I said instead, and was rewarded with the twitch of the hellhound shifter's jaw.

My devourer wasn't feeling quite so generous. I didn't think he'd forgiven Omen for his past transgressions yet. Snap's arm tightened around me. "I would prefer to stay with Sorsha. I can defend her if I need to."

Omen gave him a baleful look. "I promise I have no nefarious intentions. She'll be returned to you soon in approximately the same state she's in now, depending on what we find in those tunnels."

"I still think we would be a better pairing."

"And *I've* already given my orders. If you don't trust me to lead this group with all our best interests in mind anymore, you know where the door is."

Omen's tone had been mild, but Snap bristled. I squeezed his arm before he could continue the argument —or escalate it into something more. It'd been bad enough watching Omen and Thorn fighting over my fate.

"Hey," I said. "I can defend *myself* pretty well, as both of you should remember. I'll be fine. I'm sure if Omen has decided to get rid of me after all, he wouldn't bother making up a big tourist expedition around it."

Snap made a grumbling sound, but he accepted a kiss and simply hugged me extra hard before releasing me so I could join the hellhound shifter, who was now glowering at me. This date was off to a great start already.

Sad to say, if it had been a date, tramping around in Paris's underground tunnels late into the night wouldn't have been the worst I'd been on. It was definitely in the bottom ten, though. The cool, earthy-smelling air that filled the passages made me feel as if I was just shy of being buried alive. The low ceilings and general darkness didn't help with that claustrophobic impression.

Omen let the glow of his hellhound skin emerge to cast an orange haze over the walls of stone, clay, and— oooh, even better, a stack of embedded bones. I tipped my head toward those. "Really your kind of place, huh, hellhound?"

"I don't think I've slaughtered quite enough mortals in my time to make an entire catacomb out of their remains," he replied, which wasn't exactly reassuring considering there looked to be a few thousand bodies' worth just within view.

We walked on until we reached the spot Omen said was beneath a chocolate factory the Company appeared to be doing business out of—I had to take his word for it, since one dreary wall looked pretty much the same as any other down here. Squinting in the dim light, I couldn't make out any trap doors or other openings that might have given us a sneaky path up into the building.

"I could bring out some fire for a little more light," I said, with a hesitation I couldn't help even though I didn't like it. Tempest's remarks had clung to me like a nettle, with an equal amount of irritating prickling. If I was a phoenix, did that mean I was doomed to burn myself up with my power sooner or later?

And how much would I burn down with me if it came to that?

Omen considered me. He'd been surprisingly thrifty with the snark himself during our exploration. I couldn't tell whether he was sizing me up for destructive potential or self-confidence.

"She isn't always right, you know," he said, as if that answered my offer.

"What?"

"Tempest. Sphinxes might be known for their

wisdom, but they also speak in riddles, and sometimes they get the two tangled up in their heads. She isn't all-knowing, and she has plenty of reasons to want to shake you up." He paused, his gaze shifting to the passage around us. "And I can see well enough to say that this spot is a wash too. We're done here. Come on." He stalked on down the tunnel.

I picked up my pace to keep up with him. "You don't think I'm actually a phoenix, then?"

"Oh, I believe that part. It's the first explanation that's really made sense, what with the whole habit of inadvertently setting yourself on fire. I just don't think that necessarily means you're going to burn up much else if you happen to go down in flames. Although I'd rather not experiment to find out." He glanced back with a flash of a tight but obvious smile in the darkness. "I'm going to guess that you're much better company uncharred."

"Well, I'm glad to hear you've revised your initial opinion of me at least that much."

He laughed. "You've remained full of surprises. Thankfully not all of them bad ones."

As recommendations went, I'd take that.

"Have you ever known a phoenix before?" I asked. What had happened to other beings like me? Tempest had indicated there weren't many of us.

Which Omen's answer confirmed. "No," he said. "And the stories I've heard have belonged more to mortals than shadowkind, so I have no faith in their accuracy. It could be that only a hybrid can become one. I highly doubt Tempest has ever met one either."

Okay, I could take a little reassurance in that. She was just spouting off half-baked fables, not speaking from any kind of inside knowledge.

Omen led us through several increasingly narrow passages, which didn't help with the suffocating sensation, and then up a set of rough stairs that ended at a span of thick wood paneling.

"The sphinx isn't the only one who knows a few tricks around this city," Omen said, and pressed a knob in the wood. One of the panels swung open to give us enough room to squeeze out into a small, dusty room stacked with chairs and boxes of tapered candles.

With a waxy scent tickling my nose, I followed Omen out the doorway at the other end and discovered that Versailles hadn't used up all my capacity for awe.

We'd come out into a cathedral—and sweet chirping cherubs, what a cathedral it was. The stone ceiling arched so high above our heads I could have believed it brushed the sky. High over the altar area, intricate stained glass windows streaked lamplight from outside in patches of color across the tiled floor. The columns that stood at intervals all along the pews were immense enough that I wasn't sure I could have wrapped my arms around one even if I'd cloned myself for extra help.

I wasn't much for religion, but if any place could have convinced me of the grandeur of a life beyond this one, this would be it.

"Notre Dame," Omen intoned beside me, gazing up at the towering stained glass windows. "I'll never claim that mortals haven't managed to make a few spectacular things in their time."

Speaking of surprises... I'd never have imagined I'd hear the hellhound shifter offer any praise to mortals as a general group.

A different sort of uneasiness rippled under my skin, stirring a flicker of fire with it. I willed the unsettled heat down, but maybe it'd be easier to deal with that if I said what'd been on my mind since our confrontation with Tempest.

I lowered my gaze to the floor, feeling unusually awkward. "You know, I'm sorry. For laying into you about your attitude so much. I mean, you deserved it at the start when you were being a real asshole to me, but even after you eased off on the tests and all that—I didn't appreciate how far you've come from who you used to be and how hard that must have been. You're nothing like Tempest. I don't know how much you used to be, but you're not now. Not when you're being the ice-cold bastard and not when you let your fire out. In case you still worry about that."

From stray comments he'd made across our conversations over the past weeks, I suspected he did.

Omen sputtered a laugh, which wasn't quite the response I'd hoped to provoke with my attempt at extending an olive branch.

"You're apologizing to *me*?" he said, turning to face me head-on. "I'm the one who had you chained up in anticipation of your possible death less than a week ago."

I folded my arms over my chest. "I'm not saying that was the highlight of my life, but with what you'd heard and the hold the Highest have over you... I get it. It means a lot that you didn't toss me straight to them—that it was a decision you couldn't have made lightly." I paused. "I'm still not totally sure why you *didn't* take the free pass I gave you."

He reached to graze his knuckles down the side of my face, a whisper of a touch that set off a wave of a much more enticing heat. His eyes pinned me in place, incredulous and maybe a little conflicted but not at all scornful. "If you would throw your life on the Highest's mercy just to save two shadowkind, one of whom hadn't given you much reason for generosity, I find it exceedingly hard to believe that you'd turn around and tear down the rest of the world on a whim."

My throat had constricted. "I don't know if I'll get much choice."

"Of course you will. There are always choices. And for all your snark and defiance... you obviously care enough to make the choices that won't result in mass destruction." Omen's gaze dropped for a second before catching mine even more intently. "I should have pieced that fact together well before you had to throw yourself between Thorn and me. You haven't really made a secret of *your* mind-set. I just didn't recognize your altruism for what it was—or maybe I didn't let myself recognize it—until it was that blatant."

I swallowed thickly. "So... you're not still waiting for me to fuck up so you'll have an excuse to haul me off to the Highest after all?"

He looked honestly startled by that question. "Is that what you thought?"

"You haven't exactly been Mr. Talkative since you unchained me, even by your standards."

He stroked his hand down my face again with a tad more pressure than before. My heart skipped a beat. Then it kept right on jitter-bugging away like it was '50s prom night in my chest.

Omen's mouth had twisted. "Ah. Well. There've been things I've known I should say to you, but I hadn't quite settled on how to say them, so I may have erred too much on the side of saying nothing at all." He drew in a long breath. "I need to apologize to you. I *was* far more of an asshole to you than you deserved when we first met, and I should have let up on you sooner—to a greater extent— You've had even less say over the hand you've been dealt than I have, and it's taken you a lot less time to make something admirable out of it. You put my own efforts to shame."

The thought of the hellhound shifter apologizing to anyone, let alone me, was so bizarre that my thoughts kept spinning around his words for several seconds as they slowly sunk in. "So... being nicer to me is your attempt to pull ahead in some competition of who's the most stellar being around?"

Omen let out a huff. "I'm trying to tell you I'm sorry for not recognizing your 'stellar' qualities sooner. Do you always have to make everything as hard as possible?"

A laugh spilled out of me. I still couldn't quite wrap my head around the praise he was offering me, but I knew him well enough now to recognize the gleam of orange fire in his eyes and to note that his hand had lingered against the crook of my jaw as if he wasn't ready to stop touching me yet. I might not know how to respond to kindness from Omen, but I knew what to do with that heat.

I trailed my fingers down the front of his shirt, stopping just an inch above the fly of his slacks. "I can think of one or two things we both enjoy my making harder."

Omen let out a growl, but it was all hunger. Then he was tugging my mouth to his, his lips descending on me with a kiss so blazing it branded me all the way down to my toes.

I gripped his shirt, kissing him back with everything I had in me. No matter how much we'd squabbled, no matter how much we might both have to apologize for, there was nothing but rightness in the way our bodies sparked against each other.

Omen's tongue swept into my mouth. He pulled me tighter against him, one hand on my ass, the other sliding up my side to cup my breast. He was plenty hard already, and the feel of that solid length pressing against me through our clothes sent a shock of heat straight to my sex.

A famous cathedral wasn't where I'd have pictured getting it on with any of my lovers, least of all the most hellish of them, but not a single particle in me had any interest in pausing this encounter to move elsewhere.

Omen pushed me up against one of the columns. A

flicker of his fiery power raced between us—and my inner flames rose up to meet it like they had before. Pleasure burned across every inch of my skin.

The hellhound shifter dropped his mouth to the side of my neck, and I tangled my fingers in the short tufts of his hair, sprung wild in his abandon. The slick of his tongue beneath my chin drew a whimper from my throat.

"Tell me what you want," Omen said, his voice thick with desire and portent.

Oh, there were a hell of a lot of things I wanted, but right now only one seemed to matter. "Fuck me. Fuck me as hard as you can."

A scorching chuckle fell from his lips and spilled hot across my skin. "Just this once, I'll happily submit to your command."

Last time, he'd burned the clothes right off me. Or maybe I'd burned them off myself—it'd been kind of difficult to tell with all the flames dancing around. This time, maybe in recognition that I didn't have an easy change of clothes waiting one room away, he yanked my shirt off the mortal way and tossed it aside instead. There might have been supernatural power in the speed with which he unlatched my bra, though.

A split-second later, he'd sucked my nipple between his teeth with a spike of bliss so sharp I gasped. I held onto his hair and tugged at his shirt with my other hand. His hellish light flared all across his body, and *that* piece of clothing disintegrated into ash. Along with every other piece of clothing he'd been wearing. Lucky me.

I traced my fingers over the taut muscles of his torso,

and his devilish tail, newly freed, teased across my forearm. I couldn't resist wrapping my fingers around its warmth, lithe length. It twitched against my palm, the tip tracing a giddy line along my thigh. Then Omen was tipping me down onto the tiled floor, wrenching the rest of my clothes off as we went.

It shouldn't have been a comfortable surface to sprawl on. But before any chill from the smooth stone could penetrate my skin, a wash of Omen's fire coursed around and beneath me. It cushioned me like the fieriest of duvets.

Omen's mouth branded mine with even more heat, his body poised just above mine. "I will fuck you until you're screaming with the pleasure of it," he promised, so confidently I'd have soaked my panties if I were still wearing any. "But I'm going to take my time enjoying you so I can remember every bit. That first time was something of a blur—a blur of good things, but still."

He grazed his fangs over my collarbone, and I inhaled with a pleased hum. "No arguments here." But maybe one tiny speck of concern, now that we were taking our carnal collision a little more slowly.

As he teased those houndish teeth over my breast, I almost lost my words, but they tumbled out with my next hitch of breath. "We should probably make sure—I'd rather not end up with hell-puppies out of this."

The shifter let out a snort that somehow managed to be as sexy as everything else about him and flicked my nipple with the tip of his tongue. "Not going to happen without the same shadowkind ceremony your mother used. And seeing as only three shadowkind have ever managed that in the history of existence, I think it's doubtful I've undergone it unknowingly."

That did sound like a fair assumption. Especially considering I suspected he'd sear right through anything resembling a condom, not that I had any lying around anyway, and I *really* didn't want to put an end to this fucking before we'd even gotten started.

Omen caught my other nipple in his lips and dipped his hand between my thighs at the same time. The deeper jolt of pleasure wiped away anything else I might have said. I released a growl of my own, my hips arching to meet him. His fingers curled right inside me, hot as every other part of him and setting off fresh flames, but it wasn't half as much as I was hungry for.

"I'm going to take you apart and put you back together again, and you'll be begging for more," Omen murmured. He eased lower down my body with a kiss to my belly.

The sound that slipped from my lips in response wasn't particularly articulate, but I meant it to say something along the lines of, *Sounds fantastic to me, get on with it!* I didn't need to express that sentiment any more clearly, though, because the next second the hellhound shifter had pressed that scorching mouth of his to my core.

Oh, let the angels sing. The force of his lips and the slick of his tongue sent waves of pleasure pulsing through me. All I could do was moan and gaze up at the vast ceiling overhead, the ecstasy building so fast I might as well have been soaring up to meet it.

But Omen made good on his promise to savor the moment. Every time I started soaring toward my release, he eased up just slightly, slowing the flicks of his tongue, teasing with his fingers rather than stroking me to completion. A knot of need built in my core, expanding with each glimpse of a climax.

I clutched the short tufts of his hair, my fingers scraping his scalp. Finally, the words he must have been waiting for spilled out of me in a growl of my own. "Please, damn it. *Please.*"

I felt the curl of Omen's lips against me as he grinned. At a sharp suck on my clit and a deeper plunge of his fingers, I really might have screamed with delight. My vision whited out with a ringing in my ears as I spiraled over the edge into an explosion of bliss.

The flames I lay on rippled beneath my back as if urging my orgasm to greater heights. I'd barely caught my breath, the afterglow pealing through me, before Omen rose up over me. He hefted my hips right off the floor to meet him.

His mouth crashed into mine, smoky with both our flavors, and his rigid cock drove inside me. I wrapped my legs around him and bucked to match his rhythm, wanting more and more as the pleasure swelled through me again. Our flames crackled between us with a stinging that was all joy, no pain.

I wouldn't have thought the shifter could wring even more ecstasy out of my body, but I hadn't counted on all his special features. As our bodies rocked together at an increasingly furious pace, something glided across my ass. The devilish tip of his tail traced gleeful patterns across my skin—and slipped between the cheeks to stroke my other opening.

Another bolt of pleasure raced to join the sensations already surging through me. A gasping cry broke from my mouth.

Omen kissed me as if to drink down that sound. His cock rammed into me to the hilt, his tail teased a giddying trail from behind, and I did break—into a thousand shimmering, scorching pieces, lit up from the inside out.

As I shuddered and sank my fingernails into Omen's back and ass, he groaned. With a few increasingly erratic thrusts, he threw himself after me with what might as well have been a spurt of liquid fire.

As his muscles relaxed, the hellhound shifter lowered us both to the ground, letting some of his weight rest against me. I didn't hesitate to look into his eyes this time. The orange flare mingled with the icy blue in perfect contrast.

He gave me a sardonic smile, as if he couldn't quite bring himself to look totally satisfied even after the vulnerabilities and admiration he'd already admitted to. That diffidence was so perfectly Omen that a flutter of fondness passed through my chest.

A bittersweet pang followed it. Suddenly I was remembering how he'd talked in the palace about his time with Tempest.

I felt the need to clarify the situation, for both our

sakes. "This means more than just fucking. To me, anyway. *You* mean more to me than that." I wasn't totally sure what or how much yet, but I knew what I'd said was true.

Omen's smile softened just slightly around the edges. "I don't think anything with you is ever going to be 'just', Disaster." He dropped his head, his lips grazing my cheek, answering a question I hadn't even formed yet. "You're a finer being than Tempest ever was or could be. As many regrets as I may have collected over the years, you won't be one of them. Even if it damns us both."

An unexpected lump filled my throat. He might be giving up not just his freedom but his life if the Highest found out how he'd betrayed their orders.

I tucked my arm around his neck, and he met me for another kiss, sweeter but no less searing. As he urged my lips apart with his tongue, a lightbulb blinked on in my head. I kissed him even harder and then pulled back.

"What?" Omen asked, looking amused as he took in my expression.

I grinned up at him. "I know how we can get at the Company pricks even if they never set one foot outside."

9

Ruse

After stopping for gas just before we reached the Italian border, Omen took over the driver's seat in the Everymobile. I appreciated the release from that duty, especially since the RV had taken to randomly flashing its blinkers in time with the bells that were dinging through the rumble of the engine. Sinking into the smooth leather padding of the sofa, I got out my phone.

Sorsha sashayed over a moment later with a grin. "Any more dirt from our new hacker associate?" she asked, hopping up to sit on the table with her legs dangling.

She'd had a more buoyant energy to her since she'd come back from the search of Paris's tunnels with her latest brilliant idea. I liked seeing her lit up like this, but at times it seemed almost frenetic, as if she were racing along to stay a step or two ahead of some deeper anxiety.

I also hadn't been able to help noticing that when she'd returned all energized, the smoky smell clinging to her skin hadn't been just her natural fiery scent but a tang of brimstone that belonged to the hellhound shifter as well. How much was she buoyed by her new brainstorm, and how much by whatever the two of them had gotten up to after they must have made their peace?

It was bad enough being an incubus in love without getting jealous about my lover's other partners. Darkness forbid she ever asked for a count of how many women I'd gotten it on with over the centuries. But somehow knowing she'd been hooking up with Omen—and was clearly happy about how that had gone down—rubbed up against other anxieties of my own that had been gnawing at me.

"He hasn't come up with much in the past few hours, but being mortal, he does need to sleep occasionally," I said. "Now that we've determined there's significantly more Company activity happening in Rome than anywhere else on this side of the ocean, he'll be checking for more distinctive patterns there. We'll narrow in on family and friends soon enough."

Sorsha sighed, the swing of her legs slowing. "Of course, it'll only work if the Company employees have been allowed at least a little contact with the people they care about outside. Their boss—the mortal one or Tempest—might have them under a total communications lockdown too."

I gave her thigh a light squeeze. "Then you'll come

up with some other brilliant plan. You've been pulling out the inspiration as fast as your flames."

The Everymobile chose that moment to hiccup, a little lurch vibrating through the entire frame. Sorsha had to grip the edge of the table to keep her balance. Then, like actual hiccups, the RV hitched again. Up at the front, Omen let out a growl of frustration.

"I'm starting to think taking 'Darlene' through a rift wasn't such a great idea," I said, just loud enough to make sure he'd hear me.

Sorsha laughed, broken by another tiny lurch. "She isn't quite the same as she used to be, that's for sure. How do you figure we cure vehicular hiccups? Give her a glass of water? Jump out in front of her to scare her out of it?"

"Well, we did just fill her up with her liquid of choice, so I'm guessing that won't do it." I chuckled along with her for a moment until the fact that I honestly had no idea what to do about our transportation issues or much of anything else clouded over my good humor.

I tried to keep my smirk from faltering, but Sorsha quieted too, her gaze lingering on my face. She slipped off the table, caught my hand, and tugged me toward her bedroom. "Come here a moment."

Ready for more action, was she? My own desires woke up as I followed her down the hall. But even the familiar sensation of lust—and the less-so sensation of a sweeter affection—didn't offer much of a balm to my restless thoughts.

In bits and pieces, the others laid out their encounter with Tempest for me. All the sphinx's haughty remarks and dismissals of their concerns—and her accusation that they'd forgotten their monstrous natures. She hadn't levied that charge at me, but merely because I hadn't been there, I had to assume. The moment Snap had mentioned it with a pained twist of his mouth, I'd felt it like a jab to the gut.

Had I really fallen for Sorsha in defiance of my promiscuous inclinations? Or... had some subtler aspect of my powers simply recognized what a blessing it'd be to have an easy source of nourishment at my side for all time?

She'd been the first mortal—or semi-mortal, at least— to accept me for all I was. I could sate my hunger for pleasure night after night without needing the slightest supernatural seduction. In many ways, it was incredibly *convenient* that I'd found myself longing for a relationship of more commitment with her.

Did I love her, or was convincing myself that I did the biggest con I'd ever pulled yet, this time on myself?

I didn't want to look all that closely at that question. And showing Sorsha a good time of the intimate variety was the one thing I absolutely could do beyond a doubt. So if she wanted that from me, I'd damn well deliver it.

"I hope you know I'd intend to make this last for more than a *moment*," I teased as she shut the bedroom door behind us. "I do have a reputation to uphold."

She poked me in the chest. "I didn't bring you in here for a ravishing, although I won't necessarily say no to that once we're done talking. What's up with you? You've seemed a little out of sorts since we started this trip."

My lover was far too perceptive. I gave a quick laugh and attempted to turn the conversation around. "Have I not been attentive enough, Miss Blaze?"

Sorsha poked me again with an expression that brooked no arguments or foolishness. "You've been perfectly adoring, as I think you know. But we've spent enough time together that I can tell when you're not your usual carefree self, Mr. Charm. I've opened every part of me up to you. Don't you know by now that I'm not going to judge whatever it is that's bothering you?"

A particularly unfamiliar pang of guilt struck me with that question. Our mortal *had* opened herself up— had given me permission to read her mental state even though she'd had a terrible experience with another shadowkind manipulating her mind as a child. She'd said she loved me, and she didn't have any supernatural hunger to give her an ulterior motive.

She'd believed in me, and I'd better get into the habit of believing in her, or I'd lose her regardless of my own motivations.

I tugged her into my arms and ducked my head next to hers. She smelled only like herself now, fiercely sweet. Whatever else might be going on inside me, there was no denying that the feel of her against me released some of the tension in my chest.

"Ruse," she prodded, but her tone had gentled. I could bring that out in her too—the tenderness that complemented her fire so well.

"Omen dragged you off," I said. "He might have thrown you to the Highest to be killed. And there was nothing at all I could do to stop him or to help you. Thorn and Snap got right on the case—hell, even the *imp* might have contributed something, whether it worked out or not."

"You've helped with plenty of other things. Not everyone's talents are going to fit every problem."

"You're the most important thing I've had in my life since... since ever." As I found the words, the truth of that statement cut through me, sharply poignant. Maybe I should have been reassured to put one doubt to rest, but the certainty that my feelings were real only brought my failure into harsher relief. "If I can't do a thing to protect you when your entire existence is on the line, how in the realms could I possibly deserve you?"

Sorsha made a strangled sound and turned in my arms to meet my gaze. She touched my face, her thumb stroking over my cheek, and thanks to this miraculous love I'd found myself capable of, that touch sparked more warmth than I'd ever found in clinching genitals with those untold numbers of other women.

"You know I don't blame you for not throwing yourself in front of the hellhound's jaws, right?" she said. "There wasn't a single moment when Omen had me locked up that I thought to myself, 'Gosh, where is that incubus? He should have rescued me by now.'"

"That doesn't mean you *shouldn't* have been thinking it," I muttered.

"Well, I wouldn't want to be looking at it that way. I don't think love is supposed to be some kind of transaction where you earn enough points to 'deserve' someone. If it was... how the hell would *I* deserve any of you? For all we know, I'm going to explode in a ball of flame at any moment and take you all down with me."

She spoke flippantly, but I caught enough strain in her voice to know that wasn't a totally imaginary fear. Tempest had stirred up doubts in her too. She was worried she might hurt us.

I kissed her temple. "*I* know that's not going to happen. So does everyone else, including Omen, despite his momentary lapse in judgment. If a tiny bit of fire scalds us now and then, we're a pretty resilient lot. And some types of burning are very enjoyable."

Sorsha hummed as if she didn't quite accept my argument but didn't feel like pushing the matter. "That's not the point. I've decided *you* deserve me. I want you in my life for all the wonderful things you do bring into it. And you'd better not be telling me I don't get to make my own decisions."

The corner of my lips quirked up before I could stop it. Our mortal did have her own knack for persuasion. "Woe betide anyone who attempts that." Maybe her proclamation didn't ease my guilt completely, but maybe I should never have been letting that guilt interfere with what we had in the first place. If what I could offer was enough for her, then whether it was enough for me was only a problem between me and myself.

"I suppose I'll be forever wondering how I managed to con you into making that decision," I added, lightly enough to show it was a joke.

Sorsha rolled her eyes at me and did a little shimmy

against me with a lilt of her mixed-up lyrics. "Oh, I, I just glide to your charm, all right? It must have clean gone to my head."

I caught her jaw and drew her so close my nose brushed hers. "I'll show you a lot more than charm," I said, one promise I knew I could make good on, and captured her lips.

Why shouldn't this be enough? Making her laugh, making her sigh with pleasure... I *did* have talents none of our other companions possessed.

I kissed her harder and lowered her onto the bed. Her fingers slid down my chest while the other hand hooked around one of my horns in that way that sent an electric thrill over my skin. I was just easing up her shirt when a tiny scaly body wriggled its way between us as if attempting to join what he saw as a cuddle fest.

"Pickle!" Sorsha protested with a snicker, scooping her hand around the little dragon. Her shadowkind pet let out an indignant chirp. "Have I been neglecting you? I promise you'll have my full attention after I finish this... conversation with Ruse." As she got up to see him out the door, she shot me an amused look. "Sorry. I didn't realize he was in here."

"So much competition for your affection these days," I teased.

"Good thing I have so much to go around." She nudged me back down on the bed, leaning over me, and then paused. "There are different ways of saving someone, you know. Maybe duels to the death aren't your forte, but so many times you've bolstered my spirits when that was what I really needed. I know I can always count on you."

"Sorsha," I said, filled with more emotion than I was prepared to navigate. Getting back to kissing seemed like the simplest way to show her. But before I could bring her mouth to mine, we were interrupted again, this time by the chime of her phone.

Sorsha groaned, but she grabbed her purse. So few people called her that it was likely to be important. Her stance stiffened at the sight of the call display.

"It's Vivi. I've already put her off twice in the last few days."

The hesitation in her voice pricked at me. The woman she was avoiding had once been her best friend— I recalled the fondness her voice used to hold when talking about or to Vivi. But the longer she'd spent with us, the more she'd withdrawn. Was there anyone from her life before meeting us that she hadn't pulled away from?

If she was worried about hurting *us* in our semi-immortal state, how scared must she be when it came to people like Vivi? Did she think putting distance between her and them was the only way *she* could save them... from herself?

It wasn't right for her fears to separate her from the people she'd cared about and who'd cared about her before all this had come to light. Our mortal might be more shadowkind than she'd ever suspected, but that shouldn't mean she didn't deserve human friendship. Perhaps she needed a reminder of that to calm those fears

—a chance to talk to someone who could speak to her non-monstrous side for once.

I sat up next to her and kissed her cheek. "Answer it. I can wait, and you know I can share."

Sorsha drew in a breath and nodded. She hit the answer button. "Hey, Vivi! I know, I know. Things have been crazy, but—I'm sorry."

I propped myself against her pillow, watching the tentative smile cross her lips at her best friend's banter. A deeper contentment than I'd felt in days settled over me.

I'd done at least one thing right here. Perhaps I should remember what she'd said about there being different ways of saving. The ways I could protect Sorsha didn't look anything like Thorn's warrior strength, but that didn't have to mean they mattered so much less, as long as I spotted those opportunities when they came.

10

Sorsha

I peered up at the stucco apartment building, its thin face looming several stories above the street. Patches of orangey-brown and a paler cream color mottled the stucco, and rust speckled the hinges on the antique-looking front door.

"This is the place?"

"Unless our stalwart hacker connected the phone number he traced to the wrong address." Ruse cocked his head and then motioned for me to stand back from the door. "Wait here. I'll take the lay of the land from the shadows first. If we're lucky, we won't even need your thieving skills. The fellow up there is engaged to his Company lady, but they're not living together yet. As far as we know, he's not involved in the Company himself. There's no reason for him to be particularly protected."

Because the Company had no reason to believe the

man up there knew anything that could help their enemies—a.k.a., us. But if his fiancée hadn't let anything useful slip during their phone conversations, Ruse would simply charm the dude into forgetting we'd ever stopped by like he would anyway, and we'd see what other connections his new hacker ally could dig up from back in Paris. Thank all that was wired and wild for the internet.

Ruse stepped into the shadows of the narrow alley between that apartment building and the next—so narrow it'd have been a tight fit for me to walk down it—and vanished. While I waited for his report, I pulled out my phone to give the impression I was occupied with more than just loitering here. The three other members of my shadowkind quartet had come along, but they were staying in the darkness until we knew what we were looking for.

Too bad I couldn't text with them while they were in their shadow forms. My lips quirked at the thought of what enthusiastic observations and dour cautions Snap and Thorn would pass on.

Omen? Who knew what the hellhound shifter would think it worth saying to me. But although he hadn't exactly gotten less enigmatic, I'd felt more comfortable in whatever uncertainties he stirred up since our interlude in the cathedral.

He intended to ensure I made it through this alive, Tempest and the Highest be damned. That much I was convinced of now. And if we had the chance to steal another heated moment or two along the way... I didn't think either of us would turn it down.

Ruse reformed out of the shadows looking pleased with himself. "Not a bit of iron or silver around, at least not enough to be of any concern."

I tucked my phone back into my purse, feeling abruptly adrift. This had been my plan, but it working well meant I didn't have any part to play in it. "I guess I should head back to the Everymobile then."

"Not at all! Come on." He nudged me toward the doorway. "I've already chatted with our host enough to ensure he's open to visitors. You can't come all the way to Rome without doing a little sightseeing. And I promise you, you'll get quite the sight from up there."

As usual, his playful cajoling was irresistible, even without him turning any of his supernaturally-powered charm on me. I tramped after him into a cramped corridor that led to a rickety lift so small I was practically snuggling with the incubus inside its car. Good thing the rest of our companions could shrink to a much smaller size when they traveled through the shadows.

The lift whirred upward with only an occasional wobble. Naturally, Ruse couldn't resist the excuse of the tight space to give my ass a squeeze. I swatted his in return as he got off ahead of me, and he laughed.

I wasn't sure he'd completely dropped the whole "I should have protected you better" idea he'd expressed to me on the drive here, but at least his usual carefree flirtiness was back in full force.

"The rest of you can come out too," he announced to

the landing at large as he knocked on a door that had clearly seen better days. Just as the worn surface with its flaking white paint swung open to admit us, Thorn and Snap materialized behind me.

"Omen wanted to survey this and the surrounding buildings more closely," Thorn informed us in an undertone as we headed inside. His mouth was set at a displeased slant, his near-black eyes scanning the room we stepped into even more warily than usual.

Our charmed Italian host waved us on into a small living room with threadbare chairs, a scratched up coffee table, and a window so big the warrior could have stepped through it with arms outstretched without brushing the frame. It looked out across sprawling parkland toward the grandiose ruins of the Colosseum.

"Wow," I said, needing to catch my breath. Ruse hadn't been lying about the sights. I walked right up to the glass as if drawn by a magnetic pull, taking in the full view up close.

Snap joined me, looping his arms around my waist and pressing a kiss to a sensitive spot just behind my ear that sent a welcome tingle through me. Even the impressive view couldn't distract him from offering the public display of affection, although afterward he leaned his head next to mine, his chin brushing my temple, and considered it with widened eyes.

"That building—it's very old even by mortal standards. Thorn says he was young when he saw it newly built. I don't believe I had come into existence yet."

Shadowkind, not being the type to celebrate birthdays seeing as they weren't quite *born* and, y'know, the whole lack of concept of time in their own realm thing, didn't tend to keep very close track of their age. Snap might have been only a little older than me or decades more. But in the mortal world, he was still pretty much a newbie.

"Lots of battles fought in that place," I told him, trailing my fingertips over his knuckles. Was his embrace even more insistent than usual? Maybe seeing Ruse grope me on the elevator had woken up his possessive instinct with a fiercer edge. "Mostly for fun, though—for the people watching, anyway. Like those soccer games you saw on my TV, back when I had a TV."

And an apartment to house that TV in. I couldn't even blame my shadowkind companions for that loss when I was the one who'd set the place on fire. Of course, they'd been the ones who'd brought the Company to my doorstep attempting to kidnap and possibly kill me. But who was keeping score?

Thorn came up at my other side. "Mortals do have strange priorities at times."

I raised my eyebrows at him. "Says the wingéd who fought in some immense war for reasons he can't even remember?"

He let out a grunt as if accepting my point, but his frown made me wonder if I'd gone too far with my teasing. Or maybe something else was bothering him. He'd looked a little more serious than usual since he'd appeared, which for the warrior was pretty dire.

I shifted in Snap's embrace, and the devourer let me go with only a faint noise of discontent. I stepped closer to the wingéd and tucked my arm around his muscular one. Sometimes it was easy to forget how passionate a heart lay under all this bulk and brawn, but in some ways, my warrior lover was the most deeply affected out of all of them.

I twined my fingers with his. "Is everything okay? Did Omen notice something that made him think we could be in trouble here?"

Thorn shook his head. "Not that I'm aware of. I believe he simply meant to confirm there were no signs of Tempest's presence, as he's best equipped to identify that." He let his hand come to rest on my hip with an affectionate stroke of his thumb, but his gaze shifted to the horizon beyond the Colosseum. "There is at least one other nearby who might remember what we fought for."

Another wingéd? Thorn could sense when any of the few remaining members of his kind were nearby—that was how we'd found Flint. It made sense that he'd be encountering more of them as we jetted all across the world. He didn't seem all that happy about it, even though he'd already revealed his nature to the rest of us.

I squeezed his hand. "Maybe they'd join in, like Flint did. You persuaded him easily enough."

"Perhaps. But to have lingered mortal-side in much closer vicinity to the terrain of our shame... I'm not certain what their mindset might be."

"It can't hurt to ask, can it?" Snap said brightly, turning from the view. "Bringing more shadowkind on

board has only helped us, as Sorsha expected it would."
He leaned in to give me another peck, this time on the
temple.

"But those that do not come on board have the
potential to cause trouble," Thorn muttered.

Did he think this wingéd might outright work against
us? It was hard to imagine a being with a similar solemn
nature to his and Flint's taking a stance like Tempest's,
but then, there were a lot of ways a powerful warrior
could be destructive if he—or she—got the idea to be.

Behind us, Ruse's dupe let out a loud burst of
laughter. I swiveled to watch the incubus's
"interrogation." The wingéd left off his brooding enough
to turn with me at my tug.

Our host chattered away in eager Italian, so fast I
didn't catch a single word I even partly recognized,
although my local vocabulary was admittedly mostly
limited to "spaghetti" and "fettuccine." The man's hands
swept through the air with each exclamation. Ruse
nodded and retorted something in the same language
with a perfectly authentic accent. Apparently languages
came to the incubus naturally too.

Watching the mortal guy's gesticulations, I tried to
guess what they might be talking about. The apartment
building was growing yet another floor? Pineapple was
the best ever pizza topping? We should all hop on a Ferris
wheel for a ride?

Ruse's voice dropped, his demeanor turning more
serious. He made several statements with some dramatic
gestures of his own. I was pretty sure the jerk of his hand

was the shutting—or opening?—of a door. A flap of his hands like wings—indicating some sort of shadowkind creature? From his tone, he was getting down to business.

His dupe's smile faded too, but he responded with as much emotion as before, just sounding upset instead of excited now. He mimed something that I was going to assume was *not* icing flowers on a cake, however much it might look that way, and then what might have been an explosion. That didn't give me the impression of good news. If it'd been an explosion of joy, surely he'd have looked happier about it.

As the incubus and our charmed host continued their urgent discussion, Omen slipped out of the shadows by the bathroom doorway and ambled over to us. He caught Ruse's eye but didn't say anything. The incubus acknowledged him with a quick tip of his head.

"Do you understand what they're saying?" Snap asked him, nuzzling my hair.

"I can pick up a little, but I haven't spent much time in this country in centuries, and the language has, you might say, evolved."

"Indeed," Thorn rumbled. "And not for the better."

I nudged him gently with my elbow. "Kids these days and their crazy slang, huh?"

The warrior shot me a wounded glance, but the effect was diminished by the hint of amusement that glinted in his eyes. "I seem to manage to keep up with you, m'lady."

"So you do. In so many wonderful ways."

Omen cleared his throat in what I took as a shockingly polite way to say, *Shut up*, but I'd have shut my mouth anyway at the tense expression on Ruse's face as he rejoined us. His new friend was sitting on one of the chairs, head bowed and shaking in some sort of denial.

"His fiancée hadn't told him very much," the incubus said, his voice uncharacteristically grim. "But I was able to draw out a decent amount of information from piecing together what he has heard and seen and unconscious impressions from his mind. The Company definitely has major operations happening here. They're particularly focused on this disease they hope to spread to the shadowkind. And his woman on the inside has been talking as if they're just days away from releasing it."

11

Sorsha

Getting into the Colosseum wasn't a cakewalk, but I'd slinked through tighter situations before. With an only mildly scraped elbow from one particularly rough bit of stone I'd had to scramble over, I slipped away from the towering walls of the former stands to where Omen was standing in the moonlight on the stretch of smooth flooring at one end of the massive arena.

He had his arms folded over his chest as if he'd been waiting there for a while, but not all of us could dart invisibly through shadows to avoid all security measures. I spread my arms to say, *Here I am*, and glanced around at the space he'd decided we should use for my next training session.

The span of even terrain ended several feet away at a pit full of deteriorating stone walls and arches that rose nearly to ground level. Strange to imagine that some two thousand years ago, gladiators and beasts had battled their way across this stage... and now here I was, about to enter a different sort of battle. Whether it'd be more with the hellhound shifter in front of me or my inner demons, I'd find out soon enough.

"All right," I said. "What's the big idea? Or did you just want a place with as much room as possible in case my powers explode?"

Omen gave me a narrow look. "If you're going to play a significant role in taking Tempest out of commission, you'll need to develop that focus of yours even more than I anticipated. Since you have a lot more practice with physical rather than mental gymnastics, I figured we'd start with that." He tipped his head toward the broken ground ahead of us. "Let's see you make a circuit of the arena. No falls."

Yeah, I didn't think falling that far would have been a good idea even if he hadn't made it one of the rules. I dragged in a breath of the cool night air, a dry mossy scent filling my lungs, and made a running start of it.

I vaulted over the little metal fence meant to stop tourists who didn't have a death wish from tumbling into the depths and landed on the top of the nearest arch with only a slight sway. *This* part was a piece of cake. I'd scrambled along ledges higher and narrower than this dozens of times.

Making my way around the arena was like a combination of a tightrope walk and an obstacle course, one that mostly involved leaps and bounds. Any part of it might not have been the most difficult feat I'd had to pull off, but I'd never had to play quite such an extended game of hopscotch. By the time I'd circled back around toward the platform, sweat was trickling down my neck beneath my ponytail and my calf muscles had a few things to say about my chosen nighttime activity, none of them pleasant.

I did make it back to Omen with nothing worse than a little fatigue and a tiny ache in my heel where I'd landed on an especially obnoxious lump on one of the crumbling walls. As per usual, the hellhound shifter kept any overt signs of approval to himself.

"Good," he said in his terse voice. "We know you can survive the journey. Let's make it challenging now."

He vanished into the shadows and reappeared only as flickers here and there along the course I'd followed— where pale squares of what I quickly deduced was paper blinked into being on top of the aged stone protrusions. Omen had planted at least twenty of them before he returned to the platform, swiping his hands together with a hint of satisfaction with his work.

"You want me to light them all up?" I asked before he had to give the order.

The corner of his mouth curled upward just slightly, but that ghost of a smile was enough to bring back the memories of our interlude in the cathedral. I didn't think the heat that washed through me at that thought was the sort he'd wanted to inspire, but it *was* a lot less likely to literally burn me.

Maybe we could enjoy an impassioned work break in

here too? Make this a grand tour of fucking across the landmarks of Europe?

The flash of orange in his cool eyes suggested he might have guessed at my thoughts—or had similar thoughts of his own. But Omen was sadly very good at keeping it in his pants. He motioned to the path he'd laid. "You know how this works. Get to it. Extra points if you can light them all up on your first time around without having to stop."

"And without lighting myself up in the process."

"Yes, I assumed that went without saying."

"I don't know. Sometimes you like it when I bring out the fire up close and personal," I teased, and sprang over the fence before he could grouse about me not taking the training seriously enough.

I couldn't say I'd ever been an avid student, but I'd take this version of training over most of Omen's past methods, which had included speeding toward me in a camper van and nearly torching Pickle in an attempt to terrify me. The majestic sprawl of the arena and the haze of the night sky overhead made it easy to leave any worries that'd been niggling at me behind and give myself over to the moment.

No matter what anyone said, the fire inside me was *mine*. I was going to figure out how to work with it or die trying... and we'd just ignore the fact that the latter possibility had sometimes seemed way too likely for comfort.

I narrowed my awareness down to the little white squares that caught the moonlight, the momentum of my body soaring from perch to perch, and the flames that rose in my chest at my beckoning. Out, out, out, just a little at a time, enough of a jolt of heat to set that slip of paper and the next one curling and blackening under a bright flare.

I didn't quite manage a perfect run. My balance wobbled after one particularly long leap, and I had to stop and gather myself before I could incinerate the paper there and dash onward. But Omen was fully smiling by the time I reached him.

"You always do rise to the challenge, don't you, Disaster?" he said in a tone warm enough that I had to restrain the urge to grab him by the shirt and see what else I could make rise.

"Maybe one of these days you'll have to stop calling me a disaster," I retorted instead.

He chuckled. "Don't take it as commentary on your present skill-set. It reminds me of where we started."

"And how far we've come?"

"That too." He tapped my chin. "Tempest isn't going to know what hit her when we unleash your powers for real." Then he stepped back and sprang into the shadows again to reset his course, laying out more papers this time —because no matter how much he might like me now, I knew better than to expect he'd ever cut me any slack.

As I readied myself to race through the course again, a trickle of heat, maybe at the thought of Tempest and her sneer, prickled across my back. I smacked at it as well as I could over my shoulder. The little flames that had emerged nipped my fingers before they settled down.

Shit on a soda cracker. How was I supposed to stop the self-scorching side of my powers from emerging when half the time it seemed to come out of nowhere? If the trick was never feeling annoyed about anyone anywhere, I was screwed.

My frustration must have shown on my face when Omen reappeared. He looked me over with a particularly searching expression. "Are you good to go again?"

Asking rather than ordering—that was an improvement. I rolled my shoulders and dragged in a breath. I hadn't *really* hurt myself, now or any time before. My shadowkind powers healed me up faster than a regular human would have, almost as easily as they burned me in the first place. If a few blisters here and there came with the territory, I could handle that, as long as it meant I was taking down the baddies at the same time.

"No problemo," I said. "You can't start a fire without a spark."

"As you would know better than most. Get on with it, then."

Even with the extra targets, I made it through that round and the next without faltering and with all the papers at least singed if not turned to ashes. I'd also scalded a couple more spots down my spine and the backs of my arms, but ignoring the stinging was working out okay. If I could hide it well enough that Omen wasn't noticing, then that was some kind of improvement.

When I'd finished the last lap, I paused to lean against the railing. A yawn stretched my jaw before I could catch it. At least part of the reason I hadn't outright burst into flames was the sweat now sticking my damp shirt to my skin.

"All right," Omen said. "That's enough obstacle-course running for one night. You've come a long way. There's one more thing I think we should work on."

"Sure. What's that?" I shook the fatigue out of my limbs as well as I could, doing my best to tune out the tender spots my shirt rubbed against.

They'd heal. No big deal. I wasn't letting nerves stop me from stopping that psychotic sphinx.

"We can't forget what makes you such a formidable foe—what you bring to the table that none of the rest of us can." Omen stepped into the darker recesses of the building and pulled a sack from a shadowy nook. I thought I saw him suppress a wince, though from the heft of it, the bag couldn't be that heavy.

Then he upended the bag in the middle of the platform, and I understood. He'd brought several metal items, some silver and some iron.

I studied his face. "You hauled all this in here? You could have asked—"

He waved me off. "I can survive being in close proximity for a little time here and there. I just can't manipulate it well enough to effectively use it. But if *you* can bind Tempest with silver and iron, she won't be able to escape into the shadows like she did the last time. You can force her to hold her physical form, and then we'll have a real chance of taking her down."

"Right. So what exactly am I doing with this right now?"

"I'm having a chain manufactured that'll combine both metals and be long enough to wrap around her, but it won't be ready until tomorrow. For the moment, I'd imagine it'd be most useful for you to practice melting this stuff. Get used to how much fire you need to summon to heat the metal to that point. You'll want to meld the chain right around Tempest to be sure she can't simply shake it off."

I'd melted the silver-and-iron bars of Company cages before. This wasn't so different. I sifted through the collection of items, raising an eyebrow at a few of them. The ornate silver sugar bowl looked like it'd been stolen from Versailles itself, and the cast iron frying pan would have been very satisfying whacking into the sphinx's head all on its own. A little tricky to keep hidden until the right moment, though.

I focused on the smaller pieces first, letting the floodgates inside me ease open until the searing sensation rose to my throat. A burst of flames reduced a silver necklace to a shimmering puddle. A sharper spurt of fire liquified an iron bar the size of my thumb. The burns I'd given myself earlier prickled, but no fresh ones broke out on my skin. Two victories in one.

The frying pan proved the most difficult. I glared at it for a full minute before the flames I'd called up brought the edges and handle sagging down.

My frustration sparked an answering flare across my

hip. I swiped at it, hoping Omen was too distracted by the metal spectacle to notice.

"You won't have to work with anything that dense when we face Tempest," he said. "Good to know you could if we needed you to."

I let out a hoarse guffaw, twice as weary as before even though I'd barely moved in the past half hour. "As long as whoever I'm trying to melt that pan at doesn't mind waiting around while I work up to it."

"Hey." Omen touched my shoulder, thankfully not on any spot where I'd barbequed myself. His tone turned unusually gentle. "You've got this. She thinks she knows all, and that's her biggest downfall. She's got no idea what she's in for when you really step up to the plate."

"She doesn't really know you anymore either," I reminded him, and couldn't resist the opportunity to lean in and claim a kiss. If it was as much to reassure myself that he was still invested in this—and in me—as to satisfy a pang of desire, I didn't see how anyone could blame me.

Omen kissed me back, his hand sliding up to tease over my hair, but it seemed a world tour of landmark sex spots wasn't in the cards tonight. When he drew back, despite the hellish heat glinting in his eyes, he looked intent in his typical all-business way.

Maybe even more serious than usual. He didn't speak as we crossed the platform to the Colosseum's looming walls, or after our separate trips through the shadows, when I caught up with him on the street a block away. A pensive furrow had formed in his brow.

We'd left the Everymobile—and the rest of our crew

—parked in a lot nearby that had cleared out for the night. The city bus guise still functioned decently well. It had even adapted to the city. I just hoped no one wondered why this particular city bus featured a whirling satellite dish on its roof.

The second I stepped inside, Snap hustled to my side to escort me to the table and tuck his arm around me there. Ruse had picked up pizza to indulge in, and they'd left a few slices for the one member of the party who actually *needed* that kind of food.

After I'd downed one of those, I didn't feel half as exhausted. I leaned back in Snap's arms, letting my other hand come to rest on Thorn's thigh where he'd sat down beside me, bolstered by the presence of all four of my lovers and the other allies who'd followed us this far as well.

"From what Tempest said when we met up with her and what Ruse got from the guy here, we should make our move soon," I said, looking at Omen. "She survived an onslaught of wingéd in the past. How are *we* even going to get close enough to attack her?"

"With extreme difficulty. But it's occurred to me that we may have already hit on the perfect strategy. One that doesn't involve our own wingéd, at least not right away." He glanced from Thorn to Flint with a slightly apologetic tip of his head. "No criticism meant to present company, but the wingéd aren't exactly known for subtlety or slyness. I'm not sure we'll ever get her in a position where we could attempt that kind of onslaught again, let alone succeed in it."

"Unfortunately, I suspect I can't charm her into going along with our requests," Ruse said.

"No. But another aspect of our mortal's recent plans may point us in the right direction." Omen let out a sharp breath. "There isn't much Tempest cares about other than her own satisfaction—but she did value the association she and I had enough to reach out to me rather than simply rebuffing us. She offered us the chance to join her based on that association. I think we may be able to work with that."

The thought of cozying up to Tempest in any way made my skin crawl, but I nodded. "In what way?"

"I can put out word that I've reconsidered and I'd like to join forces with her. She'll be wary, but she'll believe it enough to meet up again. Her ego is too big for her to dismiss the possibility entirely. You and I will go alone. I'll present you as a weapon we can use for her cause, as if you're under my control. When her guard is down, you'll strike—hard enough to at least give me an opening to finish this."

"And by 'finish', you mean...?"

Antic did a little dance between the table while dramatically dragging her finger across her neck. Omen grimaced at her, but he didn't object to the gist of her suggestion.

"She should have left this world centuries ago. It's time that reprieve came to an end. As long as she remains living, she's proven herself an immense threat to mortals and shadowkind alike." He paused, his gaze settling on me. "And the Highest will be much more likely to grant *you* a reprieve if we have irrefutable proof that you dispatched her."

He was willing to kill one of his former friends—but after what I'd seen of her, I couldn't summon much discomfort at the thought. I'd burned up dozens of mortal Company lackeys so far. If they'd deserved it, then Tempest did a thousandfold more for urging them on.

Thorn stirred next to me. "I believe I should speak to the other wingéd nearby in case we require more manpower after all, concerns about our capacity for subterfuge aside."

"It never hurts to have a backup plan. Tell them what they need to hear." For the first time ever, Omen sank onto the sofa-bench across from me. He rested his forearms against the edge of the table. "Sorsha and I will need some time to go over our opponent's weaknesses. One thing I can say without a doubt—we're only going to get one chance at this trick. And if we miss the mark, Tempest *will* make us pay."

12

Thorn

S tanding in the vast courtyard, looking up at the peaked dome topping the majestic building ahead of us, an uncomfortable tightness spread over my limbs. The columns framing the courtyard and the weathered stone of their construction brought back far too many echoes of the archaic times before the war that had nearly ended the entirety of the wingéd race. The fact that Flint and I were on the verge of addressing two more survivors of that catastrophe didn't do anything to alleviate my uneasy spirits.

As we crossed the courtyard through the shadows of the buildings and passing tourists, my companion gave off an equally discomforted vibe alongside his usual dour energy. When we'd found Flint, he'd been living alone in a hut in the middle of the desert, flagellating himself mentally—and perhaps physically, not that I was inclined to check for the scars—for remaining while so many of our kind had died. That had been mere weeks ago.

I was only just coming to terms with the idea that my survival might have been the result of keen thinking on my part rather than a failing of valor. But Sorsha had been right when she'd pointed out that I scarcely recalled what we'd even been fighting about. More and more I was coming to believe that if I'd heeded my doubts back then *more* rather than less, the outcome for all my brethren might have been better.

There was no telling what we might encounter with the two wingéd I could sense in this place the mortals called the Vatican, though. For them to have chosen to linger on the rooftop in such a place did not bode well for them having moved beyond wallowing in our history. As one who might have wallowed now and then myself, I was well-equipped to recognize the signs.

But they were here, and every wingéd had a warrior's instincts and power. We needed allies now more than ever. And I would like to contribute something to our current cause beyond nearly battering our commander into a senseless pulp.

That was all the mortal woman who'd earned my heart had seen from me in recent days. How could I stake any claim on her affections in days to come, let alone as large a claim as I'd have liked to make, if all I could offer her was brutality and gore?

I'd brought Flint into our band. I could do the same with these two. Act the diplomat rather than the barbarian.

"I do not like the echoes of this place," Flint muttered as we drew close to the main building. "Why do so many mortals flock to it?"

"They weren't alive to experience the past these structures harken back to," I said. "The echoes are more fanciful than real for them."

He replied with only a grunt. Without needing to discuss our approach, we rose up through the shadows around the columns that framed the doorway, aiming for the rooftop where our brethren's presence rang out most strongly.

They'd set up their sort-of camp around the back of the intricate dome. High above the surrounding buildings, I allowed myself to step from the patches of darkness into physical form to meet them in a presentation more suited to this realm. If they wouldn't even detach themselves from the shadows, they wouldn't be much use to us in our conflict.

The warmth of the morning sunlight steadied me. "My brethren," I said, low but loud enough to carry around the pale stone. "We come to pay our respects in a time of great need."

The dual impressions shifted, coming around to the side of the dome one right behind the other. Something about their form in the darkness sent a skittering sensation through my nerves. Then they materialized onto the dingy concrete, and I understood why.

Both of the figures, one male and one female, had the same stature and might Flint and I could boast. They were also both damaged beyond the abilities of their shadowkind powers to heal.

The man stood lopsided, one of his arms missing and little more than a hollow where his right shoulder had been, the flesh there twisted into thick, knobby scars. The woman had lost her left leg from the knee down, a worn wooden post fixed in its place, but more striking was her face, where half of her jaw had been carved away.

We could form our physical features and dissolve them again as we leapt from and back into the shadows, but those features were set in our essence... and if they were damaged beyond repair, they remained so, just as a shadowkind who died mortal-side remained dead. By all appearances, these two had only narrowly escaped the latter fate.

A different sort of uneasiness rippled through my chest. Even with the mangling of her face, the sight of the woman wingéd struck me with an unexpected sense of familiarity.

One she evidently shared. Her gaze skimmed over us and settled on me. Her voice came out warbled around the remains of her jaw, but no less weighty for it. "If it isn't Thorn. Back after all these years to finally attend to the wreckage you left behind, are you?"

My lungs constricted. I drew myself up to the full extent my considerable frame would allow. "What do you speak of?"

"Oh, do you not even remember those you fought alongside? You once stood shoulder to shoulder with one

I might have called my brother, we came into being so near together and so similar in nature."

That was what I recognized. In her violet eyes, in her silvery hair, there were echoes of another aspect of the past. My own voice came out quieter than before. "You speak of Haze."

He'd been one of my closest comrades. I couldn't count the times we'd fought together shoulder to shoulder. How many times I must have deflected a lethal blow before it could land on him and the same from him for me. Until that last battle when I'd abandoned my post and failed to return in time.

The woman who'd considered him even more than a comrade simply stared at me with her stormy eyes. More words slipped from my mouth unbidden. "I searched for him. If there'd been anything I could have done—"

"You could have remained with us and fought as you were meant to," she spat out. "Instead you took a coward's way."

Not long ago, I might have accepted that judgment without argument. It would only have been how I'd already judged myself. But now, a protest rose up. "I didn't leave for cowardice. I left because I saw how many of us had already fallen, and it seemed wrong to me that we tore into each other so violently over matters none of us truly understood. I meant to prevent the battle altogether if I could."

The man guffawed. "Prevent the battle? Are you wingéd or weakling? It was our duty to stand with our brethren and respond to the call to war. That we linger at all is our own shame, but *you*—those minor scars show how little you paid."

The comment summoned the sphinx's harsh remarks from days ago—her accusation that I'd forgotten what I was. From her the suggestion had rankled; hearing the same from one of my own drove it deeper. The stabbing of guilt, my constant companion of many centuries, lanced through my gut as I'd thought it never would again. *Had* I strayed too far from what I was meant to be?

I swallowed thickly. "What is done is done. I believed it was for the best for us all—including you, including Haze. There is no glory or benefit in dwelling in the shame. We have other wars in which we are needed, where we might see a better outcome for all our kind if we respond to the call."

What remained of the woman's lips curled into an undeniable sneer. "Is that what you're here for? To call us into some new fray—what, so that you can see us cut down even more while you stand back and simply watch?"

She might have summoned up old guilts, but I hadn't lost my sense of honor. "I have already spilled more blood and protected more of my kind in these past weeks than I'd imagine you have in centuries."

At her wince, a deeper pang of guilt struck me. That statement had been a blow in itself, one that should have been beneath me. I coughed and fumbled for the right recovery.

"I do not mean to criticize. You have borne a terrible burden, one greater than my own ever was. I respect that.

It is simply that we face a far greater threat to all shadowkind than we ever encountered in the ages long past. There has never been a greater cause. I wouldn't step back from this one even for a moment, knowing how much hangs in the balance."

"It is our chance to win where we lost before," Flint spoke up in his hollow of a voice. "An opportunity to make something of the shame of our continued existence, to make it more than a matter of shame."

There, he could speak their grim language better than I could now. But our two brethren looked unconvinced. The woman worked her fractured jaw from side to side in a nauseating motion. "You betray us all that time ago and now you seek our help? Ha!"

Was clinging to her sense of righteousness more important to her than doing what was needed in this moment, regardless of who was delivering the message?

Perhaps, knowing my kind, that was a foolish question. Of course it was.

I ignored the sting of the word "betray" and focused on the now. "The existence of *all* life in both realms may be at stake. This isn't a matter of my own wants but of the greater good."

"So you say," the man remarked. "We have no one's word for it but yours and this one you've already deluded."

Frustration prickled up from beneath the guilt. "If you'll come with me, you can speak to others who can assure you the impending disaster is far too real. It would merely—"

"No," the woman interrupted. "You will not appear out of nowhere and demand an even greater sacrifice from us, you who sacrificed so little. If you truly wish to atone for the offenses of centuries ago, you will honor those fallen, including Haze, now."

Some part of me wrenched at the thought that there might be something I could do for those who'd met their deaths in my stead, as difficult as I found it to imagine what that might be. "How would you have me honor them?" I asked.

"We had a box..." She looked down at her hands. "Of mortal make, but as fine as anything you ever saw. It held what fragments we could gather of those who fell completely, including my greatest brother at arms. But a pack of griffins sensed the power lingering in those remains and flew off with it. In our deficient state, we haven't the power to challenge them and win it back."

A pack of griffins. The creatures with their mix of eagle and lion features could be formidable foes, but no match for an uninjured wingéd unless in immense numbers. "I could see to that. Where has this pack absconded to?"

"We know not," the man replied. "It was some years ago, and we weren't able to continue pursuing them. They are territorial creatures, though. No doubt they are still somewhere in this region."

By region he might have meant all of Italy or even the Mediterranean. "Years ago," I repeated, my heart sinking.

The woman let out a sharp huff. "Far less time than you've spent skulking around offering nothing in recompense. Are you only willing to lend your strength when it's *easy*?"

The words gnawed at me even though I knew they weren't true. But—what *had* I offered to make up for the losses my brethren had suffered in my absence?

"The matter we are currently engaged with is urgent," I said, groping for a middle-ground. "If you would see that through with us, as soon as we are sure of the security of the realms, I would gladly—"

"Ha!" the woman said again. "I see how it is. No, you go back to your playing at honor while we remember how the world truly is. Do you think our own matters have no urgency? The griffins tear at the remains and devour them scrap by scrap... I can feel even from a distance Haze's last fragments of energy fading away..."

Her face twisted with such agony that my stomach twisted alongside it. How long could it take to track down a roving gaggle of griffins for the sake of my old comrades? To show I hadn't abandoned all concern for them as I'd abandoned our battle?

But what might happen to Sorsha and the others if I left *their* sides for long enough to see to address this issue?

Flint was watching me with obvious uncertainty. I took in the ruin of my brethren's bodies again—the ruin I'd been able to escape by shirking my duty, regardless of the purity of my motives—and an oath tumbled out before I could rethink it.

"I swear I will help you in the best way I can, as I owe and have always owed those who fought and fell."

13

Sorsha

O men had been right about one thing: Tempest cared about him enough to agree to another meeting. It'd have been nice if she hadn't insisted on holding that meeting a three-hour drive away, but hey, why shouldn't we get in some more sightseeing now that we'd come this far from home?

We parked the Everymobile and our restless companions a couple of miles from the site she'd chosen, because Omen had promised he'd "deliver" me to her on his own, and the sphinx would sense any other shadowkind who ventured nearby. As we got out, the hellhound shifter caught Thorn's eye and pointed toward the night sky.

"You and Flint can hover in the darkness up there where you have a decent view of the tower area. As soon as any flames come out, get your asses to us as quickly as possible." He cast his gaze toward the others. "The rest of you, stay put and out of trouble."

Snap frowned and tugged me to him for a quick but demanding kiss, as if to remind me why I'd better come back. Ruse didn't look all that pleased to be left behind either, but his contribution in charming the Company woman's fiancé seemed to have eased some of his doubts about his worthiness.

"Give her hell for us," he said to both me and Omen.

Antic hopped from foot to foot in a frenetic dance around the two of us, looking like a little kid who desperately needed to pee. "Are you sure I can't do anything—cause a distraction? Get her guard down with a laugh? I haven't even seen this crazy lady yet!"

"Believe me, you're better off that way," Omen said dryly.

I had a vision of Tempest pouncing on the imp like a lion on a wobbly baby gazelle. "We can produce some laughs," I assured her. "The two of us are practically a comedy act."

She looked at me skeptically while Omen let out a resigned huff. Even if this was the most important scheme we pulled off in his entire crusade, he didn't expect me to take it with Thorn-level solemnity, did he?

At least we didn't have a two-mile trudge ahead of us. After we'd walked a few blocks, Omen hailed one of the few taxis cruising the city late into the night. As I sat down in the back seat, my purse clinked faintly.

The cab took off, and Omen glanced over at me. "Are you ready for this?"

I nodded, even though "ready" wasn't exactly the word I'd have used. I was ready to accept that there was no way I'd ever feel more prepared to face off against a shadowkind psychotic genius than I did right now, so we might as well get it over with. We'd trained more throughout the day. I knew the movements I wanted to make by heart. But neither of us could predict exactly how Tempest would behave once we had her in front of us.

Would the silver-and-iron chain in my purse be enough to restrain her voodoo? Would I manage to meld the ends into place around her in time? How much of myself would I scorch while burning her eyes blind?

All very good questions I'd soon have the answer to, whether I liked them or not.

It wasn't hard to tell when we were coming up on our destination. The Leaning Tower of Pisa caught the light from the streetlamps on its pale, slanted surface, looking for all the world like a several-tiered wedding cake a few seconds from toppling over. Here was hoping our little duel didn't give it the final shove. I'd already destroyed one city landmark in the course of this crusade.

Tempest wasn't visible when we first stepped out, but a couple of young men were standing near the base of the tower. I hesitated, not sure how we could go through with this meeting when we had mortal spectators, but the sphinx materialized out of the darkness a moment later in between the two guys without showing any concern at all. Actually, she patted one of them on the shoulder with the air of someone petting a dog.

She'd dressed differently but no less lavishly for this occasion. Tonight's robe looked like a toga, I guessed to fit the Italian theme, but not your standard white sheet. No, when Tempest wore a toga, naturally it had to be rich crimson silk adorned with an ornate golden clasp and stitched with glinting gemstone beads. While we were in view of the public—though quiet—streets, the thick locks of her bronze hair lay peacefully around her head, but as I watched, a couple of them twitched as if jonesing for the chance to fly free.

I couldn't get close to her just yet. Judging by his own sensitivity, Omen had estimated that she wasn't likely to notice the chain of noxious metals I was carrying as long as I kept at least ten feet away, ideally more just to be safe. I stopped on the grassy lawn that filled much of the yard around the tower and curled my fingers around my purse strap, resisting the urge to check yet again that I'd left the top open so I could dip my hand inside in an instant.

Omen ambled forward with an unusually casual air— but then, he *was* supposed to be convincing Tempest that he was here to make friends. He tipped his head toward the sphinx's mortal lackeys. "You brought company. I thought we were meeting alone."

"You have your semi-human toy, so I figured I was allowed two that are fully human." Tempest gave her mortal underlings a disdainfully amused glance. "Not that they serve much use here, but it does delight me to have them assist what they hate so much."

Did they know what she was, then? How could any

member of the Company of Light tolerate being ordered around by a shadowkind?

The same way we'd managed it in the past, no doubt. "You've got them under some kind of spell," I couldn't help saying, even though I'd been meant to keep my mouth shut. Omen should know by now to allow a little leeway whenever that rule was part of a plan that involved me.

Tempest let out a lilting chuckle. "Oh, hardly. I asked a riddle, and they couldn't answer it, and that bound them to protect me until the effect wears off, unless they die serving that purpose in the meantime." She gazed through her eyelashes at the man she'd patted. "If it wasn't for that, you'd want to murder me just like you do all shadowkind, wouldn't you?"

"You're a monster," the guy said stiffly. "All our work goes toward ridding this world of you and those like you. As soon as I'm out from under this magic—"

Tempest waved her hand in a bored gesture to stop him. "Yes, yes. We'll see about that." Her gaze slid back to me. "Does it bother you, semi-mortal that you are, to hear how viciously your own kind hates the monstrous side you've uncovered?"

I managed to speak with an impressive amount of calm. "Not as much now that I know they've all had someone magically pulling the strings behind the scenes."

The broken-glass laugh I remembered from Versailles tinkled out of her. "Do you think I conjured their hatred? I only gave them a purpose to put it toward, one they leapt to pursue oh so easily. I have no supernatural power that allows me to change the contents of men's minds or produce motivation where there is none—Omen can attest to that."

The hellhound shifter's expression was all the confirmation I needed. "I'd imagine you talked a good game leading them down the garden path, though," he said lightly. "You are a master of words."

"Hmm," Tempest purred. "To some extent. They certainly have no idea everything they're in for, but that's only in regards to how their goal will affect them, not us." She nudged the man beside her. "Why do you want to slaughter all shadowkind?"

"Why call them that?" he said immediately, with a disgusted curl of his mouth as he glared at her. "We all know they're monsters, like you are. They lurk in the shadows and steal from us, stalk us—we'll never be safe until they're gone from this world."

"And who told you all that about these monsters?"

"No one needed to tell me. The first Company hunter I worked under showed me. The one we trapped would have slashed us all to pieces if we hadn't acted quickly enough."

The sphinx arched her eyebrows. "And what makes you so sure we're all like that?"

"Look at what you're doing to us right now," the man shot back. "Forcing us to be here against our will, to help you, over a stupid question I couldn't answer. As soon as that magic wears off, I'm going to—"

"You know what, I can see now that bringing two of you may have been overkill. I won't force you to endure this apparent misery any longer." Tempest swung back her hand, flicked a row of knife-like claws from her fingers, and drove them straight into the side of the guy's head.

I bit back a cry, biting my tongue at the same time. The metallic flavor of blood seeped through my mouth as the same liquid seeped across the young man's head.

His eyes rolled up, and he collapsed to the ground the second the sphinx retracted her claws. She wiped her hand nonchalantly on the other man's shirt, ignoring his flinch. "There. Am I not merciful?"

They weren't wrong to call *her* a monster, in every meaning of that word. But at the same time, she'd made their human monstrousness all too clear. As much as I'd have liked to believe that I could blame the horrors of the Company of Light on this one shadowkind being, I'd met too many independent hunters and collectors over the years. That depth of hatred and revulsion could absolutely dwell in mortal hearts without any coaxing necessary. Hell, we mortals slaughtered other groups of *humans* often enough with less justification.

My own emotions flared inside me, anger and disgust at both this woman and the mortals working beneath her —and more than a little fear at the powers she *could* wield. I clamped down on a burst of flame just before it shot to the surface of my skin. It seared across my muscles all the same, and I clenched my jaw tighter against the pain.

I was supposed to be here willingly—I was supposed

to be letting Omen hand me over to Tempest for her purposes.

"No less than he deserved," I made myself say.

Tempest's eyes gleamed approvingly. "Precisely." She turned her attention to her former lover and co-conspirator. "So, you've come around to seeing the 'light', have you, my dear friend?"

I could only guess how he winced inwardly at that label. "It's as the phoenix says," he replied. "They deserve whatever hell you're going to rain down on them. And who better to help you than a hellhound? I'd rather be by your side than scrambling around attempting to protect the pathetic creatures of our kind who can't take care of themselves."

To someone who'd heard Omen speak so emphatically about what he owed the lesser shadowkind and his shame over having brought harm their way in the past, those remarks held no ring of truth. But they must have been the sort of thing he might have said to appease the sphinx back then, and they were what she wanted to hear, what she thought he *should* feel. She had no idea what he'd been through in the centuries since they'd last schemed together.

Tempest smiled and inclined her head. "I knew you'd come around. Such good timing. We're nearly ready for the grand finale."

As she'd hinted before and Ruse's questioning had appeared to confirm. Omen smiled lazily back, but his gaze had turned more intent. "Your disease is perfected?"

"Only another tweak or two. I doubt we're more than

a week away from making good on all these years of work." She rubbed her hands together and studied me again. "And for whatever other havoc we wish to wreak, you've brought me this lovely gift. How have you convinced *her* to turn against her own kind?"

"They're not my kind," I said automatically, as we'd rehearsed.

Omen nodded approvingly. "The human side of her has its weaknesses. My incubus was able to charm her into following my will. Whatever I tell her to do, she'll do."

He wished. I resisted the urge to give him my most saccharine grin and a cloying, "Yes, Master." Go too over the top and the jig would be up.

"Wonderful. You'll have to expand that influence to include me."

"Sorsha," Omen said with a hint of a sardonic drawl, "do as Tempest says."

"Of course." I smiled brightly at her, and another flare of fire crackled up through my chest. Thankfully, my purse hid the balling of my hand as I willed it down.

Keep it under control. Keep my cool until I needed to blaze. I could handle this.

"Better under your sway than following her irrational mortal compulsions." Tempest curled a finger to beckon me over. "Let's look at you up close and see what you're capable of, firebird."

Oh, she was about to experience my capabilities, all right. This was the moment Omen and I had planned for. As I walked toward her, I inhaled deeply, every muscle coiling for the perfect launch of my powers. Two more steps, one—

I shoved one hand into my purse and whipped the other toward the sphinx at the same moment. While my fingers closed around the chain and yanked it out, fire streaked through the air from my extended palm.

It didn't go the way it had when we'd practiced, though. My emotions were churning too fast and furious —the fire's warble blared behind my ears. Flames sizzled around my neck and down my spine, and the blast I'd intended to hurl straight into Tempest's eyes like the stab of a scorching dagger instead flickered apart into a whirlwind of sparks.

No. I flung the chain, aiming a heft of heat with it to guide its course and soften its metals, but my initial slip had given Tempest just enough warning for her to dodge. The chain smacked into the side of her robe but didn't quite whip all the way around her.

Omen lunged at her, shifting into hellhound form in midair, but the sphinx was already diving into the shadows. I'd swear I heard a snarl of harsh laughter echo from the darkness around the tower.

Omen vanished too. I was left with a blob of melted metal, Tempest's other trapped mortal, and the singed grass that marked my failure.

Fuck a donkey's dingus.

A burnt smell lingered in the air, and my scalded skin stung with the movement of the breeze. Fresh heat was already roaring up inside me. I strode back and forth across the grass, gulping air and tamping the fire down as well as I could. The stinging sensation spread all the way down to the small of my back.

When Omen reappeared, the two wingéd had joined him. All of them looked both weary and pained.

I stated the obvious. "She escaped again."

Of course she had. Omen had known we didn't stand a real chance without tricks up our sleeves—and I'd bungled the damn trick. My fury with myself seared even hotter than the rest of my anger, blistering the bottom of my tongue.

We wouldn't get another chance like this. She'd never trust Omen again. And in a week or less, she'd have the Company unleashing their hell on this entire realm.

Somehow, the fact that Omen didn't point out my failure made the guilt slice deeper. "We'll find another way," he said. "There'll be other options."

But this had been our best one. I'd just gotten so fucking pissed off...

"If all those shithead mortals who joined up with the Company weren't so excited to murder every being they don't understand," I started, and the blistering heat spread through my gums.

"She's collected the worst of them," Omen said. "They feed off each other's hate. They hardly represent all of your kind."

He couldn't quite make that reassurance sound convincing. I knew how he felt about mortals. In his mind, *I* was the exception, and mainly because of the shadowkind side of me. He only cared about shadowkind hurting humans because it brought more rage back down on his own people.

I couldn't stop moving, my feet carrying me to the base of the tower and back again. If I stopped, if I so much as slowed *down*, the flames surging through me might spring farther ahead—right out of me.

Thorn took a step toward me, his expression fraught. "Sorsha."

I shook my head before he could go on. "One fight lost. There'll be plenty more. There always are, right? I just need to cool off. You all go ahead, fly back to the Everymobile or whatever. I'll walk it. That should be enough."

My companions hesitated. "Something makes me think you could use a chaperone," Omen said, managing to keep his tone mild.

I glared at him, reining in the fire so well for just a moment that the searing dwindled away. "I know what I need better than you do. And what I need is a good long walk without anyone judging my every move. We all know I fucked up here. Please don't rub it in. I promise Darlene will be perfectly safe from me by the time I get there."

He paused, his face tensing, but he didn't snap back. When he replied, it was in the same mild voice. "I know you gave it everything you had, and I can't judge you badly for that. You need space to work out your judgments of yourself? It's yours. If you lose your way, call us and we'll come get you."

Not a chance I'd humiliate myself like that. I nodded curtly.

Thorn frowned. "Are you sure? I could give you space but still stay within sight, in case you should have need of me."

My loyal warrior with his determination to protect me. The worst part was, his insistence only made the fire inside me prickle more fiercely.

"Did you see any other shadowkind around, or people who might be working with Tempest?" I asked.

"No," he admitted.

"Then I shouldn't 'have need.' Give me a chance to breathe, all right?"

Thorn still looked reluctant, but he followed Omen and Flint into the shadows at his boss's gesture.

Tempest's dupe kept standing there, but I felt more like burning him to a crisp than doing anything to help him. I spun on my heel and stalked away from the tower.

With every block I covered, the fire inside me blazed hotter. My fingernails dug into my palms within my fists. I passed rows of stucco buildings, restaurant patios abandoned for the night, shadowed doorways and winding alleys. All the windows were dark, any inhabitants sleeping behind them.

Sleeping and blissfully unaware of the terrors being committed around them. Would they care even if they knew? The Company tortured and murdered shadowkind, but the whole rest of the human race happily told their ghost stories and made their monster movies and fueled that hatred, and maybe they'd have all joined in if they'd realized how real those creatures actually were.

Pricks and bastards, all of them. And I was too, wasn't I, wanting even for that brief moment to blame Tempest for their crimes? The real monsters were right here, all around us, laughing and living their mindless lives—

A wave of heat so huge it qualified as a tsunami rolled through me—and out of me. Flames crashed and caught all across the face of the buildings along the street ahead of me. More lashed down the backs of my arms and legs.

I dropped to the ground, smacking my limbs against the pavement to put out the fire. That did nothing for the inferno already swallowing up the entire block of shops I'd been approaching.

The fire roared, smoke billowing up. Glass shattered as the flames whipped higher. Cries rose to join it as people in the apartment building across the street woke to the blaze. They were lucky my flames hadn't headed in that direction, burning up them instead of store merchandise.

My gut twisted into one huge knot. *I* was lucky.

The heat that washed over me on the night wind woke up a renewed throbbing across all the spots I'd been burned myself. I froze, staring—at a fruit and vegetable market where all the delicacies my devourer would have swooned over had already blackened. At a musical instrument vendor where piano strings were twanging as they snapped. At a watch store where the melting glass faces in the shattered window showed I'd literally made time fry.

I'd done that. Dozens of people's livelihoods were being incinerated before my eyes because of the fury I'd let loose. And there wasn't a single thing I could do to calm those flames. Every part of me ached with the suspicion that if I reached with my power to try to control the fire, I'd only end up hurling out more.

So I followed the strategy that had served me so well in my career as a thief—I ran as fast as my feet would take me.

The crackling roar of the fire and then the swell of sirens dogged me long after I'd left the scene behind. As I dragged in each breath, a smoky smell congealed in my lungs. I pushed myself onward toward the spot where the RV was waiting, a heavier sensation welling up inside me, drowning the last of my inner fire.

I was a menace. How much more was I going to destroy before this battle was over? What if the Highest were right? What if I was a greater threat to both mortals and shadowkind than Tempest had ever been?

I should march right into the Everymobile and tell Omen to take me to the Highest to meet the fate I'd escaped so long.

I paused and shut my eyes. The hopelessness squeezed around my ribs, suffocating. But through it, the image of Tempest's gleaming slit-pupil eyes, of her broken-glass laugh, returned to me.

She'd provoked me. She'd figured out the best buttons to push and jammed on them like a six-year-old pulling an elevator prank. She'd *wanted* me to explode, probably way more than I actually had, so she could snicker about it afterward.

I hadn't wanted to hurt anyone. And if I gave up, I'd only be stepping out of Tempest's way. She'd like that, wouldn't she?

I'd been our best chance of stopping her, and maybe I'd get another chance.

I knew better what to expect from her now. The others were counting on me. I had to stick with this at least long enough to save the rest of the world from the brutal chaos she intended to inflict on it.

And after that... then maybe I'd feel I needed to be put down. But not yet. Too much was riding on me. Too many lives hung in the balance.

I raised my chin and started walking again. The air that filled my lungs tasted cleaner now. The sirens had faded away.

I intended to see this mission through to the end, and heaven help anyone who got in my way.

14

Sorsha

As he smoothed another dab of aloe gel over the burns on my back, Snap's hands couldn't have been gentler, but my skin was so raw that I winced anyway. He made a fierce hissing sound through his teeth.

"I'd devour the sphinx without any regrets whatsoever," he declared.

Of the many things I could have pointed the finger at Tempest for, flambéing my body wasn't one of them. This had definitely been a self-barbequing. But I couldn't quite bring myself to correct my lover, any more than I wanted to ask if anyone had heard anything about a sudden blaze in downtown Pisa last night. Denial might be a river in Egypt, but I could transport it to Italy if I wanted to, thank you very much.

None of my companions had mentioned the flashfire,

but then, we'd driven right back to Rome, and they weren't exactly avid watchers of the news. And maybe they wouldn't have thought much of it anyway. A block of shops and all their contents incinerated? Just the dangers of mortal living.

I wished I could dismiss it that easily—and at the same time the thought of ever overcoming the guilt twisting through my gut horrified me.

"If that would be enough to end her, we'd toss her right to you," Omen said from the doorway, although he'd know even better than I did that Tempest wasn't likely to let anyone toss her anywhere in the first place.

I shifted where I was lying chest-down on my bed so I could pull my hair out of the way. Snap smeared more of the aloe—my second coating since I'd returned last night —across the back of my neck. "How *are* we going to come at her next, now that she won't be accepting any friendship bracelets from you?"

"I've been thinking about that while you've been sleeping," the hellhound shifter said, as if my repose had been pure laziness and not a physical necessity. "With our best option for stealth out the window, we may need to return to your old strategy of strength in numbers. Perhaps we can round up a shadowkind or two with some ability that proves to be a game-changer."

"I think our hacker friend can come up with a few more people with Company connections for me to sweet-talk in the meantime," Ruse said, sauntering past Omen into the bedroom and propping himself against the small dresser. "Might as well wring everything we can out of them."

Thorn formed out of the shadows at the base of the bed so he could get in on the conversation too. "I could attempt to speak to my wingéd brethren once more. They were hesitant to become involved, but if I could quickly see to their concerns... It might be a simple matter." He sounded doubtful, though.

"I will aid you in whatever their demands require," Flint put in, peering over Omen's shoulder.

A second later, Antic bounded in, her kindergartener-sized body jittering with excitement. "I know! You all haven't been thinking big enough. You've only been looking mortal-side. Why don't I go through a rift and see if I can round up some real help from the shadow realm?"

Omen folded his arms over his chest. "We don't need a horde of gnomes and pixies."

"Hey, a horde can get plenty done! And I can convince beings bigger than me! One of my best friends was a sea dragon, I'll have you know."

Between the lot of them, there was barely space to move in here anymore. I made a grumbling sound and reached toward the stack of clothes beside my bed. "Whose idea was it to have a strategy meeting in my bedroom—and while I'm shirtless? Let her go through the rift. There are a hell of a lot more of you on that side than here. I'm sure she'll find someone."

"Off with you, then," Omen told the imp. "We'll see how long it takes for you to find that someone."

"Aye, aye, captain!" She saluted him and scampered back out, which didn't exactly open up a whole lot more space. I tugged on my shirt, careful of the sensitive patches of healing skin on my neck, back, and arms.

Snap rested a protective hand on my hip. "You and I could go looking for shadowkind together, Peach," he said. "I can spot the ones in the shadows—but you're better at explaining how much we need their help."

Omen gave a definitive clap. "Perfect. I'll search around the city as well, Ruse will do his charming, and Thorn and Flint can barter with their not-so-angelic acquaintances. Let's attempt to meet back here by midnight. Tempest will be rushing her plans along even faster than before now that she's seen how far we're willing to go to stop her."

Thorn's mouth twisted at his orders, even though he'd suggested the plan of action. As everyone moved to leave, I caught his hand. "Give me a sec," I told Snap.

When we were alone, the massive warrior peered down at me. "Is there more I can do for you before I go, Sorsha?" His brawn had already tensed as if ready to spring to my aid.

"I was just wondering if there's anything I can do for *you*," I said, squeezing one of those impressive biceps. "From what you said before, your 'brethren' out at the Vatican gave you kind of a hard time."

The tightening of Thorn's jaw suggested he hadn't even told us the half of it. "I'm accountable for whatever tensions remain between us, and I will resolve them," he said. "It is the least I owe them."

"I don't think you owe them anything at all. It's been centuries. You didn't even do anything wrong to begin with."

"There are varying opinions on that matter. And the past is more present in its impact on them than it is for me." He sighed and lowered his head to brush his lips to mine, his voice dropping too. "Believe me, if I could simply stay by your side at all times, I'd much rather be here."

"Well, hurry back then," I said, giving him a peck in return, and headed out after him to where Snap was waiting near the door.

Normally, I couldn't have asked for a better companion for exploring a city than the devourer. He devoured new sights and experiences as avidly as he did his favorite fruits—and human souls.

For the first hour or so, that expectation held true. Snap peered with wide eyes at the looming ruins of antiquity in the Forum, listened in with eager little hums as a tour guide described the ancient activities that had taken place there, and sampled the energies around the structures with his forked tongue when no other tourists were near enough to see.

But we didn't find any shadowkind to beg to lend a hand—the couple that Snap sensed in the shadows darted off as soon as he paid any attention to them. As we passed a gaggle of college-age sightseers who jostled against me without so much as a glance back, let alone an apology, the devourer's usual bright demeanor started to dim.

"The shadowkind are nervous of all the mortals

around," he said. "Humans haven't been all that kind to this place, even though it's their own history. I can't taste anything from the times when all this was whole and celebrated... Too many impressions of people chipping away at it, bumping against it without watching, carving words that make them laugh into it to show how *little* they think of it... Why would they do that?"

The fraught confusion in his voice brought a lump into my throat. "We don't always appreciate our history," I said. "It's harder when we don't live anywhere near as long as shadowkind do, you know. For the people seeing this now, the society who used this place was gone before any of our great-great-great-however many times grandparents were born. It doesn't feel totally real."

"I didn't exist that long ago, and I still find it fascinating."

I bumped my arm against his playfully. "Well, that's part of what makes you so special."

The compliment lit him up again, but only for a little while. We failed to gain any supporters from the creatures lurking near the Pantheon and the grand museums. Clouds clotted in the sky as we approached Trevi Fountain, and Snap shivered with the fading of the sunlight.

"Someone carved that whole sculpture without any magic at all," I said over the burbling of the water. "Pretty amazing."

"It is," Snap agreed, but the brightness of his voice diminished too. "They built so many things... and so many of them wish no being like me ever got to see them.

They would be upset that I enjoy all the fruits and the honey and..." His brow knit. "*Most* humans would want us dead if they knew of us, wouldn't they? That's why we keep our existence secret."

"Well, maybe not *dead*," I started, but I didn't really know how to follow that up. Because, yeah, it was possible the majority of humans *would* wish to see beings like my monstrous lovers slaughtered if they found out shadowkind existed. I didn't want to lie to him. But the hurt in his eyes and the gloom creeping into his words made my heart ache.

The Company hadn't killed Snap while they'd held him captive, but how much was he really *Snap* if they destroyed his sense of wonder?

A spurt of flame lanced through my insides. I coughed and barely managed to swallow it down so it seared nothing but my stomach. For my devourer's sake and my own, I groped for a lyric to spin this conversation in a lighter direction.

"Come on. We've still got to find some shadowkind to make our appeal to." I tugged on Snap's elbow and sang, "And if I only could, I'd make an eel maraud, and I'd bet him with all our aces."

"I don't think an eel would be very helpful against Tempest," Snap said, but it was with a smile to show he hadn't really taken me seriously. Good. Between two wingéd with maybe a couple more on their way, Omen dealing with a very solid specter from his awful past, and me burning innocents left and right, we had enough sombreness hanging over our group already.

Perking Snap up didn't help us find any new allies, though. We returned to the Everymobile just shy of midnight. Omen emerged from the shadows before we'd quite reached the doorway and motioned Snap inside. "I need to speak with our mortal," he said, without even bothering to ask how our quest had gone. I guessed our failure was obvious enough.

Snap bristled with a brief flare of neon green in his eyes, but his loyalty to the shadowkind who'd called him to this cause was clearly at war with his devotion to me. He paused and then said, in a careful but firm voice, "What do you want with her now?"

Omen sighed. "I'm just going to talk to her, honestly. If anyone's going to haul her off to some dire end, it won't be me. Aren't you convinced of that yet?"

The devourer looked chagrined, but only slightly. "I didn't think you'd do it in the first place," he informed the hellhound shifter, but after one more caress of my arm, he vanished into the RV.

The early autumn night was warm enough, but Omen's solemn expression sent an icy quiver through my gut. "What's the big secret?"

He guided me off to the side of the RV. Not all of Rome was so scenic—the rundown suburb where we were hiding out smelled like tar rather than gelato, and a loose door somewhere in the distance was creaking on its hinges in the breeze. The Everymobile added to the atmosphere with the rotating hubcaps it'd recently produced, which rattled like hamster wheels as they spun endlessly on.

"It's not a secret," Omen said. "I just thought I should tell you first so there's no time for misunderstandings. I've decided I'm going to approach the Highest again."

Even after what he'd just said to Snap and everything he'd said to me in the past few days, my pulse stuttered. Before I could say anything, he held up his hands. "I won't even mention you. I'm going to tell them what I've found out about Tempest and see if they'll change my final order to taking her down rather than finding 'Ruby'. And whether they will or not, they might lend some brawn to our cause. They did want to destroy her enough to sic a whole bunch of their lackeys on her before."

It made sense—enough sense that Omen obviously hadn't been able to talk himself out of doing it, as much as I could tell he disliked the idea of chatting with the beings that had put him in their leash.

"That would certainly be helpful," I said. "It's about time they pitched in rather than pitching fits."

The corner of Omen's mouth quirked upward. "We'll see. In any case, nothing ventured, nothing gained. They should have no way of discerning that I've had contact with the mortal-shadowkind hybrid they've been searching for. I didn't want you spending any time worrying about that, even if it was only the time it took to answer half a dozen questions from our companions."

I set my hands on my hips. "Me, worry?" I teased. "Do you know me at all?" But the truth was, he did know me. Enough that I had to add, "Thank you. For worrying about whether I'd worry."

He made a dismissive sound, but then he ran his

fingers along my jaw to draw me to him. He kissed me hard, the intensity of it sparking all kinds of flames beneath my skin, but only the pleasant kind.

Why couldn't my inner fire always feel this delicious?

When he let me go, another ache formed in my chest to join the one Snap's disillusionment had provoked. I couldn't help curling my fingers around Omen's before he could drop his hand. "Make sure you come back."

He gave me a full smile then. "No one's managed to crush me yet, as many as have wanted to. You're not getting rid of me that easily, Disaster."

I laughed and followed him into the Everymobile so he could tell the others where he was going, but underneath my good humored response, the ache remained.

How had I gotten to the point with this man where the thought of *anyone* getting rid of him made me want to rain fire from the sky?

15

Omen

I t said something about how eager the Highest were for any news of the mission they'd sent me on that the slathering goblin who stopped me at the edge of their vast hollow came barreling back mere minutes later with an urgent rasp that rippled through the clotted darkness around us. "They'll see you now. Come on!"

That welcome was a far cry from my last visit, when they'd left me waiting for what had turned out to be more than a day. And that time *they'd* summoned me. I'd just have to hope they'd be too distracted by the news I'd brought to sulk over the news I hadn't.

As far as I was concerned, I had no idea where a hybrid being named Ruby might live. The only human-shadowkind mishmash of a being I knew was named Sorsha, and the Highest hadn't asked me about anything to do with *her*.

Besides, Tempest had ruined about a realm's worth of lives already. You couldn't find a threat much clearer than that.

The goblin followed me all the way into the yawning cavern, where the potent if ponderous energies of the Highest beings washed over me with an itch through my shadow-side body and a twinge around my neck. They never quite let me forget the hold they had over me. I'd have preferred not to have their slathering lackey witness it, but it wasn't my place to send him off. Or to take a good chomp out of his throat, which would have accomplished nearly the same thing with much more satisfaction.

Shadowkind couldn't die in our shadow forms, but we could certainly be maimed to the point that we might as well be dead.

The Highest's penetrating attention weighed down on me even more heavily than before. The goblin dipped into a sort of groveling bow as if looking for praise for managing the incredible task of walking me the short distance from the entrance. Self-respect was not a quality the behemoths looked for in their minions.

The Highest ignored him. "What word have you brought, hellhound?" one of them demanded, her hollow bellow of a voice echoing through every particle of my being.

Oh, I had a whole lot of words for them, but I'd better choose which ones I actually said carefully. I gathered myself. "I have not encountered a being that goes by the name Ruby, but my search has turned up an even graver danger to both realms. The shadowkind you believed you dispatched ages ago, the one whose vicious tricks I admit I sometimes assisted with, has survived after all. Tempest the sphinx lives, and she has a plot more immense than ever before underway."

I couldn't make much of the muttering that passed between the pompous leviathans. "It cannot be so," another said. "Our warriors tore her to shreds. They reported as much—they would not have lied."

"I doubt they knew they were lying," I said. "I'd imagine she performed one of her tricks on them too, to make them think she'd died or that they had her at all. But whatever they tore up, it either survived despite their ravaging or it wasn't her. I've spoken to her face to face. And if anyone should recognize that menace, it's me."

One of the massive beings loomed closer with a thicker, harsher surge of energy. "How can we know this isn't *you* playing tricks on us?"

For all my own power, it took the tensing of every muscle in my body for me to resist the urge to cringe. As easily as I could have ripped the goblin—who was still watching all this, gaping dopily, the dimwit—into a pulp so mangled it would have taken centuries for it to reassemble into his proper being, the Highest could flay me to shreds even faster. The only reason they hadn't in the first place, all those years ago when we'd made our deal, was that they'd believed I was of more use to them in one piece. I had to make sure they continued to believe that.

"What possible reason could I have for making this

up?" I asked, holding my ground. "I'm on the verge of completing my deal with you. No good could come from reminding you of my old association with the sphinx if she didn't pose a real threat now."

The rumbling that followed sounded at least slightly agreeable. My hackles came down, but I stayed braced where I was.

"What is this plot the sphinx is carrying out?" the first speaker demanded. "How much danger could she pose when no word of her has reached us all this time until now?"

"That's probably what she wants you to think. She wanted to lull you into complacency." A prod to their dignity couldn't hurt. "And this scheme is so dangerous precisely *because* she's spent so much time putting the pieces in place. She intends to see as many mortals dead as she can—and knowing her and her methods, it could be more than remain alive in the entire mortal realm after she's through—and to sicken and kill nearly every shadowkind who's ventured mortal-side as well."

Another of the Highest spoke up. "You've mentioned this sickness before. You said there were mortals creating such a thing."

"Apparently Tempest has been directing those mortals—and ensuring it'll come around to bite them in the ass," I said. "But she made it clear to me that shadowkind will die too, and she doesn't care how many. I'd imagine if she can find a way to have the sickness spread all the way to *your* doorstep, she'll do her best to make that happen. She's carrying a bit of a grudge after the whole nearly-slaughtered-by-wingéd incident."

The gawking goblin gave a shudder. Really he should have been more worried about himself. Somehow I suspected his constitution wasn't up to resisting Tempest's manufactured disease.

The grandiose goliaths muttered to each other some more. It'd been a thin line between offending them by suggesting they were vulnerable and driving home the threat Tempest posed as hard as I could. They sounded as if they were taking my report at least somewhat seriously.

"You have been in much communication with the sphinx," one said finally. "We presume you convey this information to us with some concept of how she might be brought down."

For once, they'd played right into my hands. I smiled as well as I could in my hazy state and bowed my head. "Of course. It would be an honor to not only present the problem but solve it for you as well. I do think, though, that combating a being of such experience and proven power goes well beyond a typical walk in the park. I thought perhaps you might want to adjust your orders to account for that."

"In what way?"

They were going to make me spell it out, were they? Typical. "Your original instruction was for me to notify you of Ruby's location—but this Ruby hasn't caused any noticeable trouble that anyone's been aware of in decades. Tempest, on the other hand, is days away from unleashing the worst catastrophe any shadowkind has wrought on the realms. If you would rather I pursue her, I would happily take responsibility for—"

A booming laugh cut me off—and reverberated down to my bones, turning what shadowy gut I had into water. What in darkness's name was *funny* about my proposition? The question rose up with a rankling irritation, but at the same time I hesitated to ask.

I didn't need to. The same being who'd laughed turned a waft of attention onto me that fell even thicker and darker than before. "Of course you would be happy to do so. This has been your scheme all along, hasn't it? You had to invent the sphinx's resurrection so we would take your crusade more seriously. Did you really think we would fail to see through such a deception?"

Well, I probably wouldn't have if it'd actually been a deception. Now that he put it that way, it was difficult to avoid seeing how it'd appear to be a trick of my own to someone who hadn't stood face to face with Tempest in the recent days.

"No," I said, working to keep as much irritation as possible out of my voice. "Which is why I wouldn't have attempted it as a deception. She really is alive and pulling the strings behind the Company of Light. I'd be happy to take a few of your minions to meet her to confirm, although I can't promise she won't chew them up and spit them out much worse off than they were when they arrived."

"I see no reason why that should be necessary," another of the Highest intoned. "Your intentions are transparent enough. You will resume following your original directive, and you will return to the mortal realm to see about carrying it out *now*. We have waited long enough."

They might have waited decades to find "Ruby", but they'd only asked *me* to take up the search a couple of weeks ago. I guessed I didn't get any benefit of their patience.

I wasn't the type to back down without some sort of fight. "If something isn't done to stop Tempest, then there might not be anything left in the realms that's worth saving from whatever you think this Ruby is going to do. Do you really want to leave me in the position to be able to say I told you so?"

The murmur that passed between them sounded unsettled, but not concerned enough. "If the sphinx truly poses such a threat, then attend to her as you see fit. We have seen no evidence of it."

They hadn't seen any evidence that Sorsha was a threat either, other than what they'd made up in their own heads about human-shadowkind hybrids. I bit my tongue against flinging that point at them, though. It wouldn't be good for her or me to appear too invested in her.

The damned puffed-up giants. What could I say that would get through their incredibly dense skulls?

The simpering goblin was already darting to my side. "I can see the hellhound away from you so he won't bother you any further, your greatnesses," he said.

"Back off," I snapped, far less worried about what *he*

thought of me, and advanced a little closer to the Highest. "Do you want to be known as the ones who prevented a catastrophe of immense proportions or the ones who stood by and let it happen? I'm giving you the chance to be the former. And believe me, if Tempest rains down all her rage on the rest of us, I'm not going to stay quiet about your complacency."

That was a threat in itself, and a gamble I nearly regretted. A wallop of chilling fury hit me, tossing me backward like a tidal wave, head over feet. I shook myself, regaining my bearings and confirming I'd kept possession of all my limbs, and the blustering fools shoved me again. The impression of a choke collar around my throat yanked painfully tight.

Several of their echoing voices rang out together. "Begone, hellhound, and we will hear no more of this ridiculousness from you."

There was a thing or three I could have said about who was being ridiculous here, but I wasn't saving anyone if I ended up in tiny pieces scattered across the entire shadow realm. I spoke through gritted teeth. "As you command, oh Highest ones."

I loped off with only one thing I hadn't possessed before this visit: the certainty that in this war, no matter what else came of it, my companions and I were utterly alone.

16

Sorsha

"I mean, it's really no surprise, right?" I said when Omen had finished filling us in on his conversation with the Highest. "We already knew they're obnoxious and overly obsessed with me."

"Yes, silly of me to think they might be concerned by news about the re-emergence of a being they'd already decided was so dangerous they put her to death centuries ago." Omen rolled his eyes toward the Everymobile's ceiling, but despite the dryness of his tone, I could tell how frustrated he was with the ancient shadowkind that held him in their sway.

"We've taken on the Company of Light without any help from the Highest before," Snap said, stroking my hair where he was sitting next to me on the sofa-bench. "They don't seem to know much of anything anyway."

At his other side, Ruse made a vaguely obscene

gesture in the general direction of the shadowy overlords. "Hard for them to have much awareness of a realm they've never bothered to venture into."

"Right." As Pickle curled up tighter on my lap, I scratched his belly with careful fingers, putting on my best impression of being totally okay with all this. The thought of those overbearing beings ignoring Omen's totally valid warnings—of them declaring me a much more urgent threat than a centuries-old genocidal maniac who'd already been responsible for innumerable deaths of humans and shadow creatures alike—definitely wasn't stoking the angry fire inside me to uncomfortable heights. And if I decided that fire wasn't there, then it definitely couldn't justify their insistence that I be exterminated.

If pretending away reality worked for the Highest, why shouldn't it work for me?

But heat I couldn't totally will out of my consciousness prickled under my skin. I jerked my hand from Pickle's side as a particularly sharp flare seared across my palm. I'd already scorched the little dragon once, and it'd taken days for him to forgive me. If even *he* wasn't safe around me...

He was. I had it under control. With a few deep breaths and an image of the ocean I summoned into my head, the flames were retreating.

"No one's heard from Thorn yet?" I asked.

Omen shook his head. "I've yet to convince our wingéd companion of the wonders of cell phones. He did say he might need to lend his former comrades a hand before they'd agree to help us. I suppose we'll see whether it was worth the bargain when they show up."

He couldn't disguise his skepticism, but it was hard to mind when I was pretty skeptical myself. The warrior could take a physical beating without a wince, but from the way he'd looked after his first talk with those two lingering wingéd, they'd mauled something in his spirit. He'd felt so guilty about not being there for the final battle, about not *dying* there... How much would they shake his faith in himself this time?

"Once he's back, my hacker back in Paris did turn up an interesting lead we might want to pursue," Ruse said. "He's found an interesting pattern of—"

Cutting the incubus off, a swell of triumphant trombones blared through the RV with a multicolored flash of the overhead lights. As the electric panels blinked from pink to orange to green as if we were in a very cramped dance club, they caught on three figures who'd just appeared by the front door.

Antic hopped up and down with a guffaw at the unexpected welcome. Behind her, Gisele and Bow stared around them, the delicate unicorn shifter and the burly centaur looking equally bewildered.

Uh oh. As much use as we'd been putting the Everymobile to, it actually belonged to the two equines, who'd generously lent it to us to continue our quest. *When* they'd lent it to us, it hadn't been sprouting odd instruments from its roof or producing music at random moments. It seemed the vehicle was happy to have them back, but I wasn't sure how happy they'd be about the way it was expressing that joy.

Omen dashed past them to jab at the buttons on the dashboard, with a deeper grimace when he took in the smashed spot where Thorn had "disabled" the radio not long ago. Gisele's doe-eyed gaze followed him, her rainbow-streaked hair swishing over her shoulder.

"What did you do to the Everymobile?" she said, her melodic tinkle of a voice rising over the cacophony. "I thought you were going to take it for a road trip, not renovate it."

Omen managed to shut up the trumpets, but the lights kept flashing strobe-like over us. The hellhound shifter had expressed plenty of disdain for the equines when they'd first joined us, but since then they'd proven themselves capable fighters and generous allies. Worthy of guilty tensing of his expression as he groped for an explanation.

I managed to suppress a smile at seeing him put in his place by shadowkind he'd once sneered at, but I couldn't help tossing a remark of my own his way. "Yeah, Omen, why don't you tell them all about what you've put *Darlene* through?"

Bow ran a hand through his thick mohawk mane of chestnut hair, still staring befuddled at his former mortal-side home. "Who's Darlene?"

Omen shot a glare at me. Served him right for naming things that didn't belong to him. I leaned back in Snap's embrace to watch as the hellhound shifter straightened his posture.

"Never mind that." He waved to the RV's interior. "We didn't do this on purpose. We could hardly drive her across the ocean, and... she didn't come through the rifts quite the same as when she went in."

"I think the word you're looking for is, 'Sorry'," Ruse supplied helpfully.

Omen glowered at him too, but a hint of sheepishness had come into his expression that looked odd but unaccountably adorable on the powerful shifter's face. He turned back to the equines. "My apologies. I had no idea what effect the shadow realm would have on your vehicle. It's a little more... unique than it was before, but I can at least say that it seems to function just as well as it always did."

"I guess that's the important thing." Gisele peered up at the lights, which had finally faded back to their typical white glow. "Maybe some of the changes are even an improvement. I could get into the dance club vibe."

As if on cue, her partner grasped her hand and spun her around. The unicorn shifter giggled as she twirled, and some of the tension in my chest loosened. I'd forgotten the mood these two set with their easy-going presence—and there was a relief in seeing Gisele fully recovered from the injuries the Company's soldiers had dealt to her. You'd never have known that the last time we'd seen her, weeks ago, she hadn't been able to stand up without Bow's help.

"How'd you manage to track these two down?" I asked Antic. The imp had never met the equines, having joined our merry band after they'd headed back to the shadow realm to speed up Gisele's recovery.

Antic leapt up to sit on the edge of the table and grinned over her shoulder at me. "It was easy-peasy. I was ping-pong balling all over the place, talking up the cause, and they tracked *me* down. I figured there couldn't be any better allies to bring back than ones you already knew."

Bow popped open one of the cupboards. "We've still got our grass and our *grass*! I wonder what the trip to the shadow realm did to that stuff."

Omen cleared his throat. "Maybe not the best time to find out just yet."

"There are fresh strawberries in the fridge," Snap offered generously. "They're very good."

Bow retrieved the delicacies, and a moment later we were all chowing down tart berry sweetness—except Omen, who watched the whole to-do with his mouth set in a crooked line. The centaur gave Snap a thumbs up while he chewed. "Excellent pickings. Man, did I miss mortal food."

A bright smile crossed the devourer's face. He popped another strawberry into his mouth and watched avidly as the equines recounted one of their early battles with the Company soldiers for Antic's benefit, complete with physical re-enactments of key moments. Snap glanced at me and then Ruse. "It's good to have them back, isn't it?"

"The imp did well," Ruse said with amusement, and gave Snap a nudge to the shoulder. "It's good to see *you* looking this cheerful, my friend. Have we not been enough fun lately to keep your spirits as shiny as usual?"

Snap blinked at him with a hint of chagrin. "I didn't expect this mission to be 'fun'. Have I done something that bothered you?"

"No, no, not at all. I just remember the good old days when all I had to do was mix up some bubbles in the sink to get that kind of smile out of you."

The devourer beamed. "I do still like the bubbles. You stopped making them."

The incubus chuckled and gave the other man's shoulder another squeeze. "All right, something to add to my to-do list."

It *was* good seeing Snap more his sunny self again—and to see Ruse enjoying it too. The incubus might have worried about how much he could pitch in compared to the others, but he'd always felt like an essential part of this group. Maybe he was settling back into that sense of belonging after his moment of doubt.

I enjoyed the comradery next to me for a few seconds longer before the equines brought the conversation back around to our present situation.

"We'd have brought Cori too," Gisele said, "but after all that time in his cage, he was hesitant to make another trip mortal-side. As soon as we've wiped the floor with the Company, we'll tell him the coast is clear."

Omen straightened up from where he'd propped himself against the wall. "It may be more difficult than a simple wiping. We've uncovered some unfortunate information about the powers behind the Company."

The unicorn shifter's eyebrows shot up. "In what way?"

I could tell Omen was reluctant to get into that subject, but it wasn't as if we could bring our returned allies on board without giving them the full picture. He dragged in a rough breath. "There's a former associate of mine, a shadowkind of great strength, who's been pulling their strings behind the scenes. We *almost* had them beaten, but she intervened in their defense. It seems she cares very little what shadowkind get hurt along the way."

The fiery fury that had risen inside me when he'd talked about the Highest's dismissal stirred again. As he went on with his report of everything we'd heard from and experienced with Tempest, the flames danced higher despite my best efforts.

A searing sensation spread across the small of my back. Was that a whiff of burnt leather?

I couldn't let the sphinx get the better of me— especially when she wasn't even in the goddamned vicinity. I set my teeth, but every time I managed to settle my inner fire, Omen mentioned some other detail that set it sparking violently again.

He hadn't mentioned anything about my difficulties with my powers or what I was to the equines. Presumably he was going to keep the most damning aspects on the down low like he had with Antic and Flint. I'd rather not make a vivid demonstration of my habit of setting myself on fire. It wasn't as if I needed to hear this rundown anyway, considering I'd been there for most of it.

I gave Snap a kiss on the cheek so he wouldn't worry and got up. The bedroom I'd claimed as my own felt like the safest spot right now. If I moved to leave the RV completely, that would inevitably raise questions.

I might have singed the covers a tad when I flopped down on them, but without Omen's voice and Tempest's name in my ears, the heat inside me started to dwindle. It wasn't much more than glowing embers when a knock sounded on the door.

Ruse's voice carried through, lightly cajoling. "Miss Blaze?"

I weighed my options and decided I was better off inviting him in than turning him away. For all his carefree airs, the incubus had proven he could worry plenty too, given the right provocation.

"What's up?" I asked, pushing myself into a sitting position.

He slipped right in through the shadows without further prompting, as I'd figured he would. Shadowkind and their very lax concept of privacy. Snap wouldn't even have knocked.

When he saw me on the bed, empty-handed, Ruse paused. "Were you resting? I didn't mean to wake you up. I got the sense you might have left because something had irked you. Not because I looked inside your head," he added quickly, with a flash of a smile. "I *have* gotten to know you rather well in many other ways."

I had to smile back at that remark. A surge of affection filled my chest, drowning out the last of the prickling flames. The incubus did take certain requests for privacy very seriously, knowing how important they were to me, even now that I'd already given him permission to read my mental state once.

He'd wanted so badly to be there for me, to protect me. I didn't know if it was possible for any of my shadowkind lovers to really do the latter, but maybe I should give him the chance to do the former.

I motioned for him to sit beside me. "Not irked. Well, okay, Tempest as a whole is pretty irksome. But I'm totally okay with feeling that way about her. It's just, when I think about what she's doing—all the awfulness she's caused and still wants to—my powers get pretty, ah, heated up."

Ruse brushed a few strands of hair back from my cheek, offering so much tenderness in that simple gesture. "I'd have thought that was a good thing. Plenty of fire to rain down on her when the time comes."

"Well, yeah, but the time isn't now, and—" Something in me balked at admitting the rest. Sweet simpering sycamores, when had I become a *coward* of all things?

I forced the words out. "The Highest think I might end up destroying even more than Tempest will. I know Omen's decided it won't happen—I know none of you want to believe I could be capable of it—but when all that fire builds up inside me, sometimes I'm not sure they're wrong. I'm *not* in control, not completely."

"Hmm. I'd make a comment about how much I enjoy you letting loose, but I don't think that's what you're looking to hear."

I elbowed Ruse, and he chuckled. Then he slipped his arm around me and tugged me to him, dipping his head so his lips brushed my temple as he spoke.

"You've accomplished a lot of impossible things in the last few months, Miss Blaze. You've conjured love in an incubus, desire in a devourer, gentleness in a wingéd warrior, and mercy—along with a few other things, it's becoming clear—in a hellhound. Proving a riddling sphinx and some stuffy Highest bastards wrong will be the least of your accomplishments when you're through."

He spoke so confidently and with such affection that I almost believed him. Enough that even if he hadn't melted my doubts, I could shove them far enough aside to tease my hand into his hair. "Suddenly I can think of a few things I'd like to accomplish right now."

As if to punctuate that statement, a panel popped open on the ceiling above us, a plastic birdie on a spring swinging out. "Cuckoo!" it said cheerfully, like a demented clock. "Cuckoo!"

Poor Darlene. Ruse and I exchanged a glance and burst into laughter. With weirdly buoyed spirits, I drew him down with me on the bed, pulling his mouth to mine.

Here was hoping that if I soaked up all of his faith in me, I could make that certainty my own.

17

Sorsha

Ruse had only gotten in a few—incredibly delicious —kisses when Bow's voice carried through the bedroom door. "Thorn! Good to see you again too."

The incubus let out a stifled groan, teasing his lips from my jaw down my neck before raising his head. "Interrupted again. I look forward to the day when sphinx and Company alike have been tossed out with the trash so I can enjoy you at my leisure, but for now I think we'd better find out what the lunk has come back with."

Every part of me except the heat pooled between my thighs agreed. I stole one more kiss for good measure, and then paused. "You know, if you ever *need* to feed, all you have to do is—"

Ruse held up his hand to stop me. His mouth flattened at an odd angle for a second before he recovered his usual smirk. "I have no problem speaking up. Trust me, you've kept me quite satisfied, my lovely thief."

But would I always? A strange sensation ran through my chest, twinges of concern and jealousy clashing. I swallowed down the latter. Ruse was what he was, and I accepted that. I wouldn't ask this man to starve just to indulge my human notions of fidelity. And really, who was I to fuss about fidelity in the first place, when I'd been canoodling with three other men right here in this RV?

"If I ever don't—I mean, if you need more than one woman's energies to keep you sated—I understand. Cubi kind have got to cubi and all that."

Maybe I hadn't shoved that jealousy down quite far enough. Despite my attempt at nonchalance, Ruse's warm eyes softened as he took me in. He trailed his fingers down my cheek and drew me into a kiss so deep it took my breath away.

"I appreciate the sentiment," he murmured against my lips afterward. "But you don't ever have to worry about that."

Because I really was enough or because he'd be discreet enough that I'd never know? I guessed it didn't make much difference either way.

"Good," I said, and twined my fingers with his on our way out into the Everymobile's main room.

I stepped out expecting to see both of our stalwart wingéd looming in the hallway, but it was only Thorn's considerable bulk filling the space, no sign of Flint. While

Thorn's expression was often grim enough to send lesser creatures fleeing in terror, now his chiseled features held shades of pain and shame as well. My stomach twisted at the sight.

"—decided to stay with them and continue the search," he was just saying to Omen. "But my first responsibility is to you—I wouldn't be mortal-side at all if not for your mission."

A crackle of flame rippled through me. I managed to hold it in as I marched over, but I couldn't keep the searing sting out of my tone. "Those asshole wingéd tried to make you think you owed *them* more?"

Thorn's head drooped like I'd only seen once before —after we'd first gotten Omen out of the Company prison, when the shifter had laid into him for not orchestrating that jailbreak sooner. Oh, my dearest warrior. Tearing heads off was more his style than mine, but right then I wouldn't have minded dropkicking a few wingéd skulls into the stratosphere. I loved his loyalty and his sense of honor, but sometimes they didn't serve him well.

"The remains of one of my closest comrades were stolen by a pack of griffins," he said. "I attempted to locate it on the request of my brethren. I came upon several griffins and did battle, but I could not discover the object I was looking for in their midst. It remains adrift."

No doubt he had fresh scars to add to those that mottled his face and body from that battling. My hands clenched. "They should be grateful you did even that much for them. How is it *your* fault that they didn't take good enough care of this dude's ashes or whatever? Why don't they go fight a horde of griffins if it means so much to them?"

Even more strain crept into Thorn's voice. "As I related before, the wars of long ago dealt permanent damage to their forms."

Omen let out a dismissive growl. "That doesn't give them carte blanche to appropriate the one wingéd I actually like. I hope you told them to shove it."

The tensing of Thorn's stance told me he hadn't stated his refusal in terms quite that blatant. "I informed them that my duty required I return to you and discuss the situation."

And then possibly leave to go back to them? The emotion that shot through me at that thought wasn't just anger but a jab of cold-edged refusal. I didn't want to go into the battles *we* faced ahead without our warrior by my side.

"If those pompous asses think they have any claim—" the shifter started, clearly building up to a full-on rant complete with houndish snarls, but his tone had already made Thorn turn even more rigid. Lambasting Thorn's people wasn't the way to reassure him—it'd only make him feel he was betraying them even more if he stayed.

I strode right up to the wingéd, nudging Omen to the side with my elbow to cut off his spiel before he could get any more of it out. "Take a walk with me?" I said to Thorn. "I think you've had enough people telling you what to do today. I'd like to listen to what *you're* thinking."

Omen muttered something disparaging under his breath but didn't outright protest. Thorn hesitated and then offered me a smile that was small and tight but at least *there*. "Perhaps that would help me sort out my thoughts, m'lady. I would be glad of having your ear."

I followed him out of the Everymobile. We meandered into a stretch of parkland, patchy with weeds and holding a playground no one could actually use thanks to the broken ladder on the slide, the swing tossed over its support beam, and a teeter totter that had toppled right over. Tonight was cooler than past nights, the stars and moon clouded over. I walked close to Thorn to soak up the warmth his brawny frame exuded.

"It may be that I was right in questioning our wars of the past," the warrior said after a stretch of silence. "But that doesn't absolve me of all responsibility for my actions. I *did* leave at a time when others ended up falling in battle or meeting similarly harsh fates... My doubts meant leaving them to suffer."

"They might have met the exact same fates even if you'd been there," I pointed out. "You can't know how much of a difference you would have made. They were all just as strong and fierce as you can be, right? Maybe it'd have happened the exact same except you wouldn't be here to feel guilty about it either."

"That is possible. I won't deny it." The breeze hissed tauntingly through the leaves of a nearby tree, and he frowned at it. "I cannot say how much of a difference I'm making to Omen's cause either, though, can I? Why should he deserve my aid more than my brethren of old?"

"It's not just for him, is it? What good does it do chasing after the remains of someone who's already *dead*? Tackling Tempest could mean saving millions more lives than were lost way back when."

"But if I take the time to make up for past failures now, perhaps I can bring new allies to that cause as well."

"Okay, when you put it that way, I can see it's not an easy dilemma." I stopped in a clearing between the scattered trees and glanced up at Thorn. In the faint light that traveled this far from distant street lamps, his white-blond hair looked closer to silver, his tan skin duskier, his dark eyes utterly black. A furrow had creased his forehead. An ache squeezed my heart, watching him struggle.

He gazed down at me. "I have other reasons for wishing to stay, of course. Reasons that are much more selfish."

When he took on that low, impassioned tone, my pulse fluttered with giddiness despite my concern for him. "And I have plenty of selfishness too. But I wouldn't want you to stay because I put the screws to you and then have you feeling guilty about it."

"So you aren't going to make an argument on your own behalf?"

I inhaled sharply. "I want you with us. I want you with *me*. But I'll muddle through this either way. What

I'd really like is for you to figure out what you think is the right course of action for *you*. Not what will make anyone else happy. What you'll be able to look back on that will let you know right in here that you made the best decision you could." I gave him a gentle poke to the middle of his chest.

Thorn caught my hand and curled his fingers around it. His touch and the intentness of his gaze sent heat coursing over my skin. "I suppose I haven't considered that factor often in the past. What *I* think is best. What orders I would give myself, if it were up to me."

"It is up to you, you know. You're always the boss of yourself in the end, as much as I'm sure Omen—or those other wingéd—would like you to think otherwise."

"But how does one untangle one's sense of responsibility to others from one's own judgment?"

"Now you're getting into the hard questions," I teased, and lifted my other hand to caress his square jaw. "I can think of a few ways you seem to be different from the average wingéd. Maybe getting in touch with the more selfish side of yourself will help you figure things out?"

Thorn hummed as if in agreement and leaned in to kiss me. The passion of his lips claiming mine reverberated through my body. I gripped the collar of his tunic, pushing myself up on my toes to meet him with all the enthusiasm I could offer in return.

He drew back just an inch, his breath washing over me with his musky scent. "If you asked me to stay for you, I would, you know. You have proven yourself the most loyal comrade I could ask for, and so much more than that as well... I don't think I could bring myself to deny you, no matter what else was at stake."

I swallowed hard, the vehemence in his words ringing through me and waking up an answering devotion. "And if you told me you had to leave to believe you've fulfilled your purpose, I *wouldn't* ask you, as much as I might want to. I'd rather have you at peace somewhere else than torn up by guilt right next to me. Obviously if I can have both the peace *and* the proximity..."

He chuckled and kissed me again. Then he murmured, "I want to show you something, m'lady."

Before I could ask what, his body shifted against mine. His chest expanded, his body enlarging to even greater heights of brawn. A ruddy glow like embers still smoldering in a fireplace lit in his eyes. His great black wings unfurled from his back, their feathers warbling in the breeze.

He captured my mouth again with a smoky edge beneath his musky flavor, and at the same time he caught me in his arms, one solid mass of corded muscle across my shoulder blades and the other around my ass, lifting me against him. With a majestic flap of his wings, his feet left the ground too.

Between the kiss and the sensation of soaring upward, dizziness washed through me, but I was more than happy to embrace it. As the wind licked sharper over us, I kissed Thorn hard through the stutter of my heartbeat.

He hefted me higher against him, and my legs came

up instinctively to wrap around his waist. A firm bulge there was no mistaking came to rest against my sex. I dragged in a breath shaky with desire, gripped the thick strands of his hair, and let my tongue slip from my mouth to tangle with his.

Our bodies rocked together with each sweep of his wings, creating a torturous friction that brought a gasp to my lips. Looping my arms around Thorn's neck, I dared to glance down. The view knocked all the air from my lungs.

Holy mother of meteors, we were really flying. The city sprawled below me in a vast spread of twinkling lights, some of them coursing along roadways and others blinking off even as I watched as people turned in for the night.

Who needed stars when you could have a vision like this *below* you?

My life had never been more literally in Thorn's hands. If I'd slipped from his grasp, no spurt of fiery power could have stopped me from making an excellent impression of a pancake, splat on the ground below. But even as my pulse beat faster while I took in the scene we were soaring over, not a hint of that adrenaline was panic. I had a hell of a lot more faith in the warrior's strength than in my hocus pocus.

"It's spectacular." I brought my gaze back to my lover, to the smoldering wingéd visage that was even more awe-inspiring to me than the sights beneath us, and my throat constricted.

I didn't want him to leave us, for however long he

might feel he needed to—now or ever. This brutal, valiant monster was like no one I'd ever met or would again. And despite the turmoil he'd been going through, he'd offered up this moment just for me.

I touched his face, tracing my thumb over his lips before meeting his eyes again. I wasn't trying to sway his choice, but he deserved to know exactly what he was choosing between, didn't he?

"I love you," I said.

The words came out so quietly I was afraid they'd be lost in the wind. But the flare of the glow in Thorn's eyes left no doubt that he'd heard them. Even with the unearthly reverb that came into his voice, his response came out ragged with emotion. "And I you, Sorsha."

He kissed me so hard my head spun—or maybe it was that we really were spinning with another flap of his wings, spiraling even higher into the sky. A waft of chilly air licked across my neck, but it only created a perfect contrast with the heat coursing between us.

Thorn's lips traveled from my mouth to my jaw and down the side of my neck, sparking pleasure everywhere they touched. His resonant voice sent giddy tremors over my skin. "You would not hate me instead if I left?"

I shook my head against him, soaking in everything I could of the being that held me. "The fact that you wouldn't let love stop you from fulfilling your responsibilities is part of what makes you who you are. It's an honor to mean so much to you that I'd factor in at all."

He made a rumbling sound low in his throat and

managed to maneuver his hand to stroke over my breast. Bliss quivered through my chest with the swivel of his palm against my nipple. "How could my absence not wound you? It's hard enough for me to think of it."

"It would hurt, but that's okay." I thought of that moment in Omen's cave when I'd jumped between him and Thorn and thrown my life on the line to save them both. "Sometimes the right thing hurts. It's just that the wrong thing would hurt more. And whatever you do, I know it's a measure of what you need to be the man you believe you should be, not how much you care about me. You've proven all you need to about that already."

I pressed a kiss to the edge of his jaw with a little smile and sang, "Because I've had the climb of my life, no, I'd never melt this way and more."

Thorn let out a huff that sounded more amused than anything. "You and your ridiculous songs," he rumbled, and then he was kissing me again, pulling me flush against his muscle-packed body at the same time. His thickly corded erection rubbed against me through the layers of our clothes, and it was a miracle I didn't spontaneously combust from that.

If I ever went down in flames, that'd be the way to do it.

A needy whimper slipped from my lips, and my warrior knew how to answer it. Without hesitation, he wrenched at my jeans with a rasp of tearing fabric. I fumbled between us to undo the lacing on his trousers. Fuck the cool night air against my suddenly bare ass or any concern about where we'd find a new pair of pants to prevent a very revealing walk of shame back onto the RV —I wanted my lover inside me, filling me with all the power his body could offer.

Thorn whirled us in the air again and settled me over him with incredible steadiness that clashed with the storm of hunger in his eyes. As I sank onto him, we groaned together.

His cock was even more massive in his shadowkind form, but the burn of it stretching me felt so fucking good, like he was both splitting me in two and the only force in the universe holding me together. Every particle in me quivered with desire for more.

Our mouths crashed together, no room for tenderness left in our hunger for each other. I swayed against the warrior, slowly as my body adjusted to his girth and then faster as I could handle more.

Each burst of friction sent a rush of pleasure roaring through my body, along with noises wilder than I'd known I had in me. Thorn gripped my ass and the back of my head, moving with me, his strength radiating through every facet of our joining.

He plunged deeper still, and a moan spilled from my mouth into his. His wings sent us careening higher. I'd never felt anything like this, racing toward my peak inside while my body hurtled upward in unison.

The tingling of ecstasy washed through me from my core out to the tips of my fingers and toes, swelling sharper and harder. With one final thrust, it exploded inside me with such force that all I could do was cling to Thorn and shudder.

Thorn came too, with a ringing bellow that wrapped around me in its passion. His arms squeezed tighter, as if he never meant to let me go. I did melt into him then, flying high and yet perfectly grounded by this monstrous man who was still mine for at least one more moment.

18

Sorsha

"Souvlaki and moussaka, here we come!" Ruse announced as we roared away from the border crossing between Albania and Greece. Just a few cajoling words with the border patrol, and they'd been waving us through with broad smiles.

The incubus glanced back from the wheel to shoot a grin Snap's way. "Just wait until you see how many edible delicacies there are to discover here."

The devourer's forked tongue flicked across his lips. He leaned past the driver's seat to check the dash. "Perhaps we should be stopping for more gas soon? And Sorsha will need more to eat before much longer." He caught my eye with a playful glint in his.

"Yes, all for our mortal's benefit, I'm sure," Ruse teased, but I thought I could still hear a hint of tension in his voice that had been there ever since he'd informed the rest of us yesterday that his charmed hacker had found a promising lead that pointed us to Crete. Something about this venture bothered him.

The traces of phone calls and emails the hacker had dug up suggested there might be someone out on the ancient island who'd been working very closely with Tempest, though, so whatever the problem was, he'd obviously decided it wasn't worth mentioning. The next time I got him alone, I'd have to prod him about it.

I was starting to see how the ability to simply peek inside people's heads could be awfully tempting.

"Straight flush!" Antic declared, slapping her playing cards down on the table where I'd agreed to a few rounds of poker with her and the equines just to pass the time. Snap had briefly joined in until we'd switched to bidding with pennies rather than strawberries—which was really his own fault for eating them all.

Maybe that was for the best, though, because the imp was proving to be a menace. She chortled to herself as she scooped up more copper to add to her already considerable heap, and Bow let out a snort of frustration.

Omen emerged from the shadows in the hall and gave us a baleful look, but he managed not to remark again about how much faster we could have gotten to Crete if he'd stuck me on a plane and then hopped the RV through a couple of rifts. Gisele's usually sparkly temperament had become more like the glint of a sharpened scalpel the last time he'd brought it up.

"Haven't you already put her through enough?" she'd said with a jerk of her hand toward the sink, which at that point had been sputtering alternating dribbles of pineapple juice and sour milk, and the hellhound shifter had been wise enough to shut his mouth.

I had to say the pineapple juice was actually kind of enjoyable. Hey, don't judge. The warm iced tea that had been spewing from the showerhead for a few hours this morning? Not so much.

"We *will* need to fill up the gas again before we reach our destination," Omen said to Ruse. "Pick the stop at your discretion."

"Letting me play the boss? That could be dangerous." Ruse motioned Snap closer. "Grab my phone and let's look up our options for delicious satisfaction."

Omen must have made a gesture of his own, because Thorn materialized a moment later and dipped his head before making a report. "No sign of concerning activity in the area. I don't believe we're being followed."

The warrior had decided to stay the course for this potentially crucial stage of our mission, but I knew he still felt uneasy about the debt his fellow wingéd had suggested he owed them. His gaze slid to the landscape passing by the window, his face set in a pensive expression.

I passed my cards over to Gisele so she could shuffle and looked up at Omen. "If this is some kind of trap Tempest set up, she wouldn't need to have anyone following us—she'll be waiting for us there."

He grimaced. "I wouldn't put it past her to employ multiple tactics so she can keep an eye on us. We've already surprised her once."

"I know you and Thorn enjoy worrying," Ruse called back, "but I wouldn't have suggested we embark on this voyage if it looked anything like a trap. The bits and pieces connecting the Company to this guy are mostly from months or even years back. We didn't uncover any communication between them and him since he was sent off to Crete last month. Tempest didn't even know we'd be looking for her back then."

"I wouldn't have agreed to your suggestion if I thought it was likely to be a trap either," Omen muttered. "I just know that when it comes to the sphinx, more care is a much better strategy than not enough."

Antic bounced on the sofa. "Too much doom and gloom around here. Are we playing another hand or what?"

I happily indulged in another round of that distraction, even though it cost me the last of my pennies and several nickels to boot. The imp was just crowing over her winnings when the RV slowed.

Ruse pulled off at a faded gas station with only two antique-looking pumps and a similarly scruffy café next door. I couldn't read the lettering on the grimy sign over the door. The mock columns that ran along the front of the building on either side of it, designed to look like a Greek temple if those temples had been painted with red and blue stripes over the whitewashing, had gone dingy with time, and not in a way that gave them historic grandeur.

"Ignore appearances," the incubus said as he led the

way out. "This place is supposed to have the best dolmades in a hundred-mile radius."

Rather than salivating, Snap was peering at the restaurant front with a faint frown. He'd jarred to a stop a few feet from the RV. When I touched his arm, he shook his head as if to clear it and aimed one of his brilliant smiles at me. "Should we discover what these dole mad Es are?"

Ruse took it upon himself to do all the ordering, but I trusted the incubus's affinity for carnal pleasures. As he, Snap, and I schlepped the bulging bags to the RV, where the equines were basking in the sun, a man so skinny he could have passed for a signpost seemed to shimmer out of the shadow cast by an actual signpost and stalked over to Omen. I stopped in my tracks.

"What is the meaning of this excursion?" the unfamiliar shadowkind demanded in a haughty, nasal voice.

Omen reined in a bristle with visible effort. "Who the hell wants to know?"

The skinny guy, whatever sort of being he was, folded his arms over his chest. "The Highest expect you to be taking your commitment to them much more seriously. While Ruby is on the loose, this isn't the time for taking vacations."

Shit a slimy slug, they were following Omen to nag at him now? And to nag at him specifically about the being he was supposed to be reporting on... who was, er, standing right here carrying a load of dips and pitas. My pulse skipped a beat.

The hellhound shifter rolled his eyes with a long-suffering expression, but he managed to flick his glance my way with the swiftest of warning glances in the process. Trying not to look suspicious about it, I hustled onto the Everymobile.

Omen's voice followed us. "It just so happens that I'm coming this way on a very promising lead. The Highest managed to maintain some patience over how many years already? But if they'd rather that *you* take over the search, by all means. I'll just head back to—"

"Certainly not!" the lackey said in a tone of both horror and deep offense, as if he couldn't imagine taking on such a huge responsibility and simultaneously found it demeaning that Omen would try to pass it off on to him. Then the door clicked shut, muffling their conversation.

Thorn appeared for just long enough to reassure me, "It's just the one skulking around here," and then vanished, presumably to make sure that continued to be the case. My appetite had vanished too.

Ruse set his bag down on the table, his mouth slanted at an awkward angle. "If they knew," he murmured, "they wouldn't be showing up just to pester Omen about his promptness."

"That doesn't mean they couldn't find out," I said, keeping my voice similarly low. I resisted the urge to go up to the window and watch the rest of the conversation play out.

Snap stared out at Omen and the walking signpost with an anxious flick of his tongue. His shoulders came up. "If this being tries to come after you…"

"I'm sure it'll be fine," I said, with much more breeziness than I actually felt, and flopped down on the sofa.

Pickle scrambled onto my lap. I ran my fingers absently over his back between his wings. How closely were the Highest's minions watching us? What if they happened to stop by right when I was fucking up my powers again?

Heat sizzled from my fingers, and the little dragon yelped.

"Pickle!" I cried, forcing my voice into a whisper. "Pickle, I'm sorry."

He darted away to the bedroom with his wings pressed flat to his sides. My stomach knotted. Thinking about worst case scenarios had practically made me create one.

"I'll go out and see if Omen needs a little help talking his way out of this," Ruse volunteered, "seeing as making friends with strangers isn't typically on his to-do list. You stay put, Miss Blaze." He couldn't quite hide the worry in his gaze before he slipped into the shadows.

Snap sat down next to me and examined my hands. My palms had only turned mildly pink. He hurried to get the aloe anyway, despite my protest that I'd probably heal in an hour or two anyway.

"I'm looking after you in every way I can," he said, and shot another glance toward the window with an uneasy air that I didn't think was just about our unexpected visitor. "No matter what I have to do."

Something in that phrasing gave me a clue. I tugged

him down beside me. "I don't think you'll be called on to devour that lackey. *Can* you even use that power on shadowkind? Anyway, if he needs offing, I'd imagine between Omen and Thorn, every vital part of his body will be 'off' in about five seconds flat."

Snap only managed a glimmer of a smile at my joke. He sighed and tucked my head under his chin in his favorite pose. "I've never tried on a shadowkind. But I would, for you. If it's to defend my beloved, there's nothing monstrous about that."

I pulled back to peer up at him. "Are you worrying about that again? You haven't done anything wrong. You are what you are, and you've used your nature when you've needed to."

"Not only then." He let out a breath like a shudder and hugged me tighter. "That place—the colors and those columns all in a row—it looks a little like the place where I took my first devouring."

Ah, that explained a few things. I rested my arm over his and stroked the back of his hand from knuckles to wrist. "That time was an accident, wasn't it?"

"Does that make it less horrible or more? It was the first time I'd ventured through a rift into the mortal realm —I didn't know what to expect. There was a man in an alley yelling and smashing bottles. It bothered and confused me. Unsettled me. I didn't know why he would do that, and I wanted him to stop, and before I even realized what I was doing, I was already swallowing his soul. Feeling all the agony that I was putting him through. Wanting more."

"And then you punished yourself for that mistake by hiding away in the shadow realm for ages to make sure you never did it again. It's not like you just brushed it off."

"I know. But..." He tipped his head close to mine again. "The sphinx may do evil things, but she's wise about a lot too. She said we were only pretending not to be monsters, that we can't just ignore what we are forever. I wish I could. I wish I hadn't liked it. I wish I didn't still feel pinches of the hunger now and then. I'd like to just be your beloved and one who can taste impressions to help with our mission, and that's all. Even if you can accept how I am, I don't know if *I* can."

Was that why he'd been even cuddlier than usual the last few days? I turned in his arms to offer him a kiss. He kissed me back with such sweet tenderness that it was impossible to picture this man as some kind of savage beast.

"I just burned my one-hundred-percent innocent dragon because I still haven't gotten a handle on my powers," I said. "If you can forgive me for that, then I hope you can forgive yourself for not having full control over every impulse. You're doing a much better job keeping your urges in check than I am."

Snap let out a huff. "You've had much less time to get used to them."

"But much more practice *using* them. And I'm still fucking up. We just... We do our best, right? No one goes through life never wanting anything that could hurt someone else. You decide what's most important, and act on that as well as you can, and that shows who you really are." I kissed him again. "And I think you're pretty damned fantastic."

He hummed and nestled me against him, his gaze returning to the windows warily. The voices had fallen silent. I hoped that meant Omen had sent the skinny lackey off—with or without assistance from our companions—and not that the prick was investigating to make sure the hellhound shifter had been true to his word.

Fuck the Highest for hassling Omen when they wouldn't help him with the actual catastrophe we were facing. Fuck Tempest for messing with all of my shadowkind lovers' minds.

The anger nibbled at my nerves, but Snap's adoring warmth around me stopped it from flaring into a real fire.

The equines tramped on board first with a defiant air, followed by a skipping Antic, then Thorn and Ruse, and finally a scowling but no longer impeded Omen.

"He's gone," the hellhound shifter said before I had to ask. "But I can tell they'll be sending more. Bloated self-important jackasses. I don't know how much warning we'll have."

I forced a smile. "I'll work extra hard at keeping my flambéing tendencies tamped down."

As Omen took over at the wheel, the atmosphere stayed subdued. Gisele and Bow retreated to the master bedroom with a joint of their "other kind of" grass. Antic tried to coax Pickle out of my room and sulked when he didn't respond. The rest of us eyed the bulging bags that held our lunch, but none of us moved to open them.

Ruse had pulled out his phone. He tapped at it, swiped through some pages, and tapped some more, his expression getting noticeably stiffer with each passing minute.

"Have you realized that place actually only had the *second*-best dolmades in this half of the country?" I said after a while, just to prod a response out of him.

The incubus chuckled without much humor and shoved his phone in his pocket. His gaze shifted to the window, but the haziness in his eyes suggested he was thinking about something far beyond the view outside.

"I told you once about a particular mortal woman I occupied myself with back in the mists of time," he said, painfully droll. "It happens that she lived not far from Athens. As do rather a lot of her descendants now."

A prickle ran down my spine. He meant the first mortal woman he'd thought he'd fallen in love with—the one who'd rejected him. "Are you planning on doing anything about that?" I couldn't help asking.

A bittersweet smile played with his lips. "I was thinking if the timing works out, I might make a brief detour to pay a call on her granddaughter."

19

Ruse

A s he hefted his motorcycle—or as he liked to call it, "Charlotte"—off the back of the RV, Omen couldn't quite restrain a frown. He set it on the darkened road where we'd parked on the outskirts of Athens and gave me an evaluating look, as if he thought I might break his treasured vehicle just by standing next to it.

"Don't spend too long on this side trip," he said in a terse but even tone.

I offered him a jaunty tip of the cap that hid my horns. "By the time you've found yourself a ship, I'll be right there to talk us onto it."

"I'm going to hold you to that."

He got back into the RV, but Sorsha wasn't in quite so much of a hurry to see me off. My mortal love trailed her fingers over one of the motorcycle's handlebars and then turned her unusually pensive gaze on me. "Are you sure you need to do this? Are you sure you *want* to?"

She'd so generously given me her blessing to fulfill my appetites freely, but I thought I caught a whiff of possessiveness or perhaps a more general uneasiness in her demeanor, potent enough that I didn't need to extend my supernatural abilities to pick up on it. But then, we couldn't help our emotions, could we?

I touched her cheek, reveling for perhaps the hundredth time as I hoped to hundreds more in the way her bright copper eyes lit up at that simple caress. "There's nothing this woman could stir in me that you don't a thousandfold more."

"You don't know that yet. You haven't really had the chance to compare before." Sorsha let out a rush of breath. "It's not really that anyway. I just— I know how much she hurt you. Well, the woman this woman will remind you of. No matter what happens, no matter what you see or what she says if you talk to her, it doesn't change anything about who you are."

"Maybe it does," I said.

The gleam in her eyes flared, and I felt a waft of heat she must have suppressed before her anger condensed all the way into flames. "She barely knew you. She didn't bother to. And her granddaughter has no idea at all what—"

"I know. That's not what I meant." I teased my thumb over Sorsha's chin just below those tempting lips. "What happened back then has stuck with me, though. You've seen that, or you wouldn't be rising to my defense

—very admirable of you, of course. That fragment of my history has held like a splinter under the skin of my soul, as much as I have a soul, and I think confronting it might be necessary to finally pulling it out. I'd like to be who I am without it."

Sorsha made a face at me, but her tone was light. "Well, fine, give a perfectly understandable reason so I can't grumble about it anymore." She leaned in to steal a kiss as deftly as she'd stolen so many other things in her career, not least of all my heart. I let my mouth linger against hers, absorbing one last bit of love and courage to carry with me.

As she left me, I swung my leg over the bike. It wasn't the first time I'd borrowed Omen's ride, and my body settled into place on the seat easily enough. But despite my reassurances to Sorsha, my spirit was not at all settled as I revved the engine and took off through the crisply warm Mediterranean dusk.

Sorsha's emotions weren't the only impressions that had snagged on my incubus senses. From all around, more and more with each passing day, faint ripples of anticipation skipped across my skin from indistinct directions. Ripples with a vicious edge.

I couldn't say for sure what they were. Possibly it was merely a global epidemic of emotional indigestion. I suspected, though, that I was picking up the violent hopes of those who knew about the Company's goals and weren't currently shuttered behind steel and silver. Those who knew that Tempest was only days from reaching that goal.

It wasn't just Sorsha who needed me. It was the companions I'd promised to help in this mission and all the shadowkind who'd wither away if the sphinx got what she wanted. Maybe I wasn't all that fond of every one of those shadowkind, but I wasn't the type to wish them dead either. I vastly preferred it if they stayed alive and at a distance where they wouldn't weigh on my limited conscience.

And if I was going to make sure of that, I'd damn well better be at my best. No niggling splinters of shame and doubt, no nagging memories I should have put to rest before Sorsha had ever come into my life.

Danae had lived in a hilltop villa with a view of the distant sea—the sort of home I'd now have said looked more believable as a movie set than in reality. But it was still here, the pale stucco walls of the house rising amid the bushes no longer in bloom. A few cracks and patches of repaired plaster showed here and there that hadn't existed before, but the place was in much better condition than Danae herself would be these days, wherever they'd laid her old bones to rest.

I left Charlotte at a safe distance and traveled around the matching garden walls through the darkness. The gnarled old olive tree I'd once playfully called to my one-time lover from had gone as kaput as she had, but I found a rocky protrusion a few feet from the wall that allowed me nearly as good a glimpse into the yard. As I clambered onto it, my chest tightened.

If my memories of Danae were a splinter, then that shard of noxious wood was digging into my gut right now, prodding out trickles of embarrassment and shame. The way she'd looked at me when I'd made the proposition that we take our relationship beyond mere physical pleasures—the way she'd *laughed*...

What should it matter now? I was here, and she wasn't. My capacity for love had endured after all, despite my nature, despite her dismissal of it. Still, I braced myself as I peered into the garden, preparing for a more wrenching wave of pain.

The current owners had changed the landscaping quite a bit. The only feature I recognized was the marble fountain dribbling water in the center of the space. The poor cupid poised over the pool had lost his head, which gave the whole piece a much more macabre look.

A newer wrought-iron bench stood nearby beneath the shade of a lemon tree, and the bushes stood scattered across the terrain in abandon rather than their former neat order. The varying shades of green in their leaves made for a delight of color even without their flowers. An herbal scent carried on the breeze thickly enough that I could taste it even from the shadows.

The sky had deepened into the indigo of night, but a few windows on the villa still gleamed with light. I was about to slip over the wall to spy through the glass when the woman I'd come to see saved me the trouble by strolling out.

It had to be the granddaughter—Demi, the miraculous internet had informed me. She was a tad taller and a shade slimmer than her grandmother had been, but her hair shone the same honey-brown, loose across her shoulders. Here and there the light caught a strand of gray—she was a decade or so older than Danae had been during our... acquaintance. But that only meant there were a few more lines around her graceful features, which held an echo of the woman who'd come before her. I could have believed I was seeing Danae herself in her middle age.

I took all that in—and my pulse beat evenly onward. The shame had faded away into the tranquility of the night. No jab of loss or regret ran through me. I couldn't even say I felt a twinge of anger at the reminder of the woman who'd seen me as little more than a very animated, multi-featured dildo.

No, mostly what I felt was a mild curiosity. How far had the apple fallen from the tree?

Not all that far in some respects, if the book she held was anything to go by. She lifted the canvas-covered volume, the frayed ribbon placeholder dangling, and spoke in a low, sweet voice. Reciting the lines to a play—one of Aristophanes', if my sketchy recollection served.

She must have picked up that hobby from her grandmother. That was how I'd fallen for Danae—watching her stride around her garden, making impassioned speeches and cracking the best of ancient Grecian jokes. She hadn't wanted to act professionally, just to live out those scenes at her leisure, enjoying the poetry and the drama. Finding more depth in them than she'd ever been willing to see in me.

Should watching a woman so like her go through the

same motions have rankled me? It didn't. Instead, a strange, serene certainty washed over me.

Demi *was* merely going through the motions, just as her grandmother had been. Neither of them had ever really passionately declared a challenge to combat or plotted the demise of unspeakable enemies or bantered with scurrilous rogues. I'd fallen for the roles Danae had admired, but she'd only been playing at them.

Sorsha was every bit the fierce and unshakeable woman contained in those roles—and more. The love that had grown in me in her presence ran right down to my core, as true as anything. She was as tangled in my being now as the roots of that lemon tree were with the earth.

And I wouldn't have had it any other way.

Whatever splinter had remained from the follies of times past, it crumbled away with that understanding. I drew back from the wall without a moment's hesitation and returned to the motorcycle.

It wasn't hard to find my companions, even though they'd driven right through Athens down to the harbor. When I reached that area, I opened my supernatural senses to the energy I'd recognize as Sorsha's—not pushing hard enough to get more than a taste, just enough to direct me.

Long ago, I'd let the scraps of desire I'd read in one woman's mind convince me that if I only told her how much more I'd wanted, she'd find the same longing in herself. Now I didn't need to scour my love's soul for an answering emotion. I had a woman who offered up her affection with every word and gesture she directed my way.

The Everymobile was parked outside a closed fish shop. Its tour bus guise was thrown off a little by the tinsel it'd decided to sprout along the edges of the roof, which wavered up and down even without a breeze to carry it. It was definitely for the best that we hadn't braved another trip to the rifts. It might have come out decked with a full set of holiday lights.

I left the motorcycle around back and traveled in through the shadows, only stepping out by Sorsha's door. I could tell she was inside the bedroom, but it gave me an inexplicable pleasure to honor her privacy with the small gesture of knocking. "I've returned with all my parts intact, Miss Blaze."

"I should hope so," she said dryly, but when I slipped inside, I found her smiling. She looked me up and down as if confirming that claim for herself and gave my hair a fond ruffle. Her hand lingered over one of my horns in a way that never failed to send a thrill through me before it dropped to her side. "You look happy. Was she everything you expected?"

"She was exactly what she should have been, which was nothing I have any interest in anymore. I'd have had an awfully dull time of it if she'd been open to my full range of charms after all."

I winked at Sorsha, and she laughed, but maybe the remark rubbed up against that thread of jealousy a little too closely. Just for an instant, flames coursed up over her hands, nearly translucent but hazy with heat. They vanished so quickly, with no change in her expression, that I wasn't sure she'd even noticed her power had snuck out.

I took hold of the hem of her shirt and tugged her to me, tilting my face so my forehead rested against hers. Our mortal exuded so much strength and fire it was easy to forget she had her own vulnerabilities. She hadn't asked me this, and she shouldn't need to. It was a pleasure and an honor to say it for its own sake.

"In case I wasn't clear enough earlier, there's no one I need or want other than you."

The corners of her lips curled upward again, and she met my kiss with that smile. But I knew even as I enjoyed the moment that it wasn't enough. She had worries far beyond my part in her life.

She needed more than *me*... Maybe more than all four of us, despite all we could offer. She was a being of two worlds and uncertain abilities with possible apocalyptic potential.

All we could speak from was the shadowkind side. I could see that she got whatever other perspective she might need too, couldn't I? The sort of help she never would have allowed herself to ask for.

Whatever Tempest was going to throw at us in the next few days, Sorsha had to be at her best to meet it too.

When I left her, I stepped outside and pulled out my phone, but it wasn't to do any more digging into my own past. It was to bring up the number of the most vital presence from Sorsha's.

"Hello?" said the voice that answered, energ
cautious at the same time.

I leaned against the RV's side, tipping back my h
to watch the tinsel waving in its manufactured breeze
"Hello, Vivi. It's your best friend's favorite incubus. How
would you feel about embarking on a little trip?"

20

Sorsha

I braced my legs to keep my balance on the swaying dock and eyed the seafaring vessel Omen had pointed to. "*This* is the ship you got us?"

The boat was big enough—that wasn't the problem. But more of the hull's white paint had been scratched or worn off than was left on, which made me wonder just how intact the wood was beneath that. Aged beams jutted every which way around the small cabin, making the ship look like a mutated narwhal.

"She's an old fishing boat," Omen said, aiming a pleased glance at his find. "Outfitted with a modern motor, but still with all the other trappings. I thought we should make use of the time we'll be at sea to get in some more training, and props are always useful for that. Unless you've got something better to do?"

I dragged damp, salty air into my lungs. I guessed if

there was anywhere I could safely practice my fiery skills, out in the middle of an immense body of water would make the top of the list. "I suppose you've already named her?"

His lips curved upward, and he waved down the length of the boat. "I didn't need to."

Curling lines of blue swept through the patchy white paint, the letters spelling out *Penelope*. I had to admit it was an Omen-esque name if I'd ever heard one. I cocked my head at him. "Now I see the real reason you bought her."

He waved off my remark and motioned me on board in one smooth movement. "Let's get going, Disaster, while you've still left the harbor in one piece."

I stuck my tongue out at him and darted across the plank that led onto the ship. Not wanting to draw attention in case Tempest's lackeys or some other member of the Company asked around, the other three shadowkind in our crew had leapt on board out of sight in the shadows.

We were back to our original quartet, leaving the equines and Antic back in Athens with the Everymobile. If we hadn't returned from Crete within three days, they were meant to launch a rescue mission. I'd expected Antic to complain about being left out, but she'd danced around with so much joy at the thought of being a potential rescuer that she might even have been hoping we were heading into a trap.

It was going to be a long voyage, but Omen had vetoed any talk of planes for this final part of the journey.

"Too many records, too tight a space." As if we had a whole lot of places to flee to out in the middle of the sea. I definitely couldn't have gotten in any training on a flight, though, and maybe the rhythm and hiss of the waves would settle my nerves more before the confrontation ahead.

Omen cast off, and I gamely raised my hand in greeting to the other boaters we passed to show we were perfectly normal people off on a pleasure cruise, if on a somewhat unusual ship for that job.

When the harbor had dwindled into blobs in the distance, Ruse, Snap, and Thorn materialized on the deck. Snap leaned over the metal railing that was mounted along most of the starboard side and drank in the sea scents with a blissful expression. Thorn immediately clambered up to the top of the tallest post with its bedraggled sail still wrapped around it, where he'd get the widest view for surveillance.

Ruse flopped into one of the deck chairs, his face slightly greenish and his hand resting on his stomach. "Never been a huge fan of water travel," he admitted.

I sat down next to him, tipping back my head to soak up the Mediterranean sun. "You could stick to the shadows. Plenty of them around."

"That actually makes it worse. Which is a pretty mean feat considering I barely have a stomach in that state."

"I suppose that means this picnic lunch is all for me, then."

As I rifled through the large bag of edible supplies

we'd brought for a bottle of lemonade, Snap hustled over with a sound of mock consternation. "*I'll* take Ruse's portion."

The incubus felt well enough to laugh. "That's no surprise."

The devourer gave me the sly look he was starting to perfect, turned adorable by his beaming grin. "You'd make yourself sick too if you tried to eat all of it, Peach. I'm simply keeping your best interests in mind."

"Of course you are," I said with a playful swat. "But it's hardly lunchtime yet. We just had breakfast."

The next sound Snap made wasn't so joking in its consternation, but he settled for only plucking a plum out of the bag. He perched on the railing, long legs dangling over the water, and hummed happily as he bit into the fruit. "*I* like the sea."

"You're welcome to it," Ruse muttered, but after a stretch of calm waters and the soothing rumble of the motor, he'd come back more to his usual color.

For the first few hours, Omen focused on sailing, which apparently he had some experience with, and left the rest of us to lounge—or, in Thorn's case, to broodingly eye the horizon. I knew that reprieve wouldn't last. Not long after we'd dug into our picnic lunch, the hellhound shifter emerged from the cabin, considered the vast sprawl of endless blue all around us, and snapped his fingers at me.

"All right, Disaster. Let's see what we can do to mitigate that catastrophic nature of yours."

I licked the last few flecks of icing sugar from my

, bougatsa dessert off my fingers. "I'm not the
.1e here, dog-breath. How about a 'please'?"

He glowered at me and dipped into a little bow.
"Would Her Highness kindly allow me to continue
teaching her how she might avoid incinerating herself?"

"That's more like it." I got up, stretching my arms and
then cracking my knuckles—and trying not to notice that
three other gazes had focused on me with varying levels
of concern.

Snap sprang from the arm of the deck chair where
he'd been cozying up to me. "If there's any way I can
help—"

"I've got this," Omen said dryly. "She isn't going to
leave your sight, so you can ensure I leave her in one
piece."

Was the devourer worried about what Omen might
do to me or what I might do to myself? At this point, it
was hard to say which of us was a larger threat to my
well-being. Ruse might have even straightened up a tad as
if preparing for some kind of intervention, and Thorn
was peering at me instead of the horizon now.

I folded my arms over my chest. Okay, so I'd let loose
a few more flames than usual in the last couple of days,
but we did have a psychopathic, immensely powerful
shadowkind who might be launching a double-genocide
any moment now, so who could blame me for being a
smidge wound up?

How immense a genocide would we be facing if I
didn't get those powers completely under control?

I shoved that question aside and nodded to Omen. "Got some more bits of paper for me to charbroil?"

"I thought we'd try something different for a change. We're just going to spar. And by 'just', I mean fists and feet only. No supernatural powers. You let your fire out, you automatically lose, no matter how pissed off I made you. Oh, and to add a little challenge..." He leapt up onto one of the railings with a nimbleness I wouldn't have expected from his well-built frame. "Touch the deck with both feet, and you also lose. Should we make it the most wins out of five, or do you need more chances than that to get warmed up?"

As I climbed onto a wooden beam that crossed the stern, I raised my eyebrows at him. "You're assuming I'll even need five. I'm the one who spent most of the past few years scrambling across rooftops and through windows."

Omen smiled at me with a gleam of his teeth. "I suppose we'll see."

He didn't give me any more warning than that. The next thing I knew, he'd launched his muscular frame right at me.

I dashed down the pole protruding from the stern, swayed, and hurled myself upward to grab one of the salt-gritted ropes so I could swing over the hellhound's head. Ruse let out a whoop of appreciation, but all I'd done was flee, not land any blows. I spun around, ducked the fist speeding toward me, and managed to jab my heel into Omen's calf before he dodged.

I stalked after him along the pole, both of us over the

open water now. "What's the rule about wet dogs? Does that count as a loss too?"

"I guess it'd better," Omen said, and threw himself at me.

I nearly did perform a spectacular belly flop then. It was only by a hair's breadth that my fingers snagged on a ridge on the upper hull, giving me just enough leverage to toss my leg back over the railing.

As I scrambled back up, the hellhound was already barreling toward me. I dashed along the railing and hefted myself onto a rope near the bow.

My foot skimmed Omen's face, just shy of a strike— and he caught my ankle. With a yank, he sent me tumbling onto the deck. I hit the worn wooden boards ass-first.

Sprawling on my back, I waggled my legs in the air. "Technically my feet didn't touch it."

Omen snorted. "And here I thought the spirit of the rules was clear. But if you're determined to be a cheater as well as a thief..."

The words should have rolled right off me. It wasn't as if I hadn't been called worse—hell, *he'd* called me worse several times over. But something about that accusation struck a spark inside me, and I had to clench my hands to will back the flare of heat before it burst from my skin.

All the more reason to play along with this training. That inner fire had damn well better learn to stay tamped down until I called on it with a purpose.

"Fine," I said. "I'll just have to whoop your ass the other four times."

Omen's icy eyes glinted. "Come and try me."

I had to say I didn't think the rules were exactly fair. Omen might not have been bringing out his own hellish fire, but his speed and dexterity were several cuts above mortal standards. Not that I was going to complain that I couldn't keep up with him to his face. A gal's got to have some self-respect.

I'd just have to be more tricksy.

We exchanged more feints and parries around the edge of the boat until I saw my opportunity. I dropped low, hooked my arm around the railing, and heaved both of my feet into the side of Omen's legs.

He groped for balance, but not fast enough. This time the smack of flesh meeting wood wasn't my own. I pushed myself up straight, grinning down at him, as he dusted himself off.

"We're just getting started," he promised. "You need to be able to hold yourself in check and bend those flames to your will when you're face to face with Tempest, and she isn't going to be half this easy on you."

"Bring it on," I shot back, but something—maybe the mention of Tempest—sent another jolt of heat through me. This time it coursed up through my ribs and into my shirt before I quite got a grip on it. With a hitch of my pulse, I slapped my arms against my sides to smother it.

Omen didn't comment, but a flicker of tension passed through his face, his mouth tightening into a brief frown.

Before I could do more than take a breath, he sprang at me again.

The momentary loss of control must have rattled me. Omen threw his swipes and punches with brutal fury, and each time his knuckles clipped my body, another spurt of anger threatened to break the surface of my composure.

Stop it! I thought at the fire searing from my gut up to my chest. *He wants to rile you up. He's not really a threat. Chill out already.*

My mental commands didn't have much effect. I banged my knee against a board while dodging a roundhouse, and a sputter of flames licked over my hand, blistering my fingers.

Omen didn't see—my hunched torso had hidden the lapse from view. *Not again. Stay the fuck* inside *me,* I ordered the roiling energies.

Both to distract myself and to annoy my opponent, I danced backward with a little musical accompaniment. "And if you only scold and spite, we'll be holding on forever. But we'll only be faking a fight—"

Omen growled and charged at me, cutting me off as I had to fling myself at the ropes to escape. My feet skimmed the deck by mere inches, but I wrenched myself up and around fast enough to clock him in the back of the head.

He teetered but caught himself and whirled around to leap after me. The singing hadn't boosted my spirits as much as I'd hoped—or really at all. Gritting my teeth against another waft of flame, I scrambled across the netting. I kicked Omen in the shoulder, let out a hiss when he hauled on my leg so hard he almost dislocated my hip, and finally made it within jumping distance of the opposite railing.

"Come on, Disaster," the hellhound shifter said, hurtling after me. His voice was taut, his face set in an expression that looked as uneasy as it did fierce. "Is this how you're going to fight all those Company bastards and the sphinx who's egging them on—by running away? Didn't they *kill* your guardian? How many more are you going to let them murder?"

"I'm not running away," I snapped, and reversed course to throw an uppercut he neatly avoided. My sneakers squeaked on the metal bar. "Isn't it called fighting smart?"

"Doesn't look so smart to me. We don't have time for pussyfooting around the problem now, do we?"

"I know that." Holy humping harpies, was he pissing me off. Even more fire crackled through me. Every muscle in my body went rigid, holding it in. "I'll be ready."

"Are you sure? You've got to tackle it head on, before we come right down to the wire. Maybe I shouldn't expect any better from a being who's only half—"

Before he could even finish that sentence, the fire blazed up so sharp and sudden my vision hazed. All I could see was the glare of the flames; all I could feel was every inch of my skin sizzling and charring. The pain shocked the air from my lungs.

A solid force slammed into me. I crashed into the

placid ocean head first, salty water bubbling to a boil around me for an instant before it doused the flames.

I came up sputtering—and feeling the prickle of raw patches all across my skin. My ponytail drifted over my shoulder into view, its tip burnt black. Nausea pooled in my stomach.

Omen had tossed himself into the water along with me. He shook the moisture from his hair in a gesture that was undeniably dog-like and glanced over me with a gaze that was all man, lit with his own orange heat. His mouth twisted.

"That was a low blow," he said. "It should have been beneath me."

It took me a second to process that he was apologizing and another to realize the apology was for the comment that had provoked my inferno, not for the unexpected swim. I glanced up at the boat, taking in the scorch marks streaking across the mottled paint, and my stomach lurched again.

I'd almost burnt up our sole mode of transportation with no land in sight, and Omen was apologizing to *me*.

My tongue turned leaden in my mouth. I'd failed. I'd been a fucking disaster.

But what was the point in talking about that when Omen knew it just as well as I did?

After a fumble for words, what fell from my mouth was, "Well, now we're both beneath the boat. Maybe we should fix that?"

Thorn had flown down from the mast. As he leaned over the railing, the smoldering darkness cleared from his eyes and his wings vanished. A moment later, Ruse and Snap joined him, looking equally worried. Now we had a whole party celebrating my ineptitude. Wonderful.

Omen swam closer to me. The damp darkened his eyelashes, making his gaze even more piercing, but it wasn't chilly right now. Treading water, he examined one of my forearms and then the other.

The red patches were already fading back into their usual pink. "Your healing abilities are heightening as quickly as your fire is," he remarked.

"Oh, joy. More time to burn alive if there's no convenient ocean to throw me into."

His eyes met mine, stormy with an emotion I couldn't read. "Maybe I've been going about this wrong."

"What do you mean?" What fresh hell did he have in store for me now?

But he brushed his fingertips over my soaked hair, sparking a much more welcome heat, and it occurred to me that *he* might be worried about me too, however much trouble he had showing it.

"I've been trying to push you to the brink," he said. "Get you used to the sensation so you can control it. But maybe this power isn't something you can control that way. Maybe the answer isn't suppressing your anger but making sure it's focused on the right target."

I arched an eyebrow at him. "Trying to keep it off of you, hmm?"

This once, he didn't rise to the bait. "No," he said, all seriousness. "I'm trying to keep it off of *you*. Whatever the Highest or Tempest or anyone says, there's nothing wrong with you. You don't deserve the shit they're trying to put you through, so you sure as hell shouldn't be putting yourself through even more. You're incredible."

"I'll second that motion," Ruse called from the deck.

"Fantastic," Snap murmured in eager agreement.

A smile stretched Thorn's lips. "I couldn't have expressed it more eloquently."

In the face of that deluge of admiration—prompted by the being who'd once been my biggest critic, no less—I didn't know what to do with myself. My mouth opened and closed and opened again only to sputter sea water back out. One thing I definitely had to keep doing: treading this damn water. No matter how distractingly tender my hellhound shifter had unexpectedly become.

Omen glanced up at our audience and then back at me, his hand lingering against my jaw. "I'm not sure just saying that is quite enough. It could be that you don't avoid destruction by ignoring everything that's against you—you do it by remembering everyone who's for you. So how about instead of tossing you around, we try grounding you instead?"

I blinked at him, and a snarky response fell out before I could catch it. "That might be a little difficult considering there's literally no solid land in sight."

One side of Omen's mouth quirked up. "Then it's a good thing I had a more metaphorical 'grounding' in mind." He motioned overhead. "Thorn, could you toss a net down—one that's fixed well to the ship. And then the rest of you can toss yourselves in. Our mortal deserves a group effort."

Was that the first time he'd ever referred to me as *theirs?*

I didn't have much time to puzzle over his unexpected compliments or his intentions before the warrior had heaved a heavy length of net over the side of the boat. As Omen drew me through the cool water over to it, the others leapt in after us. No big deal for them if they left their clothes on—they could rematerialize them from the shadows dry the second they got out. Although from my glance at Snap, it appeared *he'd* decided to simply chuck off all garments right from the get-go.

Omen tugged my attention away from the pale gleam of Snap's naked body with an insistent press of his fingers beneath my chin. He looped one arm through the net. "To make sure Penelope doesn't go astray," he said with that same crooked smile, and guided my mouth the rest of the way to his.

I felt all kinds of naked with my body coming to rest against the hellhound shifter's in the water, our clothes plastered to our skin, his lips branding mine. The traces of sea salt that lingered on those lips gave the kiss an extra tang—and so did the knowledge that this was the first time he'd ever made a public display of his affection in front of his companions.

Ruse let out a low chuckle. Three other bodies drifted around mine, their warmth encircling me in the cool water. Omen released my mouth, keeping his head tipped close to mine. "You're ours. We won't let you lose yourself, Phoenix."

Ours. The word tingled through me, too sweet for me

to bother with protests about whether I belonged to anyone at all. I knew him well enough by now to be sure he didn't mean it that way. I belonged *with* them, and I had no arguments about that at all.

And they were all here with me—the men I loved.

Naturally, the incubus took the initiative to move things along first. As Omen brought his mouth to the crook of my neck, Ruse leaned in to capture my lips. The shifter eased to the side to give him more room.

Thorn's massive form had come up behind me. He circled my waist with his hands and trailed one up to cup my breast. His fingers flicked over my nipple one by one, drawing it to a stiffened peak through the wet fabric with quiver after quiver of pleasure.

Another hand, slender and lithe, traced the curve of my thigh. Snap pressed his mouth to my shoulder, with a little nip to shift my shirt collar so he had access to more skin.

I didn't know if this would ground me the way Omen had hoped, if it would do anything at all to calm my inner flames when I needed them under control, but I couldn't have imagined a more enjoyable strategy. All of my lovers had joined together to share and adore me. The fire coursing through me now held only bliss.

They stayed clustered around me, their mouths marking my skin with their own heat, their fingers teasing every inch of my skin with giddy waves that echoed the rocking of the sea. Thorn wrenched off my shirt and bra and flung them over the hull onto the deck; Snap pulled me higher in the water to slick his forked tongue over my breast. As Omen sucked my other nipple between his lips, Ruse's hand glided between my legs to stoke the sharpest blaze my body was capable of when they had me like this.

My hips swayed with his caress, pleasure pulsing through me. Omen swallowed my gasp with another kiss. Thorn ran his fingers down my spine and nibbled my shoulder blade with startling delicacy.

I fumbled with Ruse's shirt with one hand, refamiliarizing myself with Snap's lean chest at the same time. The incubus paused just for an instant, and his clothes vanished as the devourer's had. When he flicked open my fly, Omen helped him peel off my pants.

Too much desire was flowing through me and around me to leave room for patience. I hooked my legs around Ruse's to pull him closer. As he teased the tip of his cock over my clit and farther downward, a needy whimper slipped from my mouth. Snap caught me in a kiss, and the incubus plunged right into me with a rush of the headiest delight.

Thorn was fondling my breasts again from behind, holding me in place to meet Ruse's thrusts. Omen grazed the sensitive skin of my throat with the tips of his houndish fangs. I reached down his body, now nude too, and wrapped my hand around his erection. The shifter groaned against my neck.

My hips bucked with Ruse's, my mind glazed with the pleasure—so much of it—they were conjuring across my entire being. As the incubus hit the perfect spot inside me, Snap dipped his hand between us. His fingers found my clit. The devourer kissed me again, circling that nub of nerves in time with the delicious pounding of the incubus's cock.

Thorn pinched my nipples. My fingers squeezed tighter around Omen's cock, jerking it faster as I careened into the breathless surge of my orgasm. A cry broke from my throat with the force of the release, which crackled through me with a brilliance no flames could match.

The hellhound shifter thrust into my hand, his own breath stuttering. Ruse spilled himself into me with a groan. I was still floating on the bliss of that first release when he withdrew and Snap pushed in front of me with all his possessive determination.

"My peach?" he murmured in a tone that left no doubt about what he was asking.

I squeezed his shoulder. "Please."

He penetrated me so swiftly and deeply that a fresh gasp propelled from my lips. A gust of heat against my wrist and the crush of Omen's mouth on mine told me another of my lovers had reached his own peak. I groped behind me, and Ruse guided my hand through the water to Thorn's groin with a knowing hum.

"Sorsha," Thorn rumbled as I clutched his rigid thickness. His mouth seared against my cheek. I twisted my head so I could receive his kiss where I wanted it most.

No, I didn't feel grounded at all. I was soaring as much as I had that night with the wingéd, buoyed now by all of the four monstrous men who offered up their fondness in such different but delectable ways. My body arched and rocked between them with the shifting currents, Snap drove deeper still with a hungry panting, Omen's tail flicked across my ass, and I was coming again, ricocheting up to the clear blue sky.

Snap buried his face in my neck and shuddered with his own release. Thorn followed with a groan moments later. We drifted there, twined and sated, our own circle of ecstasy in what might as well have been an otherwise empty world.

Would this extraordinary encounter tame my fire? I didn't know, but right then the bonds between us felt too potent for any sphinx or murderous mortal to tear them apart.

It was evening by the time we docked the boat and started up the rocky terrain to the location Ruse's hacker had pinpointed. By the time Ruse pointed out the shabby cabin from which Tempest's mortal lackey had been doing his work, night had fully set in.

"From what we've gathered," the incubus whispered as we crept toward the building, "she's had this fellow investigating ruins that were constructed with protections to repel shadowkind. Looking to see what secrets the ancients might have wanted to keep from monstrous eyes."

I studied the thin glow that seeped from the cabin's one dingy window. "She must think whatever he could find will be important to completing her plan, or she wouldn't have him still poking around out here rather than behind Company building walls."

Thorn reappeared next to us, back from a quick scouting. "There are plates of silver and iron in the walls of that place, but it's fragile enough that I should be able to smash it with only minor discomfort."

"Not exactly subtle," Ruse said.

"We don't have time for subtle—and if this mortal is as wrapped up in Tempest's affairs as it seems, he might contact her at any sign of interference before we have a chance to carry out a longer plan." Omen wiped his hands together. "So, let's see some crashing."

Thorn gave us a grim smile, squared his massive shoulders, and hurtled toward the cabin. I'd seen him smash through concrete walls, so this wasn't a surprising feat. Adrenaline hummed through my veins all the same.

The warrior rammed into the side of the cabin fists first. The weathered wood creaked and crumpled. Jaw clenched against the toxic effects of the metals around him, Thorn grabbed the startled middle-aged man standing inside and wrenched him out from under the teetering roof.

The rest of us were already hustling over the hillside to meet them. I spotted the gleam of a thin silver-and-iron-twined band on the man's index finger and pushed myself faster. As soon as I reached him, I snatched his hand and tore the ring off.

The man flinched with an oddly faint cry. A second later, Ruse was at his side. The incubus fell into his cajoling tone. "Hello, friend. We're here to help you escape the fiend who's held you in her sway."

The usual glaze didn't come over the man's gray eyes. He attempted to shove away, but Thorn still gripped his shoulders firmly.

A momentary frown crossed Ruse's face, but he soldiered on. "We only want what's best for you. We'll sort this all out—you don't have to worry about a thing."

The man thrashed in Thorn's hands again, totally unaffected. Then he made a desperate gesture at Snap, as if assuming the sweetest looking figure among us was most likely to be on his side.

Something about the movement of his hands struck a pang of recognition. Understanding clicked in my head.

A rough chuckle fell from my lips. "Tempest didn't bother to hide him for a reason. She knew no shadowkind could charm him with a little sweet-talking."

Omen shot me a sharp look. "What are you talking about?"

I motioned to the man. "I'm pretty sure that gesture he just made was sign language. He can't hear a thing Ruse is saying—he's deaf."

21

Snap

"Look at it," Ruse said, waggling his phone in the mortal man's face. The glow of its screen showed a message the incubus had typed. "Doesn't it make you want to follow my every command?"

The man who worked for Tempest jerked his head to the side, unable to move any farther than that thanks to Thorn's strong hands holding him in place.

We'd gone inside the partly smashed cabin, taking spots around a rough wooden table now scattered with splinters from the wall the warrior had bashed through. Thorn had the man planted in a chair while he loomed from behind. Ruse sat across the table from him. Sorsha and I stood on either side of the incubus, watching the proceedings, while Omen paced the small space by the cabin's kitchen. Without even looking at him, I could tell the hellhound shifter was just as unhappy with the situation as our captive looked.

"Would it work even if you *could* make him read it?" I asked.

Ruse grimaced. "I don't know. I've never tried to charm through visuals before. Persuading with my voice is what comes naturally. It'd be easier to tell if we could force him to read in the first place. Even if our stalwart lunk here holds this asshole's eyelids open, we can't make him focus on the words."

"Try this." Omen tossed a piece of paper and a pen onto the table. "Your handwriting might contain more power than words typed on some mortal device."

"If he'll read *that*." Sorsha leaned over the incubus's shoulder. "Write the letters really big so he can't help seeing them."

Ruse chuckled to himself. "Like I'm trying to teach a child how to read." But he scrawled across the sheet of paper in as broad strokes as it would fit. *KEEP READING WHAT I WRITE.* "Might as well cover that hurdle first."

Thorn gripped the man's head to turn it toward the table, and Ruse brandished his message like a flag. The man appeared to glance at it, but all he did was screw up his face into an expression so sour it made my tongue curl up. He whipped his hands through the air in more of those gestures that were his own way of speaking. I didn't understand the physical language, but I got the distinct impression he'd told Ruse to shove his paper—and possibly other things—up his anus.

If the incubus's charm was having any effect, it definitely wasn't making the man any friendlier. I bent over the table, flicking out my tongue to capture more definite impressions. Perhaps we didn't need this fellow's help. I might be able to glean something useful about his investigations for Tempest without him offering any cooperation at all.

The man didn't seem to have used the table for his work. I caught wisps of fingers closing around a hot mug with a whiff of coffee smell, laying out a knife and fork for a simple meal of grilled meat, and resting a book against it as he contemplated a story of men on horseback shooting at each other while wearing large hats.

Moving away from the table, I tested the cupboard beside it, the narrow bed with its scratchy blanket, and finally circled around Omen to check the kitchen. With each flicker of sensation that rose up, the fragments I'd gathered formed a patchy picture of the man's life here—not vivid or comprehensive, but something.

"He's been here for a while," I reported, taking a taste of the walls between comments. "Long enough that he's gotten bored with it. He imagines a woman who lives in some other place—she smiles a lot, and he thinks she is very pretty. He gets annoyed when he sees her with a man that puts his arm around her."

I frowned, sorting through the emotions I'd picked up from our captive's reminiscing. "I think maybe she is mates with someone else, but he wants her to be his. He keeps working because somehow he believes the sphinx will help that happen."

Sorsha wrinkled her nose and aimed a glare at the man. "He's helping Tempest so he can force some woman to hook up with him? What a catch. And the Company calls you all 'monsters'."

Those impressions left me uncomfortable too. They didn't help us defeat Tempest, though. "I can't get much sense of his work. He leaves early and comes back late, tired. Walking a lot, and digging. Maybe he's been looking for something?"

I knelt by a wicker basket in the corner where a rumpled shirt slumped over the rim. My tongue darted through the air above it, and a tingle of past excitement raced through me, spurring my own. "He found it. I can't tell what it was, but he was eager to tell Tempest about it so he could finally leave."

Omen's head jerked around. "Has he already told her?"

"I think he's told her some things, but he still had to go back and uncover more of whatever it was." I tipped my head to the side as if that would knock the jumbled impressions into a more coherent story. It didn't work.

At the table, Ruse had flipped the paper over and pushed it and the pen toward the man. He gestured to them emphatically. The man's lip curled. He snatched the paper up, crumpled it with a few twists of his fingers, and hurled it at the incubus's face.

"All right," Ruse said, standing up. "I think we've determined that my charm doesn't extend to the written word or pantomiming. What now?"

Perhaps if I tried the clothes the man was wearing

right now? I edged over beside Thorn and bent my head.
A ripple of the deeper, chilling hunger nibbled at my gut.
I closed my mind to it and inhaled more impressions.

"It's too present," I said with a jab of regret. The blare
of emotions the man was experiencing right now
drowned out any subtler information. "He's angry and
frustrated—and a little scared. But that's when he thinks
of the sphinx discovering we've found him, not so much
of what we'll do."

Omen growled under his breath. "We haven't got any
leverage. There's clearly nothing he cares about in this
place other than his own life, and you can be sure he
knows Tempest would slaughter him in epically painful
fashion if he betrayed her, so *us* threatening to kill him
won't do much."

Sorsha's mouth twisted. "He's got to know something
useful if he's been working so much for Tempest.
Whatever he uncovered here might be what's allowing
her to finally unleash the sickness the Company created."

Omen's gaze veered to me and then away again. He
hesitated, which was so unlike our leader that I turned to
study him.

"There is one way," he started, measuring out his
words.

All at once, our captive jerked forward. With our
attention on the hellhound shifter, Thorn's grasp on our
captive must have loosened just slightly. The man's knees
banged the underside of the table, and he swung up a
small gun that must have been fixed there.

The warrior slammed him toward the ground. The

gun went off with a *boom* that shattered the quiet of the night and clipped the ragged edge of the wall behind Sorsha.

He'd almost killed her. That bullet would have hit her in the forehead if it'd flown a few inches to the right. Without thinking, without *feeling* other than the swell of vengeful horror, I threw myself between my beloved and her attacker.

As I loomed over the slumped man, my rage simmered down to a duller anger within moments. He couldn't stage any further attack while he was pinned firmly under Thorn's bulk.

Omen kicked the gun off into the night, none too gently. He glared down at the man. "No, you don't value your life all that much, do you?"

Even with the initial jolt of my protective instincts fading, a ball of hunger remained at the base of my throat, gnawing rather than merely nibbling now. My jaw itched to let loose the needle-like teeth that could pierce this man's skull and siphon away his soul shred by shred.

I sucked in a ragged breath, and Omen glanced at me. Something in his expression sent a shock of comprehension through me.

He didn't want me to subdue my hunger. When he'd said there was a way, he'd been going to suggest that I use my power. That I flay our captive's being down to the barest essence, for all the torment it would put him through, to see everything he'd been and done.

If the man refused to communicate with us and Ruse couldn't wheedle him into doing so, devouring him was the obvious answer. It would tell us more in a matter of minutes than we might get out of him or his home... ever. And what this lackey knew might make the difference between saving hundreds of millions of other beings, mortal and otherwise, untold amounts of pain.

Still, my body balked. My tongue quivered over my lips, and the hunger rose up my gullet. How could I know whether I was making this decision out of justice or monstrousness?

My voice came out in a croak. "Tell him. Make him understand that he'll die if he doesn't agree to share what he knows. He should have a choice." Even if we were already sure of which one he'd make.

"Snap?" Sorsha said softly. Her hand slipped around my forearm, a gentle warmth. So much gentleness my beloved could offer despite all the fire and strength in her as well.

She wasn't concerned about herself. She'd shown she loved me regardless of whether I turned to this power. It was only my own well-being she was worried about—how I felt about going through with this act.

"I'm not going to order you," Omen said. "It's *your* choice too. I'll just point out that there's a lot on the line. Sometimes there isn't any answer that isn't at least a little monstrous."

The truth of those words settled in my chest. Sorsha squeezed my arm, and the resistance inside me started to melt.

Yes. Avoiding devouring this man would likely sentence all those other beings to their own horrifying deaths. Would letting that devastation happen be somehow more humane of me simply because I hadn't carried out the destruction through my own jaws?

This was what my beloved and my friends saw in me: not a monster giving in to viciousness, but a shadowkind with an ability that could reverse an immense catastrophe. I could do this. I was *meant* to do this. And I found I could think that without cringing for the first time since that night long ago when I'd sunk my teeth into my first meal's skull unknowingly.

Why had I joined Omen's cause at all if I wasn't going to give this mission everything I had?

While I'd grappled with myself, Ruse and Thorn had conveyed the situation to our captive as well as they could with motions and scribbled words. He shook his head against the floor with a defiant scowl. Inhaling slowly, I crouched beside him.

"You are helping to hurt many people who've done nothing wrong," I told him, in case some of my meaning might travel into him even if he couldn't hear my voice. "I must hurt you to make sure those horrors end. It's what I was made for—I won't deny it. Sometimes it takes a monster to fight monsters."

I knew in that moment through my entire body that as long as I cared about this realm and mine and all the beings in them, I wouldn't ever let my monstrousness overwhelm me.

Greenish light glittered across my vision. I gave myself over to the change into my full devourer form. The stretch of my limbs and sprouting of sharper teeth came over me as though I were breaking free of a blanket that had been wrapped around me suffocatingly tight. A burn that was almost pleasant spread through my muscles.

Part of me would enjoy this act, as horrifying as it was. That was all right too. The enjoyment could belong to the good I knew I was doing even as I mourned the agony that came with it.

My jaw gaped open. Pulled by a mix of determination, justness, and the swelling hunger, I clamped my teeth shut around the man's head.

I'd forgotten how intense the rush of images could be. Sights and sounds and, oh, the *tastes* surged through me, so vivid they might have swept away my sense of purpose if I hadn't held on tight.

Yes, the rush of a young boy racing across a field to an ice cream truck—and the creamy sweetness flooding his mouth afterward—was meant to be savored. Yes, I could allow a moment's satisfaction from his internal scream as I scoured through the memory of his teenage self smashing someone else's prized violin into the smallest pieces his heels could produce. But farther, deeper, there would be the answers we needed.

There would be a sphinx and awful promises and mysteries unraveled. And I could devour until I found them.

The moments I'd been searching for hit me unexpectedly: a flash of amber eyes, graceful movements of bejeweled hands that I couldn't follow, a caustic sense of agreement racing through the man in response. Tall towers, deep caverns, dry heat and damp darkness, chambers lit by an artificial glow. Glints of the metals he could pass but his master couldn't tolerate. Writing, carved or painted, that he snapped photos of or copied with painstaking precision.

Spurts of triumph. Maybe this time would be enough. Maybe this time.

I lingered over every morsel as long as I could, inhaling every detail and marking in my own memory. The man's silent wail of agony wound through the images brittler and harsher, until—*snap!*

My hunger severed the last thread. Nothing remained inside his husk of a body.

I heaved myself backward, falling into my regular mortal body as I did. Emotions still churned through me, some of them mine and some of them my victim's, but the strongest sensation that expanded in my chest was relief.

The words spilled out of me. "He found writings— stories about shadowkind weaknesses. Rumors of poisons and other toxins. It wasn't enough. She wanted more. There were claims of mortals sickening shadowkind and sickening themselves in turn. Ways to protect against that too. He saw just a day or two ago— *To shield against the weaknesses one or the other possesses, you must contain both their strengths.* I don't know what that means, but Tempest was pleased when he told her. And... something about a place with many large rocks. He found a painting of it. Energies could resonate from it. I think she decided to unleash her disease from there."

"Large rocks?" Sorsha repeated. "A mountain?"

I reached back into my mind's eye. "No. One rock here and one there, many of them, standing in a circle. A large circle, with a smaller ring inside it. Some of them were stacked on each other like... tables."

Ruse's eyebrows leapt up. He tapped at his phone and held it toward me with a photograph on the screen. "Like this?"

My breath caught. "Yes. That's the pattern."

"Stonehenge," Omen murmured. "If that's where she plans to launch her catastrophe from, she must be working out the final details close to there. We'll just have to—"

With a *boom* that rang through my ears, the roof over our heads exploded in a shower of shingles.

Thorn bellowed and leapt up from the limp corpse. Orange light flared across Omen's body. Shouts volleyed all around us—a glittering net heaved through the air— laser-like whips streaked across the darkness.

The wingéd warrior ducked, dodged, and bashed his fists into the faces of two of the attackers who appeared to be careening down the hillside in a wave. I spun around, grasping for some sort of weapon—

But we hadn't been their main target after all—not the four of us shadowkind. Two figures were lunging at Sorsha from behind. One of them jabbed something into the base of her neck with a crackle of electricity that made her body spasm before she could land her first punch.

I leapt at them, not caring that all I had to defend her were my bare hands, which weren't half as suited to the job as Thorn's. The brutes were already propelling her sagging body out onto the rocky terrain. I shoved one of them aside, but it was too late. As I reached for my beloved, a feline creature swooped down on vast wings to snatch Sorsha up in her paws.

A whip lashed across my shoulder. Ruse knocked the helmet off my attacker with the clang of a cooking pot. Omen tore past us all, his hellhound claws gouging the man's stomach open as he sprang.

She was already gone. Bodies lay broken and bleeding around us. A few figures who'd seen the turn of the tide fled into the night. And the sphinx had soared off into the blackness of the sky, not a hint of her or her precious cargo in sight.

She'd taken Sorsha. My fingers curled into my palms as every particle of my body cried out in horror. What did Tempest mean to do with her?

I'd devour every member of the Company if that was what it took to save her.

22

Sorsha

I woke up curled into a ball, my knees pressed to my forehead, every muscle still tensed with the memory of the electric shock that had knocked me out, as if it had happened only seconds ago. Even my hands had clenched tight to my chest. And, nestled against my palm—

Footsteps tapped toward me. I jerked my hand up to swipe it over my mouth and tentatively raised my head.

I was locked up in a cage like the ones I'd seen in Company facilities before: a solid metal floor rigid against my shoulder and hip, bars gleaming all around me in the stark light. But they mustn't have been silver or iron, which wouldn't have affected me anyway, because Tempest was now resting her hands against those bars as she peered between them at me with her catlike eyes.

With her that close, the razor-edged chill of her

innate power walloped me harder than it had in our meetings before. My pulse hiccupped, a tickle of my inner heat flaring in response.

I directed that first jolt of flames into my cheek. The sensitive skin stung, but the sphinx didn't give any sign that she'd noticed anything amiss. Her plump lips had curved into a smirk.

I didn't have much room to straighten out my posture. The roof of the cage stood only a foot above my prone body, and I couldn't have stretched my legs toward the walls without banging my feet on the bars. Tempest and her Company lackeys must have had quite the time squeezing me in here.

More fire stirred in my chest. If she thought I was simply going to lie here quietly—

"Throw your power around if you must," the leonine woman said. "It won't get you anywhere. I'd vanish into the shadows before I got more than a sunburn, and nothing else in here will smolder."

My gaze slipped beyond her to the wider room. Sweet twinkly trash cans, she wasn't kidding. The entire space looked as if it were constructed out of steel, from ceiling to floor and every piece of furniture in the place. There wasn't much of that anyway—a lab table behind Tempest and a smaller table laid with similarly glinting instruments next to it.

I *really* didn't like the look of those.

The flames in my cheek had smoothed the lump there into a thinner mass that tucked against my gums. I flexed my jaw and decided it was safe to speak. "Where'd you get this place—from the set of some low-budget alien horror flick? I'll skip the probing, if it's all the same to you. With the way you treat your guests, it's a wonder you're not more popular."

Tempest chuckled at my sarcasm, her languid voice turning the sound sultry. "You could have been a proper guest if you hadn't attempted to incinerate me on our second meeting. But look at all I've done for you regardless! I had this entire space constructed just for you, my darling phoenix."

Well, that was certainly some level of obsession. I shifted my weight, my arms already starting to ache from the awkward position I was lying in. "Any particular reason I'm getting this star treatment? I'm assuming it wasn't just so you could taunt me."

If she'd wanted me dead, I'd already be kaput. She'd had me helpless while I was knocked out. Instead I was here, so clearly she needed something from me... How exactly did she think she was going to get it?

Hopefully not with that spread of torture tools, but knowing how her Company tended to operate, I suspected those hopes were worth about as much as the ashes I'd like to leave this place in. It wasn't so much a matter of whether I'd face a version of those extra-terrestrial bodily excavations as how soon.

"You met one of my instruments," the sphinx said. "I suppose you didn't learn enough from him to connect the dots. That's quite all right. The less you know, the easier it'll be to take it from you." Her smile somehow turned even sharper.

Psychotic bitch. A fresh flare of anger erupted within my ribs, and flames crackled across my back. I gritted my teeth, biting back a hiss and yanking the fire inside me as well as I could.

Tempest cocked her head with a twinkle in her eyes as if she found my erratic powers highly amusing. "Just FYI, in case you get any ideas of martyrdom: if you start letting off too much smoke, your cage is rigged to douse you with rather a lot of water. You're not getting away from me by that avenue either."

I had no hope at all of getting through to this maniac in my current state, but I couldn't help prodding at her non-existent conscience anyway. "Does it really not bother you even a little that you're *helping* people who hate you and every other being like you? How are you winning when getting what you want depends on years of giving them what they want?"

"Ah, but once I have this, so many more mortals will sicken and fall than ever enjoyed carrying out my business. This realm will never recover. Forever is worth quite a lot."

"So then what? You get to sashay around, gloating about how horrible things are for eternity?"

Her eyes glittered piercingly. "I'm sure I'll find plenty of ways to occupy myself."

More frustration was trawling through me, dredging up flames with it. "They think you're all monsters, and you're proving them right."

"Who says they're wrong? I'm a monster. I'll own

that. And no one is going to stop me from being just as monstrous as I please."

She stepped back with a sway of her hips. The dress suit she wore today wasn't quite as extravagant as her robes from our previous meetings, but she'd still managed to find or manufacture one with diamonds stitched in patterns across the collar of the jacket and the hem of the skirt. They sparkled against the deep violet silk. She waved a hand that was just as sparkly with all the rings it was laden with.

"It's time for you to give me the last piece I need to make this scheme come together. Isn't it lovely that *you're* the one making my apocalypse possible? I'll leave my lackeys to it. Oh, and before you get any ideas about them, I should mention that it's not only your cage fitted with water pipes."

She vanished into the shadows under the larger table just as at least a dozen sprayers clicked on overhead. In an instant, a deluge filled the room, as if a thunderstorm had broken over it. The heavy drops rattled across the tables and gurgled down a drain I hadn't noticed in the far corner of the floor.

The angle of the spray meant plenty of it leapt between the bars to splatter my skin and clothes, but getting soaked was the least of my worries. The door opened just long enough to admit five figures wearing plastic visors to protect their eyes from the worst of the spray. In seconds, the downpour drenched the rest of them, from their hair to their tan uniforms.

The burliest three of the bunch advanced on my

cage. I braced myself, ignoring the growing throbbing in my cramped muscles. The moment one of them unlocked the front of the cage, I whipped my legs forward—and discovered my ankles were bound together with just half a foot of chain between them.

I still landed a kick, but it didn't hit quite as hard as I'd meant it to. One of the other burly dudes grabbed my legs before I could haul them back. I punched and thrashed, not really expecting to prevent whatever they were going to do but intending to extract every bit of discomfort I could for the indignity and the pain they were no doubt about to inflict on me.

My inner fire wasn't any help. As the thugs manhandled me over to the waiting table, water rained down on me. All the furious heat that wanted to leap from my body instead sizzled against my skin, scalding me briefly before more spray washed the boiling liquid away. Maybe a few flecks gave my captors a blister or two, but nothing that made them so much as wince.

They shoved me down on the table on my back, wrenching my arms into place at my sides. Steel cuffs snapped over my wrists, ankles, waist, and finally my neck. The edge of that last one dug into the tender skin at the top of my throat, an ache forming there when I swallowed.

The deluge was still pounding down on me, blurring my vision and filling my ears. I let my lips part just slightly to drink a little down in sips. I wasn't going to be able to fight anyone if I let myself get dehydrated as well as imprisoned. Lord only knew when Tempest might decide to feed me.

The two figures without quite as much beef on them stepped up on either side of the table, rivulets slicking down their visors. One held a scalpel from the smaller table, the other a syringe. "Preparing to take samples while subject is conscious," the first one said, her voice warbling through the falling water. "Bags labeled A."

As she pressed the scalpel to my forearm, I bit back a yelp. A stinging sensation rippled over my skin. It felt as if she dug out a sliver of my flesh—she dropped a solid scrap of red into a baggie. Then she tugged up my shirt to slice into the muscles over my ribs.

My heart thumped harder. She dug the blade right between two of those ribs, and the pain splintered right through my chest. I couldn't quite hold back a strained whine.

I hadn't been able to shake Tempest's resolve, but these people—they weren't ancient monsters with no concept of morality. They were my fellow fucking human beings.

I tipped my head so I wouldn't drown by fully opening my mouth and spat out the words. "I'm a person just like you are. I think and feel just like you do. I'm not some mindless beast that goes around ripping apart innocent people. How can you think it's okay to torture me like this?"

The lab techs kept working without so much as a blink. You'd have thought they were deaf like the man in Crete if they hadn't been talking to each other.

"Shin bone," the man reminded his colleague, and she reached to pull up my pant leg. My ankle jarred against the cuff with the instinctive urge to wrench away. An even deeper pain radiated up through my leg.

"I was born in Austin, Texas," I said into the rush of artificial rain. "When I was a little kid, I loved ice cream and watching the bats fly over the bridge. I went to school —I learned all the presidents' names, how to write an essay, and that we're supposed to treat each other with respect even if we have personal differences. I've fallen in love. I've had my heart broken. I'm *human*, for fuck's sake. You're carving up a person."

Not that it was any more okay when they did crap like this to a shadowkind. But my captors clearly didn't give a shit how much like them I was. They'd happily destroy me just as they'd destroyed so many other creatures—even their own people, when they'd thought their opponents were getting too close to the truth—just for the chance to exterminate a whole realm of beings, most of whom hadn't done any more damage than the average human.

How could they hold so much hate? How could they let it burn out every bit of compassion in them?

Or maybe human beings weren't all that compassionate to begin with. I wasn't fully one myself, was I? Were all mortals capable of turning this sociopathic if given a nudge in the right direction?

"Listen to me!" I shouted, my voice breaking with a cry as the scalpel slashed the tip off my baby toe. Rage whipped up inside me and surged from my body—only to meet the falling water with a hiss of dissipating steam. My tormenters stepped back just for a second as the scalding droplets cleared, but for all the notice they gave me, I might as well have been a malfunctioning radiator rather than a living, thinking being.

Thinking for now. As they closed in on me again, the man raised his syringe. "Now to take the unconscious samples. Bags labeled B."

"No!" I said, managing to choke back a sob.

He jabbed the needle into my neck just below the cuff. Darkness unfurled over my mind. My awareness narrowed and spiraled down, down, into cool blackness— but not quite so fast that I missed one last remark the woman made, with a sigh as if slicing and dicing me was cramping her style.

"This had better be enough to get that cure."

23

Thorn

The imp eyed us as we moved out of the shadows into the interior of the Everymobile. "That was a fast trip." She had the impudence to curl her lip in the slightest pout, as if she were actually *put out* that we hadn't fallen into enemy hands.

That was, most of us hadn't. My jaw clenched in the wake of yet another wave of rage and loss.

"We returned through a rift," Omen said curtly. "Seeing as we needed to move quickly—for the same reason as we were able to make use of a rift without worrying about the Highest."

Gisele's gaze had already traveled over the four of us. She leapt up, the ferocity that appeared incongruous with her petite frame sparking in her eyes. "What happened to Sorsha?"

Those words brought the little dragon scuttling out of

the bathroom. Pickle peered at us, his wings trembling at half-mast, and let out a snort that sounded of both consternation and anxiety.

"Tempest took her," Snap said, his usually bright voice turned dagger-sharp. Impassioned fury had been radiating off the devourer from the moment we'd regrouped. "The sphinx was too swift—we were overwhelmed by the Company attackers—we have to get her back before they hurt her!"

I didn't want to see what state it would bring him to if I acknowledged that the sphinx and her murderous Company had likely already harmed our mortal in some way. My hopes centered around recovering her *alive*.

They'd held Omen for months when they'd captured him, conducting their torturous experiments. But that had been while they were still determining the shape of their plans. Tempest had indicated she expected to see those plans through in mere days now. Had she even wanted Sorsha for some use or simply to deprive us of all our mortal offered?

My hands balled into fists of their own accord. If Tempest had been following the second reasoning, she'd have been motivated to end my lady's life the moment she could. If she had—if she'd taken Sorsha from us in the most irrevocable possible way... I would see the pieces of that venomous being's body torn apart bit by bit and scattered to the ends of the earth before I was through. I would rend the wings from her back and stuff them down her throat. I would—

Our commander spoke up again. "We can't be

completely sure of where Tempest will have taken her, but from what Snap gleaned from the man in Crete, it sounds as though the sphinx intends to be near Stonehenge in the near future. If she thinks our mortal is going to play some part in her scheme, it seems most likely she'll be in southern England." Omen grimaced. "Which hardly narrows our search down."

Ruse's fingers were flying over his phone, which he'd pulled out the moment we'd emerged. "Better than scouring all of Europe. I've already gotten my hacker on the job, pulling more details on the suspicious activity he's already dug up in that region. He should be able to help us get a more specific location."

Snap shifted on his feet, the neon green of his shadowkind form whirling in his eyes. "We can't just stay here waiting. We've got to start our own search as quickly as we can."

Bow got up too. "We'll be right there with you." The centaur glanced at Gisele. "Do you think it'll be safe to leave the Everymobile here for however long we're gone?"

Mortals did have a habit of getting finicky about any vehicle sitting in the same spot for what they deemed was an inappropriate length of time, which from what I'd gathered often wasn't very long at all.

Gisele frowned and then tossed back her hair. "Let's not risk it. We might need a good getaway vehicle once we're there anyway. And it'll be nice to give Sorsha a familiar place to recover in as soon as we've rescued her. The Everymobile survived one trip through the shadow realm—I'm sure she can handle one more, when it's this important."

Omen's lips twitched with a hint of strained amusement. "We'll do our best to keep the trip short for minimal side effects. Perhaps all her new features will revert back to normal on the second time through." He motioned to the driver's seat. "Would one of you prefer to do the honors? The nearest rift isn't far."

Gisele hopped up behind the wheel. With a look of utter determination, she hit the gas and turned the RV in the direction he indicated.

The portal between the mortal realm and our natural home was invisible to human senses, but I assumed all of us could sense the faint vibration rippling through our bodies that heightened the nearer we came. This one lay over open waters just beyond the shore, around a peninsula from the harbor. The quiet of the night allowed us to veer down a darkened side-road and heave the vehicle out of the physical world into the shadows, all of us gripping its walls to speed the transition.

We propelled it toward the rift, the thrum of the opening pulling us in like a vacuum. We'd just shot through into the amorphous world on the other side, a thick chill condensing around my being, when a familiar voice carried through the churning darkness.

"Thorn! I was just coming in search of you."

It was Flint's deeply melancholy tone. We all stopped, and I turned to face my fellow warrior. His presence loomed large and weighty in the murky atmosphere.

"What is it?" I asked with a flicker of hope. Had he decided to rejoin us? Was it possible the other wingéd from Rome might aid us in this battle after all?

But as he drew nearer, my hopes were extinguished with the impression I got that he was bracing himself. He wasn't pleased with what he was about to say.

"Our brethren wish for you to attend to them. They have great need of your attendance."

Irritation prickled through me before I could catch it. I shouldn't resent those who had given so much of themselves while I'd escaped our past essentially unscathed. And yet—if I accepted this delay, how scathed might my lady be by the time I reached her?

Omen made the decision for me before I had to grapple with my conflicting responsibilities. "Go. See if you can stir them into getting off their asses and pitching in before Tempest sends the whole world to hell. It'll take us some time to find out where Sorsha's being held anyway. You can smash your way through to her when you get back."

Yes. I could meet both responsibilities—and perhaps turn one into part of the solution to the other. I nodded to Omen and set off in a different direction from my companions.

It would have been difficult for me to explain to a mortal how exactly we ascertained which rift led where and how we reached those rifts in our own realm. The portals floated here and there with hints of the sensations that waited on the other side. One could spring through any at random for a trip of unexpectedness or focus on the place one most wanted to experience—and somehow or other, arrive at the appropriate portal without any great passing of time.

Flint already had a clear course in mind, having just come from what was now our destination. As we barreled through the murk, I felt his attention settle on me. "Your mortal—or somewhat mortal—companion. Something untoward has happened to her?"

"She has been stolen by our greatest enemy, the one who means to end most mortal and shadowkind existence if she has her way," I said. "It is possible that our lady's capture may even help bring that catastrophe about. By every indication, the destruction the sphinx intends to inflict on both worlds is imminent."

The other wingéd asked nothing more, but his presence beside me gave off a more palpable uneasiness.

"What is this urgent matter our brethren have sent you to me about?" I asked.

"I think it would be better for them to explain. They didn't share all the details with me, only said it was your trial to bear."

That phrasing didn't sound particularly promising. I managed to hold in an ethereal sigh. Those who had fought valiantly deserved better than my disdain, regardless of my impatience.

We emerged over a roadway only a mile or so from the palace the mortals considered holy where my brethren had made their home. As if they wished to think of themselves as some sort of "angels." That idea rankled me as we hustled on through the shadows that were starting to split with the brightening dawn.

The two with their mangled bodies were poised on the rooftop as if they'd been standing there awaiting my return since the moment I'd left. Both of their expressions looked even more grim than I recalled. And here I'd found Flint overwrought. With every one of my kind I encountered, I discovered new depths of dourness.

"You took so long in your rambling adventures I started to doubt you still had any sense of duty at all," Viscera said in her wheezing voice before I could even greet them.

My hackles rose at the attack on my honor. I held my temper in check. "I had urgent matters to attend to, as we discussed. It was hardly for my enjoyment. And an even more critical matter faces us now."

"Faces *you*," Lance said. "Do not include us in your foolishness."

"It isn't foolishness. All our fates may depend on the outcome of the next few days." I dragged in a breath and squared my shoulders. "What is it you need from me? I'll help you however I am able."

Viscera raised her broken chin. "We believe one of the griffins flew by here and dropped the box they stole, allowing what little of its contents remained to scatter. I can sense the fragments of my brother's being all around. But we dare not venture into view in our physical forms to collect them. The mortals would flee in horror."

A shudder ran through me at the thought of my former comrade's remains abandoned in that way, but I couldn't restrain the question that rose up. "Could not Flint—"

"*You* fought beside my brother. You will recognize the bits of his essence. The rest we can worry about later. You will go forth into the city and collect all you can of him."

I glanced down at the courtyard below with its framing of bleached columns. "Where exactly do those fragments lie? I will gather them immediately."

"The wind has blown them through the streets far and wide. It may take some doing, but we will bring what still exists back together."

They expected me to hunt all across one of the largest cities in the world for the tiny particles of our long-dead comrade's essence, all while a vicious menace of a shadowkind brought about a near-Armageddon?

I peered at my kin, suddenly wondering if any of this story were even true. To lie to a fellow wingéd would be shameful... but she'd already proven how little she thought of me. How could it be that these griffins had happened to pass by at exactly this time?

"Well, what delays you?" she demanded.

The thinning thread of loyalty that had brought me here fractured with an ache that shot straight through my chest. As I drew myself to the fullest my height could reach, the memory of Sorsha's arms around me came back to me— her warm voice in my ears, telling me I could leave her if I truly felt that was right, if it would satisfy my conscience.

That was how devoted brethren ought to treat each

other. Trusting their judgment of their own needs. Giving them room to make choices. Not scolding them like some sort of *child* for mistakes made centuries ago that might not even be mistakes.

"I fought as hard as I could with your brother all those ages ago," I said. "And I left the battle for his and the rest of your sake as much as my own. There was no betrayal or shame in it, and I will claim none now. My first duty is to the beings alive who stand to suffer and die if I don't act, and that includes both of you and so many others—and it isn't finding scraps of one long snuffed out that will save any of you."

Both of them were gaping at me now. Lance tried to puff himself up in some image of righteousness that now only looked ridiculous to me. "Then you forsake all your—"

I cut him off with a glower. "I forsake *nothing*. I go now to fight for so many more than died even then, and if *you* had any honor, you would be doing the same. It's up to you whether you show what wingéd are meant to be or wallow here in the pain of the past. I've made my decision."

I waited with a thudding of my heart in my chest. They hesitated and then shrank back into their wounded stances, and I knew it was hopeless.

They were hopeless. I could see that now. They weren't the final bastions of our kind but a pale shade of what we used to be, what we'd always striven to be, and it had nothing to do with the ruined bits of their bodies but of the lapses they'd allowed in their souls. I intended to do better than that.

"Fine. You've distracted me enough with your demands." I swiveled on my heel and caught Flint's gaze. His stern face had blanched in shock. "Are you staying to wallow with them, or will you stand by me and the rest of our kind when it matters most?"

The other wingéd wavered too, but only for an instant. The duck of his head hid a wince of humiliation. "I should have stayed with that fight to begin with. You're right, as you were right before. We must do what we can for all the other beings who now face so much danger. I apologize—"

"It doesn't matter," I said. "You chose what you thought was right, and then you changed your mind. It's an asset all thinking creatures possess... even those two."

I shot one last glance over my shoulder, but the ragged wingéd hadn't budged. So be it. With a nod to Flint, I hurtled into the shadows.

Long ago, I hadn't found a way to be what my companions then needed. This time, I refused to let them down—not Sorsha nor Omen, nor any of the others I meant to save.

24

Sorsha

The next time when I woke up, I was still clamped to the lab table. Aches ran all through my back and limbs from the awkward position I'd been lying in, sharper in the spots where the experimenters' tools had cut into my body. The lights had dimmed, giving the room a hazy, dream-like feel.

The deluge from the sprinklers had stopped, although the clothes still clinging damply to my body were proof that I hadn't imagined it. The experimenters were gone. Had they noticed—? With a stutter of my pulse, I probed the base of my gums with my tongue and relaxed slightly. Thank hamstrung hippos for that smallest of small mercies.

Had they left me on the table because they weren't quite finished carving me up? At least that would mean Tempest hadn't gotten what she'd wanted yet. I'd sooner cuddle up with a cockatrice than make this quest of hers one bit easier for her.

The last words I'd heard from the Company scientists tickled through my head. *To get that cure.* I wouldn't have understood why the sphinx thought I had anything to do with curing anything if it hadn't been for Snap's devouring of her lackey in Crete. What was it exactly that he'd said the dude had found...?

A warbling sound broke through my reminiscing: a voice, not much more than a whine that sounded more animal than human, wavering from the direction of the door. Then a gasp of pain and a hoarse plea: "You don't have to— I came here because I—"

That was Snap's voice, its usual brightness tarnished. My limbs jerked against the restraints automatically— and the steel cuff around my left hand popped open.

I started at it for the space of a few heartbeats, barely believing it. How could Tempest's people have been anything less than perfectly careful? But they were mortal, and as I'd imagine she'd have grumbled hundreds of times, mortals were infinitely fallible.

Lucky for me, shadowkind were far from perfect too.

I lifted my arm with a wince and fumbled with the cuff around my neck. It only took a matter of seconds for my groping fingers to snag on the latch and wrench it open. A moment later, I'd released the cuff around my other wrist and then my waist as well.

I shoved myself upright so fast my head spun, both with dizziness in the aftermath of whatever sedative my tormenters had injected me with and the lance of pain that shot up my spine. My breath caught just shy of a sob. I gritted my teeth and snatched at the cuffs around my ankles.

Snap's voice was getting more distant but no happier. Had the others come to break me out and been trapped? Damn it. But maybe I could turn the tables on these Company assholes one more time.

I swung around and lowered my feet to the ground. As I eased my weight onto them, my legs wobbled and then held with the stiffening of my calf and thigh muscles. My gaze fell on the smaller table, but its spread of torture instruments had been cleared off.

Oh well. Slicing and dicing wasn't my typical style anyway. It was barbequing time.

My hand was just coming to rest on the door handle when the fading whimper rose to a scream. I flinched, the hairs on my arms standing on end. The shriek carried on, quavering and hitching. It didn't sound as if they were simply tormenting my devourer. It sounded like they were *killing* him.

My throat constricted. I yanked at the door handle, but it didn't budge. Of course they'd have locked that.

I closed my eyes, groping for calm despite the rattle of my frantic pulse in my ears. I knew my way around a lock. If I just melted the right bits—if the sprinklers overhead didn't trigger from the concentrated heat—

An even more piercing cry sent another shock of urgency through me. I pressed my hand over the lock area and let anger mingle with my panic. How *dare* they hurt my lover. They would pay—all of the assholes here would pay in every way I could make them.

Heat flared across my collarbone, sharp enough to sear, but my fiery voodoo surged toward my intended target as well. I thrust more in that direction, wanting to reduce every mechanism in there to goop.

The shrieking had faded into a sputtering gurgle. Would I even make it to him in time?

I gritted my teeth and hauled at the door. It flung open to reveal two drenched scientists standing right on the other side.

My stomach lurched, but I didn't have time to move so much as an inch. One of the experimenters was already slashing a scalpel across my forearm; the other slammed a container over the cut. A container that caught the rush of smoke that streamed up from the wound in my adrenaline-spiked state.

Fury clanged through me alongside the jolt of understanding. My inner fire whipped out in a blaze— but before it had done more than sizzle across the moisture flecking my attackers' faces, a fresh downpour burst from the sprinklers both in the room behind me and in the hall, this time icy cold.

My breath rasped at the sudden smack of frigid water. The scientists were already fleeing with their ill-gotten plunder, and the burly guards from before barged in to replace them. I only managed to land two blows before I found myself tangled up so tightly in one of those glittering nets that I could barely wiggle my pinkie. I couldn't even congratulate myself for the blood trickling from the one nose it appeared I'd broken.

Snap's voice had vanished. But it had never really been him, had it? Or at least not him now. As the guards rolled me out of the net back into my cage, the remaining pieces clicked together.

The Company had captured my devourer before. The bits I'd heard of him actually speaking, they must have recorded while they had him in their facility. The screams and shrieks might have been from then too or simply been sound effects they'd picked to reasonably match his tone. It wasn't as if I could have identified anyone accurately from that cacophony of agony.

They'd set me up. Tempest must have decided she needed the shadowkind essence I only bled when I was particularly worked up to manufacture her cure. Had she known for sure it would come out when I was frantic, or only been experimenting after I'd bled like a mortal during the initial torture? Maybe one of the Company assholes had noticed me leaking smoke during one of our battles. Shit.

It still might not be enough. She obviously hadn't figured out how to transform what she was getting from me into whatever exactly she wanted.

The cure...

Maybe Tempest wasn't quite as impervious as she wanted us to think.

For what felt like a millennium or two, I sprawled there in my cage. When I attempted the same melting trick on the lock at its base, the sprinklers went off in an instant, and all I got for my trouble was another freezing shower. After that, I pulled my knees up to my chest for warmth and willed my teeth not to chatter.

If Tempest *had* gotten what she wanted from me this time, what did that mean for my chances of surviving the next day? Or even the next hour?

She couldn't be sure of her "cure" when she'd never made it before—or unleashed this disease before—right? I didn't think she'd take the chance of offing me until she was one hundred percent convinced she had no further use for me. Of course, if that meant living out the rest of my days in this cramped box, death didn't sound all that bad. Especially if Tempest went down with me.

My chilly reflections halted at the shimmering of a figure into sight just beyond the bars. The sphinx herself had returned. To gloat, it appeared, judging from the coy tilt of her head and the smirk curling her lips. I willed a small spurt of flame along my gums, ignoring the burning sensation of the flesh there.

"You really thought I'd give you a chance to escape," she said, her voice languid with amusement.

I wasn't in any mood to go easy on her ego. "Hard as it might be to believe, you don't actually come across as all that smart."

Tempest shrugged, but the twitch of her eyelid suggested I'd irritated her at least a little. Not the greatest victory ever, but give me a break. At this point I couldn't be much of a chooser.

Unfortunately, she knew just how to needle me in return. "How does it feel knowing you've provided the final step in the plans you've been trying so hard to interrupt?"

"Pretty crappy," I said breezily. "How do you feel knowing that you weren't quite stealthy enough to stop me from figuring out what's going on here? *To shield against the weakness one or the other possesses, you must contain both their strengths.* You're trying to find some part of my essence to protect you from your own disease, because *you're* not strong enough on your own."

A spark flashed in her eyes. She managed to keep her tone even. "Not *trying.* I've succeeded. There's nothing left that stands in our way. My people are ready to let loose our sickness tomorrow, and I'll get to watch and laugh while both they and the ones they wanted so badly to destroy crumple in its throes."

Using my smoky essence had worked, then? Or was she just trying to fake me out to set me up for some new trick?

"You seem to take a lot of pride in being a traitorous butcher," I remarked. "And here I thought you were all about brains and brilliant schemes, not random slaughter." I let my voice lilt into a skewed lyric. "Shows your lies, living so grand, darling. Do you mean to start cheating? Is your plunder planned?"

Another victory: warping songs appeared to annoy Tempest just as much as it had Omen. "Shut up," she said with a wave of her hand that was clearly meant to be casual. The momentary narrowing of her eyes showed the truth. "I can't imagine how Omen and his lot put up with you for as long as they did. I'd expect they'll be pleased to find out you're no longer their burden to carry."

If she thought I was going to believe that after everything I'd been through with my shadowkind men, she was even more off her rocker than I'd figured. I rolled my eyes at her. "I think you'll find it's the opposite. But why don't you invite them over to see who's right? I'd like to watch that visit go down."

She chuckled. "Perhaps you will. When I hold the only protection against this sickness, I hold all the power. Do you think I won't have them bowing to me if their survival hangs in the balance?"

Of course. If even *she* couldn't withstand the disease on her own, no other shadowkind would either.

Would my lovers compromise their principles to save their own lives? I wouldn't blame them for appeasing Tempest for long enough to guarantee their immunity if they eviscerated her afterward. But I already knew that Snap would never willingly back down, not once this woman had become my murderer, and I couldn't imagine Thorn putting his survival over his sense of justice. He'd already spent centuries beating himself up for remaining alive after the last war he'd waged.

She'd destroy not just me but possibly all of the beings I loved as well. A larger surge of fire shot through the nonchalance I'd been trying to convey. I clenched my jaw, but heat crackled just under my skin with a stinging wave of pain.

"You see," the sphinx said, her voice dripping with vicious sweetness. "You really could have been something, my phoenix, but that mortal side of you hasn't got the power to aim those talents properly. Such a shame."

"Or maybe the only shame will be how quickly we'll snuff *you* out," I retorted. "You can't see everything. We've already screwed up your plans at least a dozen times."

"And yet not badly enough that it stopped me from getting to where we are now." Her smile came back, thinner now. She motioned to her broad forehead. "It's not just these two mortal-esque eyes that I see with, but my inner eye as well. And a sphinx always glimpses the answers one way or another."

My gaze locked onto that smooth plane of skin beneath the fall of her gleaming bronze hair. That was where her supernatural wisdom came from—a third eye within her mind?

A jitter of excitement quivered through me. Tempest turned with a swish of her dress and vanished, leaving me alone again—but with a resolve I hadn't found until just now.

Omen had told me to fight her by blinding her. I could still do that. I had the tools right here, and now I knew which eye she truly relied on.

The only question was whether I'd get a chance to make use of that knowledge before she brought both realms to their knees.

25

Omen

T he rumble of a departing jumbo jet grated against my nerves. I shot a narrow look at Ruse where he was watching the stream of arriving travelers pouring out of the airport's security area. "Remind me again why you thought this diversion was a good idea? How is having a mortal tagging along going to help us extricate Sorsha any faster?"

The incubus tsked at my impatience, but I could tell from the tension in his jaw that he wasn't impervious to the same worries. "I told her she should join us. Maybe she won't be much help getting Sorsha out of the facility, but whatever *our* mortal has been through, having additional moral support can't be a bad thing."

"You don't think the four of us are enough for her?"

Ruse met my gaze, abruptly more serious than I could ever remember seeing him. "She's been struggling. I know you've seen it too. That's what our little escapade on the boat was about, wasn't it? I'm sure she'd say she's perfectly satisfied with all the wonders we shadowkind can provide... but she *is* half mortal too. There are things she thinks and feels that we can't wrap our heads around —as much as I'd like to become her be-all and end-all."

He put that desire into words so effortlessly, as if there was nothing at all embarrassing about an incubus— or any shadowkind—wanting to devote themselves to a mortal. Which I supposed there wasn't. But I couldn't imagine the same sentiment ever falling from my mouth quite that easily.

After all, I still wasn't entirely sure that my presence in Sorsha's life wouldn't be what brought about her ruin rather than what raised her above it. It was *my* former colleague who might have already ripped into her in who knew how many ways.

I just hoped I still knew Tempest well enough to have made an accurate guess of where she was working from, given the data Ruse's computer expert had looked up— and of the likelihood that she'd kept Sorsha alive. Surely she wouldn't have bothered knocking Sorsha out and dragging her off if all she needed was a corpse?

But who knew with the sphinx, now or ever?

I inhaled slowly and squared my shoulders, keeping a tight grip on the composure I'd spent so long cultivating. We weren't really squandering time. The others were investigating the facility we'd set our sights on—a supposed coat factory on the outskirts of West London, less than two hours from the standing stones—while we picked up our mortal's best friend from Heathrow, just a few miles away.

And I definitely wasn't letting myself dread finding out what this woman was going to have to say when she came face to face with the beings who'd lost her once-close companion.

Ruse perked up. A moment later, I spotted a figure with a recognizable burst of black curls atop a sleek white blouse and slacks. She actually *smiled* at the incubus when her gaze caught on him. She hustled over, dragging her carry-on—and slowed at the sight of me.

I'd barely exchanged five words with this mortal woman during our single meeting, but apparently that and whatever Sorsha had reported about me had made an impression. And not a good one.

She kept coming, though, and stopped in front of us with a determined expression that gave me some hint as to what she and Sorsha had in common. "Is this all I get for a welcoming party?" she said, cocking her head. "Where's the rest of the crew?"

"Attempting to confirm Sorsha's location to make sure that when we go charging in to rescue her, she's actually there for us to rescue," I said.

"Hmm. Or, if you're lucky, she'll rescue herself before you all get around to it."

Knowing my recent lover as well as I now did, I had to admit that was a possibility, as daunting an opponent as the sphinx could be.

"We'll see." I eyed Vivi carefully. She might be Sorsha's best friend, but she was still a mortal with all the potential weaknesses that could entail. My voice dropped. "You do understand the full situation, don't you? That Sorsha is as much shadowkind as she is human?"

If that news had frightened the woman when she'd first heard it, she gave no indication of fear now. All she did was shrug, aiming a glower at me that dared me to challenge her. "I just wish she'd felt she could open up to me about it on her own. Hopefully after this..." Her chin came up defiantly. "Maybe I didn't know exactly that the whole time, but I've always believed she's something special. Why do you think I came all this way? Human, monster, polka-dot potato bug—she's still *Sorsha*, and I'm here for her, whatever I can do."

Her vehemence convinced me that this one matter, at least, wouldn't be a problem. I motioned for her to follow us. "Come on, then. We can go meet up with the others and see what they have to say."

When we reached Darlene in her current state, Vivi raised her eyebrows but was polite enough not to remark on the RV's appearance. I had the feeling one more trip through the shadow realm would render the vehicle completely useless as a disguise.

Her tour bus form now looked more like a touring vehicle for rock stars... Rock stars who'd revamped it while on acid. Neon yellow streamers fluttered around all the windows—we'd tried trimming them off and they'd just grown back—and the exhaust pipe had expanded to the size and shape of a trombone. Unfortunately, it also *sounded* like a trombone when the engine started up.

The inside had gone through a similar makeover. The formerly white leather sofa was now decked out with stripes of gold shag—an update the equines had actually approved of. The faucet emitted no liquid at all but only a screeching electric guitar sound. And the fridge was now baking anything put inside it like an oven.

Basically, we were shit out of luck if we wanted a cold beverage anywhere around here.

Pickle scampered over at the sound of our arrival and snorted indignantly when his master didn't appear alongside us. Vivi stared at the little dragon and then shook her head. "Okay. That's not even the weirdest thing I've seen in the last couple of weeks. Is it part of the crew too?"

"He's Sorsha's pet." Ruse snapped his fingers at Pickle, beckoning him, but the creature lobbed a puff of smoke at him and turned tail. "I think she figured you'd disapprove."

"Of keeping a shadowkind beastie like a cat? That is... a little unusual. But I'm sure she had her reasons." The mortal woman flopped down on the sofa, her fingers curling into the patch of shag next to her. "What exactly is this shadowkind that's captured her now?"

Since the incubus was the one who'd insisted on bringing the mortal on, I left it to him to make all the necessary explanations and slid onto the driver's seat. There was a certain reassurance in maneuvering the massive vehicle with the power of my hands on the wheel. That was, until I noticed my new hangers-on were still, well, hanging on.

The skinny goblin who'd hassled me at the gas station in Greece was propped against a lamp post, ogling Darlene as we cruised by. Up ahead, I spotted a gargoyle on the top of a building that had shifted position just slightly to keep us in view.

Did the Highest really think that I'd deliver Ruby to them faster if they simply irritated me enough? Maybe we could enjoy some goblin shish kabob after we were done crushing Tempest and her schemes.

If I lived long enough after that to have a final meal. With the way these pricks were tailing me, chances were they'd figure out what Sorsha was during that battle and report my transgressions back to the Highest in a blink. And darkness only knew what kind of army they'd send after *her* while they were annihilating me.

I pulled up behind a dreary-looking business hotel where we'd agreed to meet and tried to tune out Ruse regaling Vivi with his extravagant tales of our adventures —the more intimate bits edited out. The incubus had some small sense of propriety. I wasn't sure Sorsha would appreciate him filling in her best friend with even that much detail, but she could take that up with him when we got her back.

When, not if. Even if it *was* over my dead body.

It was less than an hour before our companions emerged from the shadows around the furniture. Antic kicked things off with a squeal, leaping onto the table in front of Vivi.

"The other human is here! I love your hair. Does it grow all twisty like that naturally?"

The woman looked a tad taken aback before she found her voice with a laugh. "The braided parts, no, but this?" She fluffed the poof at the back of her head. "That's what God gave me."

"It is good to have you joining us," Thorn said, with a frown at the imp that suggested he didn't approve of her frivolous questions, and turned to me. "Everything we observed fits the information Ruse's contact conveyed to us. The building has been recently outfitted with iron and silver protections all through the outer walls—so much that we couldn't get close enough to touch them while in the shadows. Snap was able to pick up impressions from the gate and from a few pieces of litter."

The devourer nodded. "I also caught an impression of one of the workers talking about their boss bringing in a monster who could create fire. That's got to be Sorsha."

Between that and the extensive sprinkler systems we knew had also been ordered for installation in the building, I was inclined to agree with his assessment. I steepled my fingers in front of me. "All right. So, how do we get in? Are there employees guarding the place or coming and going that Ruse can con?"

Bow shook his head. "We didn't see anyone go in or out while we were watching. There was a delivery that looked like food, but it was placed in a storage box embedded in the wall. We figure there's got to be an opening on the inside for them to bring the supplies in."

I grimaced. "And I assume that's got those noxious metals all around it."

"Naturally." Gisele tapped her lips. "Do you think

the sphinx is giving all the orders from the outside? How could she handle being surrounded by all that silver and iron?"

"It's a big building. If it's only the outer walls, she may be able to work in the center of the space with only mild discomfort. There might be an entrance on the roof or underground that allows her access without passing too closely to the protections." I glanced at Thorn. "I assume you couldn't examine the roof because you couldn't get close enough to use the shadows on the way up."

"And I could hardly fly up there visibly," the warrior acknowledged. "But we could assume there's a less protected spot up there and build our plans around that."

"No. I don't like counting on an assumption. She may not be using the roof at all—it would please her to pick the option that suits her form less well just to confuse us. And no doubt whatever entrance she uses will be heavily guarded regardless, with those on the inside having all the advantage. You've smashed through reinforced walls before. I don't suppose—"

Thorn was shaking his head before I'd finished the question. "I considered that myself, but I don't think I could summon enough strength to break all the way through so much of those metals with their weakening effect, not to mention the steel reinforcing the walls as well. An army of warriors could batter their way through, no doubt, but even with you and Flint and Bow... I don't think brute force will be the answer with our current numbers."

"That's fine," I said quickly, not wanting him beating himself up any more than he already had for failing to convince the other two wingéd to come on board with our mission. We'd gotten by without brute force before. Our mortal herself had come up with all those pacifistic plans—well, pacifistic by our typical standards.

But there were no employees for Ruse to charm, and even if we had the time to ferret out a loved one or two beyond the factory walls, what could they possibly tell us that would present us with a way in?

An army, Thorn had said. The words resonated through my thoughts and clicked into place. My mouth opened automatically with a rush of inspiration and an almost furious delight. "What if we—"

I cut myself off with a clenching of my teeth. *No.* That was the kind of viciously daring plan I'd have taken the same delight in centuries ago—the kind that had stirred rages in my victims and brought down suffering on innocents' heads. I'd been done with that past version of myself for so long. What the fuck was I thinking, nearly giving over to it on a moment's whim.

The others were watching me now. I should have kept my mouth shut.

Vivi crossed her arms over her chest. "Whatever idea you have, spit it out. It's got to be better than the nothing cherry on a nada sundae you all have come up with so far. And I didn't come all this way to watch you *not* get my bestie away from this maniac."

"I'd prefer we stick to plans that don't stand an equal chance of sealing Sorsha's doom."

"It looks like her 'doom' is guaranteed if you don't do anything, so fifty-fifty odds sound good to me."

I restrained myself from baring my teeth at her, feeling my hair ruffle with a current of frustration. "Maybe those who won't be involved in the actual rescue attempt shouldn't be spouting opinions about it."

"Maybe you shouldn't have invited me here if you didn't want to hear my opinions," Vivi shot back. "Do you actually care about Sorsha or only about making sure you don't look bad if your plan has a few hitches?"

A *few hitches*? She had no idea what she was talking about. But even with that knowledge, something about her words cut straight through me.

Even after everything we'd been through, some part of me wanted to deny that I cared about our mortal. Not because she didn't deserve that caring, but because when *I* cared... that was when all the hellish inclinations in me came out to play, and the outcome wasn't generally pretty. The way I got by, the way I made sure I didn't lead anyone into a shitstorm of my own making, was by tamping down on every emotion I had in me and focusing on pure cold strategy.

It hit me then in a way it hadn't before that Tempest had been wrong about me. I'd never forgotten I was a monster. I'd spent the last few centuries with that fact at the forefront of my mind and doing whatever I could to chain the beast inside.

But Sorsha hadn't seen my beast as a monster—or if she had, it'd been one she'd embraced as much as she had Snap's cruel hunger and Thorn's brutal strength.

She'd lain beneath me on a bed less than ten feet from where I currently stood with my jaws clamped around her throat and told me she wasn't afraid of me. How many times had she asked to see me fierce and passionate rather than the "Ice-Cold Bastard," as she liked to put it?

I'd changed so much about myself since my days with Tempest, but somehow I hadn't managed to alter that one most basic thing: the belief that whatever I did and whoever I was with, if I gave in one inch to my baser nature, everything would go to hell, and most likely sooner rather than later.

Somehow I had the feeling I knew exactly how Sorsha would respond to that. *Who's to say a little hell is a bad thing?*

I did care about her, and the reserves of rage and power I'd held in check were beyond even Tempest's imagining. Wasn't it time to put all that hellishness to good use, for the sake of the woman I—

Yes.

I spun on my heel. "I have to bait the hook. Wait here. The rest of you, do whatever you need to so you're ready to storm that factory the second we get our opening. I doubt it'll take very long."

"Omen?" Snap said, his eyes widening, but I didn't stick around to answer questions. If I was going to do this, I was going to do it now, before the Ice-Cold Bastard's judgment reined me back in.

Bringing in new allies. It was exactly the kind of plan Sorsha would have loved. One I could admit I might never have thought of if she hadn't wriggled her way so far into my mind.

My lips curled into a wry smile. I doubted she'd ever have expected me to pull off quite this spectacular a magic trick, though.

I loped through the shadows a short ways and then emerged to amble down the street, scanning the buildings around me. Stop and smell the flowers. Buy myself a chocolate bar. Give every appearance of not having a care in the world except indulging myself at my leisure. Yeah, that would rile them up quickly enough.

Footsteps tapped along the sidewalk to catch up with me. A banshee fell into step at my side, her chin raised at a haughty angle. "This is not what the Highest ordered you to do. Get on with your quest."

I waved the candy bar at her. "What makes you think my quest doesn't require plenty of chocolate?"

When she glared at me, I took the final bite, allowed myself a few seconds to enjoy the sticky sweetness, and tossed the wrapper into a nearby trash bin. "Actually, I was hoping to get your attention. I figured it'd be faster than heading to the nearest rift. I've found out where Ruby is, but it won't be easy getting to her. Tell the Highest they'd better send their best—and lots of them."

The minion sucked in a startled breath. "Where? I must inform them at once."

"A coat factory not far from here. It's heavily fortified, though. You can check it out for yourself before you make your full report." I rattled off the address, gesturing in the general direction.

The banshee dove into the shadows and raced off like a bullet. I watched her go, a strange flavor creeping through my mouth—a metallic tang that was both terror and exhilaration.

Time to burn it all to the ground and see who was left standing. And if this didn't work out the way I hoped, I suspected Sorsha would applaud the effort even as she fell.

26

Sorsha

It started with a distant crashing. My ears perked up, and I raised my head from where it'd been resting against my tucked arms.

A thud reached me next, still muffled but not as faint as before—then a shout and a grunt like someone taking a punch to the gut.

I pushed myself as upright as I could get in my cage, eyeing the door to my room. Was this another trick to get a reaction out of me? But it wasn't as if I could do much with the cage properly locked this time. I'd checked the latches before I'd laid my head down, and I rattled them now just in case. They didn't budge so much as a fraction of an inch.

More thumps and booms filtered through the walls. A cry, thin and fraught with pain, pierced my eardrums. My body tensed.

This racket could mean good things for me—it could be my allies breaking in—but it could also mean a whole lot of bad. Maybe some other shadowkind had found out about Tempest's plans and meant to inflict their vengeance on everyone in the building. Maybe her own allies had figured out she was double-crossing them and were wreaking havoc out there. Who knew what other enemies she might have accumulated over the centuries who wouldn't have any reason to spare me?

Instinctively, I ran my tongue along the seam of my gums, restraining a wince at the scalded flesh there. I might not have much in this ridiculous horror show of a lab room, but I'd kept the tools I'd come in here with. Sweet chomping chimps, let me get the chance to use them.

A clang reverberated down the hall, followed by a snarl I wanted to think sounded familiar. Before that could amount to anything, the last familiar face I'd have wanted to see wavered out of the shadows into the dim light.

Tempest's gleaming locks were writhing about her head in an agitated state. As she unfastened the door to my cage, her leonine face remained in a rigid mask of resolve. I braced myself—but I couldn't make my move here. I needed my fire to finish things off, and I had no guarantee anyone had disabled the sprinklers.

"What's going on?" I asked as she gripped the door. "Not having such a good day after all?"

She grinned at me fiercely, showing catlike fangs. "There's still been plenty good about it, and I don't intend to lose that now." She yanked open the door and flicked a pair of handcuffs around my wrists so quickly I didn't have time to dodge them.

My ankles were already chained again. I put up the best fight I could, attempted to knee her in the shoulder or elbow her in the face, but physical combat with all my limbs restrained and aching stiffly wasn't exactly a piece of cake.

Tempest hauled me out of the cage to tumble to the floor. As I squirmed around so I had some chance of defending myself, she loomed over me, her shadowkind form taking over.

Her face still looked almost the same, just even more feline with a broadening of her cheeks. Her body expanded into that of a massive lion. Tawny wings burst from her back with a hiss of their long feathers. She clamped her muscular forelegs around my chest and stomped on the floor just beside the lab table.

With a whirring sound, a panel in the tiles pulled back. Letting out a breathy chuckle, the sphinx dragged me into the darkness beneath.

I only caught a glimpse of the passage we dropped into: just a few feet wide and high with packed dirt walls, the length of it falling into total darkness ahead of us. Then the panel snapped shut again, blotting out all light. The earth smell that filled my nose wasn't remotely pleasant: pungent clay with a rotting note that turned my stomach.

Tempest managed to bound through the darkness while still holding me pressed to her thickly furred chest with one foreleg. When I tried to thrash free, her claws dug into my side deeply enough for the jolt of pain to shatter my breath.

"I'm not sure what use you think I'm going to be when you're abandoning everything else you've been working on," I said, fighting to keep an agonized rasp from my voice.

"If you'd rather I tore out your throat and was done with you, that can be arranged."

"Somehow I don't think you'd be getting this cuddly if you were willing to throw me away that easily."

"Perhaps, but I'm willing to be convinced." Her eyes flashed in the darkness. A more cloying rotten-meat scent spilled with her breath over my face. "You must know by now that I don't put all my stock in any one person—or place. I might be a sphinx, but I can play hydra too. No matter how many facilities the fools destroy, there'll be more popping up in their place. I'm *everywhere*."

The vehemence in her voice turned my blood to ice. She really believed there was no way she and the horrors she'd set in motion could be stopped. Had she already unleashed her sickness on the world, and all she was doing now was protecting the source of her cure in case she needed more?

If she'd already hurt my lovers—

I clamped down on the flare of heat that thought provoked before it could sizzle from my skin. This wasn't the place to play my last gambit either—I had no idea what protections she might have built into this tunnel. But as soon as I got my opening, she was going to regret every bit of the pain she'd inflicted and urged others to inflict, no matter how eagerly those mortals had leapt to the task.

Heat seared across my tongue. I swallowed hard, gritting my teeth, and aimed it along my gum. I'd *better* be ready.

All at once, Tempest heaved upward. A large circle of metal swung up and over to bang against asphalt. Still clutching me tightly, the sphinx clambered out into the cool night air that drifted through a vacant parking lot. A ratty shopping bag coasted by us.

It wasn't the most glamorous escape route. I guessed I was cramping poor Tempest's style.

Not for long, it seemed. With a sweep of her wings, we lifted off the ground. Yells and a metallic crunching sound careened from somewhere down the street. I'd better figure out exactly what mess we were leaving behind before I took my shot at destroying the woman who'd set it all in motion.

Twisting my head, I made out a big brick building with lights flashing in some of the windows. Immense, monstrous silhouettes charged in and out of view. One wall was crumpled in across most of the left side. A few human figures scrambled through the rubble. As I watched, a shadowkind of some sort sprang at one and slashed through his neck. Several more creatures tore from the darkness in pursuit of the others.

I hadn't seen any being I recognized yet. Maybe this really didn't have anything to do with my crew. Where in Pete's name would Omen and the others have found themselves this many new allies so fast—if the hellhound shifter would even have considered sticking out his neck to ask without me badgering him about it?

Tempest wrapped her other foreleg around me again now that her wings were doing most of the work. As she soared higher into the air, the pressure squeezed my ribs against my lungs. My voice came out more strained than I liked. "Pissed off a whole lot of beings this time, did you?"

"They don't even know what they're intruding on," Tempest muttered. "Nitwits, the whole horde of them. Bashing their way in, yammering about some ruby they were looking for. If I'd had the time, I'd have directed them to a fucking jewelry store and introduced a diamond cutter to their vital organs."

I just barely bit back a startled laugh. Ruby—that horde of shadowkind was looking for me.

And who knew of me as Ruby other than my closest companions... and the minions of the Highest, who wanted me dead to the point that they'd spent twenty-five years scouring the mortal realm for me?

Omen had stuck his neck out, all right. I never would have expected him to go this far. Technically, he'd stuck *my* neck out too, but it wasn't as if my life hadn't been under plenty of threat as it was. He'd used the Highest's forces as his own tool to crash Tempest's party.

I *had* kept telling him that getting his fellow shadowkind in on the cause was our best bet of coming out on top. Nice that he'd finally embraced my approach whole-heartedly.

Of course, all his efforts would amount to jack shit if I

let this psychotic sphinx carry me off to conduct her nefarious schemes elsewhere.

Tempest must have sensed the readying of my muscles. She glared down at me. "Throw one whiff of flame at me and we'll find out whether you can survive a trip into the shadows, phoenix."

What would happen if I didn't? Would I die as she wrenched me into the darkness, or would she find herself losing her grip on me?

We were swaying with the beating of her wings at least thirty feet above the ground now. The odds of surviving a fall weren't in my favor. But at this point, all that mattered to me was that my captor *didn't* survive.

Even with all the rage scorching my insides, I might not be able to completely destroy her on my own. If Omen could use the Highest's minions, there was nothing stopping me from borrowing his strategy in turn.

"You think you know everything, but you have no idea," I told Tempest, and sang another mangled lyric at her. "Not very smart, and you're insane, you can shove your mad game."

"Big talk from a little birdie in the clutches of a cat."

"We'll see how long that lasts." I tipped back my head and bellowed at the top of my lungs, propelling a jet of fiery power alongside the words. "Hey, you beastly bastards! The Ruby you want is right here!"

My voice rang through the air, and the spurt of flames blazed across the night sky to mark our spot like a signal flare. As I blinked the after-glare away, a mass of shadowy figures surged from the ruined brick building toward us.

Tempest spat out several words that sounded deeply profane in a language I didn't know and dug her claws into my sides again. A warble of her frigid energy penetrated my skin as she made good on her promise to try to yank me into the shadows with her.

Even if I survived the trip, in the shadows I couldn't hurt her. I had to keep her here. I had to pin her to the fabric of this physical world. And luckily I'd shaped myself just the means to do that.

"Hey, Tempest, there's something else you should know," I shouted, and dug my tongue along my gums, where trickles of my supernatural fire had masked any noxious vibes the tiny instrument might have given off.

She swung her head down, her eyes glittering viciously. "What?"

"Your lackey in Crete had a very nice ring."

A ring I'd melted into a tiny silver-and-iron spear. I flicked the miniature weapon between my lips, clamped my teeth on it to hold it steady, and slammed my mouth into the sphinx's forehead with all the force I could muster.

As my jaw jarred against the bridge of her nose, the dull end of the needle scraped my tongue, but the sharpened point drove home.

A screech tore from Tempest's throat. She flailed her head from side to side as if trying to shake the sliver of toxic metals free, but it held in place, smack in the middle of her treasured third eye. Blood welled around the puncture point.

My makeshift weapon prevented her from shedding

her physical form, but it didn't make that form any less deadly. With an ear-splitting howl, she raked her claws down my side and raised a paw as if she meant to slash my face right off.

A glimmer of hellish orange was streaking toward us through the darkness below. I sent up a silent prayer to the universe that the owner of that glimmer would reach us in time and yanked back the barriers that'd been tamping down my inner fire.

The flames erupted from my body like I'd been drenched in gasoline and torched. They flooded every inch of me, stinging and scalding—and they roared across Tempest too. Ignoring the pain as well as I could, I focused every bit of energy I had on hurling more and more heat across and into her leonine body.

The claws on her extended paw drooped and melted with the intensity of the heat as her foreleg fell. The shriek that rattled from the sphinx's throat then was nothing but agony, no room left for rage. Her other foreleg moved as if to wrench away from me, but I flung my arms around her charred, furry body and squeezed as tight as I could.

The sickly smell of burnt flesh—not all of it hers— filled my nose. Her wings flapped weakly, trailing flames taller than she was, and then we plummeted.

As we dropped, the fire streamed over us like the tail of a meteor. Then the heat glazed my vision so thickly I couldn't see anything but the flickering light. I choked back a sob at the throbbing digging down to my bones and propelled even more of the raging inferno at my captor.

This was for egging on the mortals' hate. *This* was for Luna's death. *This* was for the torments Tempest had encouraged her lackeys to inflict on so many shadowkind, including my devourer and my hellhound. *This* was for the new horrors she'd meant to enact on them and so many mortals too.

Let her burn. Let her burn until there was nothing left of that sadistically cavalier fiend than the barest scraps of ashes—and let them blow down into the foulest sewer in existence for good measure.

Her body started to disintegrate in my hands. Cinders sloughed off into the sizzling wind. She tumbled from my arms just as I collided with someone else's.

I smacked into a broad chest, a familiar smoky scent with a hint of sulfur washing through the blaze. Arms glowing with a magma-bright light embraced me and eased me the rest of the way to the ground, but their fiery heat didn't scorch me further. Instead, they absorbed the flames that had been ravaging my body.

The pain snuffed out along with the fire. As I looked up into my protector's face, only a dull prickling sensation continued to ripple over my skin.

Omen smiled at me, the charcoal gray and glowing orange fading from his skin. "You defeated her. That was spectacular. And here I thought I'd get to come charging to your rescue for once."

I beamed back at him, feeling slightly delirious. The sharpest flames might have dwindled, but the fire inside me was raging on, its heat crackling through me. "Don't sell yourself short. Your brigade gave me the opening I needed."

I turned on shaky legs to stare at the blackened corpse that had fallen beside me. Tempest's wings had smashed into crisp chunks when she'd hit the ground; one of her hips had fractured, blackened all the way through. The silver needle had melted into a gleaming blob in the blackened mass that had once been her head.

She'd defied death before. I wasn't taking any chances, thank you very much. I nudged the sphinx's side with the toe of my sneakers—and her entire charred rib cage crumpled in.

Triumph flared inside me next to my still-smoldering anger. I aimed a kick at her head and watched it burst into burnt dust.

Omen stepped up behind me and took one of my hands, raising it over my head. When I lifted my gaze, my pulse stuttered. A swarm of shadowkind had surrounded us—the horde Tempest had ranted about. The Highest's minions.

Omen pitched his voice to carry. "The phoenix Ruby has destroyed our true enemy! You saw what the sphinx was preparing in that building. You witnessed how the mortals she conspired with attacked every shadowkind they met. This being has ended all of that. Ruby is our *hero!*"

Holy glittering guacamole, was that gambit actually going to work?

Plenty of the gazes that had fixed on me shone with hostility. But they hesitated, many of them turning to look at the largest beings among them, who started murmuring amongst themselves in harsh voices.

Omen tugged me back toward him. He twined his fingers with mine, his other hand rising to my cheek. The pale blue eyes that met mine were anything but cold.

"So, you took my advice for once," I couldn't stop myself from saying.

The corner of his mouth crooked upward. His thumb traced the line of my cheekbone. "There's a first time for everything. You're not *always* wrong."

I made a face at him. "If they're not convinced, they'll kill you."

"It'll be worth it."

He said it without a hint of hesitation, and a strange flutter passed through my chest. Naturally, rather than figure out what to make of that, I kept shooting off my mouth. "Oh, yeah? Because I seem to remember plenty of times not at all long ago when you were doing your darndest to get me *out* of your—"

"Shut up just this once in your life, Disaster," Omen murmured, tipping his head closer, and I didn't think anyone had ever said those words more sweetly. "They'll have to rip me to shreds before they get one piece of you. I'd put my entire existence on the line for you all over again in a heartbeat. I told you that you've made an impression—in more ways than one." He did hesitate then, his fingers going still against my skin. "I love you."

I'd never anticipated hearing those three words fall from the hellhound shifter's mouth. A giddy warmth spread from around my heart, swallowing up the fiery rage as it came. Still, one last question tumbled out. "Even though I'm partly human?"

Omen chuckled. "*Because* you're partly human, it seems. Don't let it go to your head."

"I know better than that." My fingers curled into his shirt just below his collar. "I love you too."

He answered me with a kiss, so fierce and demanding it made my knees wobble. What our spectators made of that, I had no idea, but I couldn't say I cared. This indomitable, passionate man was *mine*, the missing piece in the quartet I hadn't known I needed, and I'd never felt more at home than in his arms in that dismal parking lot.

When he drew back, I grinned up at him for a moment longer. Then I glanced toward the crowd to search for the rest of my shadowkind lovers. It wasn't a matter of *whether* they'd be here but only where. My gaze skimmed over the mass of figures—

And with a whine that rang through my ears, a gleaming bolt of metal pierced the darkness and rammed into Omen's back.

27

Sorsha

The metal projectile stabbed right through Omen's heart, the pointed tip tearing through his shirt as it burst from the middle of his chest. A plume of smoke so thick it hid his face gushed up from the wound. His body sagged into me.

A cry wrenched from my throat. "Omen? *Omen!*"

My frantic appeal did nothing to stop his legs from crumpling. I clutched at him, but my attempts to steady him only sent the rest of him falling to sprawl on the dirty asphalt. The smack of his back hitting the ground drove the stake through farther.

A fucking *stake*, made of silver and iron, like some kind of three-in-one multipurpose monster-murdering device for mortals who couldn't tell the difference between vamps, werewolves, and fae.

I dropped to my knees beside my lover, searching his

slack features, but the concentration of those metals ripping through his most vital physical organ was enough to murder even a hellhound.

Omen's head lolled to the side, his eyelids twitching. The faintest wheeze whistled from his lungs—and then every part of him went limp, oblivious to my shouts and my shaking of his shoulders.

More smoke billowed up in a congealing cloud. The color had already drained from his lifeless face. He looked more like a wax figure than a man—a man who'd once contained so much snark and power—a man *I'd* have put my own existence on the line for if there'd been the slightest chance—

Fury surged through me, scorching hot. It blotted out every thought except one question burning through my mind: Who did this?

My head jerked up. Fire blazed from my body in every direction, but most of it downward. The rush of searing flames propelling me up into the air—up over the swarm of shadowkind gathered around us, up into the night sky, glaring in the direction from which the stake had flown.

A woman was crouched on the rooftop of the low building that stood between the parking lot and the taller brick structure that had been Tempest's hideout. She was decked out in the standard Company armor, shoving another gleaming bolt into a crossbow.

My hands clenched at my sides, my fingers branding my palms with their scorching heat. *Die.*

Before she could end another shadowkind life, a

surge of flame shot up from beneath the woman's feet. In seconds, it had swallowed her completely, even her shriek of pain. Her body crumpled much like Omen's had, the fire still eating away at it, but watching her form shrivel and blacken didn't tame the rage coursing through me one bit.

A thumping of footsteps reached my ears through the roar of the flames that held me. A mass of Company lackeys were running toward the crowd of shadowkind. One of them was fumbling with a plastic box, yanking it open and drawing out one of several laboratory vials—

Tempest's disease. Of course her death wouldn't stop the asshole mortals who had no idea that her creation would end them as quickly as the shadowkind it infected. Of course their first thought while their colleagues lay dying and their building in shambles was to unleash that horror on the world.

Not today, motherfuckers.

Burn. Burn them all to the fucking ground.

More fury flared through me, and flames erupted all through the swarm of would-be exterminators. I squeezed my fists tighter. The glass of the vials melted, fusing together and snuffing out the deadly microbes that floated within.

That wasn't enough either. Who knew how much more of the Company's vile invention was still stockpiled in that building—or in other facilities across the world? How many sites and people held the information to recreate it?

They all had to go. Every last one of the pricks who'd

dreamed of ridding the world of shadowkind, who'd tortured and slaughtered for their own satisfaction, and the empire they'd built could damn well die with them.

My flames raced along the sidewalk to the smashed-open building. The roar beneath me propelled me higher still. More fire burst from my back with a stinging sensation that was offset by the rush of satisfaction as crackling flames swept through the air on either side of me to form wings.

They'd messed with a fucking phoenix, and every last one of them was going to burn.

I poured my rage toward the brick structure, and an inferno as sizzling as the bonfire inside me engulfed it. The taint of all those vicious intentions crawled over my skin. Without questioning it, I simply knew that I could follow that trail.

My awareness expanded through the darkened sprawl of the world below. An apartment here. A warehouse there. A blast of flames, and they were nothing but charcoal.

My rage spilled out along lines of communication and connection that shone clearer to my heightened senses with every passing second. It burned through the fraying threads of self-control I'd been holding onto so tightly, but what the hell did I care?

None of these pricks had cared one bit about who *they* were hurting.

My hellhound shifter, lying dead on the ground below me. Luna, shattering herself apart to avoid their capture. All the scalpel incisions and needle injections, all the slashing knives and suffocating nets, all the crashed cars and battered bodies.

But that was what humans did. One monster did them wrong, scared them, or screwed them over, and they thought that gave them the right to commit genocide on every being remotely like it.

A laboratory in Berlin. A processing office in Madrid. My attention sizzled across the ocean all the way to the shores I'd left behind, the hot spots lighting up like the pins on the map we'd seen in the shoe museum in Chicago.

The fire was gushing out of me in waves now, and I could see it all in my mind's eye: Good-bye, a few dozen Company employee houses in San Francisco. Sayonara, an entire condo building in Queens.

My reach was infinite, my fire inexhaustible, and every one of them was going to pay.

Burn. Burn. Burn it all down, until there's nothing left but ashes.

Glaring light dotted my vision. The stench of bubbling tar and frying varnish filled my lungs. Whatever grip I'd had on myself had gone up in smoke. There was nothing in me or around me but my fiery fury, like it was always meant to be.

My skin crackled and blackened; my stomach steamed. That was fine. If I had to burn myself up to take every douchebag who deserved it down with me, so be it.

More and more buildings succumbed to my flames. More and more bodies crumbled into cinders. My soul screamed in vengeful triumph. More, more, *burn it all...*

The trails I'd traced petered out. Every person who'd contributed to the Company's horrors, every place where they'd conducted their cruel business, every device that had contained their secrets had been swallowed up in the fire of my fury—but it still wasn't enough.

An ache consumed me from throat to gut, rage churning through it, roaring to be set free.

Why should the Company be the only ones to take the blame? How about all the other mortals out there who would have attacked the shadowkind if they'd known about them—which was pretty much all humans, wasn't it?

What about the shadowkind themselves who'd only hurled themselves into the fray not to protect their fellow beings but to destroy *me*? Who'd slaughtered my parents—ripped my father's head off and thrown it out a fucking window—for the sole crime of creating me?

Hell, what about the damned Highest who'd send their minions on that wretched quest? Did they think they were so invulnerable, lurking in the depths of the shadow realm?

Ha. With the prickling of the fire through and around me, I could taste how easily I could reach through the rifts and rain my searing fury across the darkness until it barbequed their ancient souls.

They thought I was a force to be extinguished? I'd show them who'd get eviscerated.

The flames were already leaping higher—from the smashed brick building to those neighboring it, across the parking lot below me to smack into one brutal being and another. I sucked in a scalding breath.

I really could do it. I could burn both the realms down and myself with them, and when I emerged from the ashes, maybe it would all be reborn into something better. Seriously, how hard could it be to do better than the shitshow we had now?

I gathered the fire swelling ever wider inside me, ready to spew it as far as I could cast it—and a voice penetrated the warbled blare in my ears. A bright, sweet voice ragged with an emotion that made my chest clench up.

"Sorsha! Sorsha, please, can you hear me?"

Then another voice: a chocolatey baritone that'd turned strained. "You're not in this alone, Miss Blaze."

And another: a deep ragged rumble. "We'll fight whatever battles need fighting, m'lady. Just tell us what you need."

The flames around me faltered slightly. I sank a few feet with a lurch of my stomach, and made out three figures hovering in the air in front of me, their forms lit by wavering orange light.

The light of my fire. Of my vast, violent blaze.

Thorn's massive wings swept through the air, holding himself and the two men he was supporting aloft. Ruse had his arm stretched out to me, a desperation in his roguish face I'd never seen before. Snap's eyes flashed brilliant green, wide and frantic.

"My peach," the devourer said when I met his gaze.

"Don't go. I promised you I wouldn't leave, no matter how upset I got—don't you leave me."

I wasn't leaving. I was here, and I would still be here when the fire ravaged me to the bones and spewed me back into being. It was everything else, everyone else— couldn't they see how rotten our worlds had become?

Omen's voice echoed up from my memories. *Remember everyone who's for you.*

Those words choked me up and provoked a fresh wave of anger at the same time. As the flames around me leapt and dipped again, another winged figure soared into sight.

It was Flint, but he wasn't alone. He was holding... Vivi. My best friend, clinging tight to the warrior's bulging arms, her face turned ashy and soot staining her typical white outfit. My pulse hitched.

She gave me a bright smile that was all too familiar. "Sorsha, you don't need to do any more. You knocked those assholes flat. If there are any left, we'll take them out, however many we need to, like shooting rats in a barrel of dynamite. But first let's cool off and figure out where we stand. Please come down?"

Down. Down. Down to the place where my most recent lover's corpse lay slumped; down to where the Highest's horde stood waiting to lay judgment on me. My teeth gritted. Flames lashed around me.

But I couldn't drag my eyes from the figures in front of me. As I stared at them, more images rose in my mind.

It was also the world where my devourer delighted in everything from extravagant hotels to a simple banana;

where we'd discovered his capacity for desire together. The world where my incubus had offered every pleasure he could imagine to leave me satisfied, not just bodily but in mind and heart as well. The world where I'd fought side by side with my wingéd warrior while he let his strength buoy mine rather than supress it.

The world where my bestie and I had passed cartons of Thai food back and forth on her couch in front of our favorite cheesy movies, where we'd laughed and danced together and made plans for grand adventures we hadn't yet seen through.

Could I burn down the realms and spare the few who held a piece of my heart? Could we even hold onto any of the happiness that had brought us together in the wreckage my raging fire would leave behind?

All those people out there, all the beings drifting through the rifts—so many of them had laughed and delighted, fought and loved too. There were so many other parents, other guardians, other lovers and other friends who'd be mourned.

Maybe some of them were monsters. Maybe we were all monsters. But that didn't mean there was nothing good in us.

Scalding tears pricked at my eyes. I didn't want this. I didn't want to spread nothing but pain through the realms. Who would I have to be furious with then except myself?

I could make Omen right about one last thing. I wasn't like Tempest, not at all.

As the rush of heat beneath me dwindled, my fiery

wings did as well. I glided to the ground, my body seeming to contract in on itself.

My clothes hung in singed scraps, my skin equally charred. When I shuddered in the sudden cool of the night air, the blackened bits fluttered off me like moulting feathers, revealing unmarred flesh beneath.

Even in the dim light from distant streetlamps, I could see that I'd scorched the parking lot around me to an even darker shade than the pavement had been before. Tempest's ashes had dispersed in the inferno. As my companions drifted down to join me, my gaze came to rest on Omen's slumped form, which had somehow held its shape.

His body lay on a streak of silver and iron. The heat of my flames had melted the crossbow bolt so thoroughly that the liquid metals had rippled across the lot to pool in a nearby pothole. His clothes, burnt into a solid mass, hid the wound on his chest, but I knew exactly where the fatal stake had struck him. I knew—

His chest moved.

It rose and fell with a shallow breath, and my heart just about leapt up my throat to do a dance number on the asphalt.

"Omen?" I threw myself to his side. His body shuddered, and the carbonized layer coating his form cracked and began flaking off like mine had.

My fire hadn't burned him. Of course not. It never had before—he was a being that thrived on fire. The flames I'd poured down had melted the toxic metals from his body and absorbed right into the gap of his wound. Had—had they—

My hand shot to that spot in the middle of his chest. The remains of his shirt disintegrated, and my palm rested against a solid plane of hellhound-shifter flesh, only a white blotch of a scar showing where he'd taken the wound.

Naturally, that was when he opened his eyes.

For a second, Omen blinked at me as if he needed to clear his vision. A faint furrow creased his forehead. Then a thin smile crossed his lips. "Can't resist the opportunity to cop a feel even in the middle of an apocalypse, huh, Disaster?"

"You fucking bastard!" I said, which wasn't really fair, since I doubted he'd *wanted* to get himself killed. But he probably figured out I didn't really mean the insult from the enthusiasm with which I threw my arms around him right afterward.

Omen let out a hoarse chuckle, lifting one arm to return the embrace. Another hand squeezed my shoulder. A third rested on my back, and a fourth brushed over my hair. My other three lovers knelt around us, welcoming me and their commander back.

"Are you all right?" Snap asked, a question that might have been for either of us or most likely both.

For my reply, I lifted my head from Omen's shoulder to pull my devourer into a kiss. Then Thorn's broad arms were tugging me to my feet as the hellhound shifter heaved onto his. Vivi leapt to my side, looping her arm around mine, and I hugged her just as hard as I had my lovers.

"You came a long way to watch me burn down the world," I said.

A startled laugh spilled out of her. "It was an epic performance, but I don't think I want any repeat showings."

"Good, because neither do I." The fire inside me felt subdued in a brand-new way, like the vast calm of the ocean after a monster of a storm.

I *had* been going to end the world... but I hadn't. And now that I'd walked up to the brink and taken a good hard look at it before stepping back, I couldn't imagine ever allowing myself to be pushed even close to over it. That vast calm was *mine* now. I was a phoenix reborn as something better, even if it hadn't worked quite the way anyone had predicted.

"I'm just glad you're okay," Vivi said.

I hugged her even tighter. "Me too. Thank you for helping talk me down."

"Any time, bestie. All you've got to do is say the word."

It seemed that was true. I'd been awfully worried about how she'd react if she found out what I was, but she'd seen the worst of me tonight, and she was still here. Maybe it was time to stop worrying.

About Vivi, anyway. Omen's gaze slid past us to the crowd of shadowkind, slightly thinned by my recent torching but still a whole lot larger than our little cluster.

Larger and taking some tentatively threatening steps toward us now that the torching was over.

"I'm getting better by the moment," the hellhound shifter said to Snap, "but I'm not sure how long this lot will allow that to last, though. I don't suppose our equines and imp came through with their part in the plan?"

"We haven't seen—" Ruse started.

"Ruby!" one of the larger minions bellowed, raising an axe, and just then a clatter of racing hoofbeats echoed down the road.

Gisele and Bow led the charge, Gisele gone full unicorn and Bow showing off his centaur form. Antic perched on Gisele's gleaming back, brandishing her tiny fist in the air.

And with them came dozens more shadowkind, rippling out of the shadows into the physical world and careening toward us in a wave.

They rushed through the crowd of minions, most of them small enough to skirt between the beefy legs, the equines jostling to make room as need be. Before the Highest's lackeys could raise much protest, one familiar figure in the oncoming swarm stepped in front of me and swiveled to take in our audience.

It was the equines' friend Cori. "This woman rescued me from the clutches of mortals who'd tormented me," he shouted over the growing clamor. "She risked her life to break open our cages and usher us all to freedom."

"She broke me out of a laboratory where I was being held," another being piped up. "I would have died if the mortals had their way."

More voices rose, one after the other.

"She fought through silver and iron to break us out and let us return home."

"She burned the place where the mortals caged us so they couldn't torture any more beings."

"I thought I'd never reach the shadows again until she came for us."

The lesser beings in the crowd of new arrivals chittered and barked in their own versions of language with what sounded like a cacophony of agreement.

A lump filled my throat. It didn't seem possible that the equines could have rounded up every being I'd ever saved, and yet there were also dozens more here than I'd realized I'd rescued. All the collectors whose homes I'd slunk into, all the Company facilities we'd razed to the ground...

I guessed it had added up.

As the barrage of testimonials faded, Thorn cleared his throat. "And she took down the shadowkind responsible for encouraging the worst group of mortals in their horrific dealings—the sphinx called Tempest, which the Highest failed to subdue centuries ago."

Omen took my hand and held it up as he had when he'd first reached me. "The phoenix has burned, and it is Sorsha, not Ruby, that remains. You can tell the Highest how badly they screwed up... or you can tell them, truthfully, that Omen the hellhound dealt with Ruby and no further threat from her remains."

Another round of muttering commenced, but at least no one was waving an axe in my direction for the moment. Some of the minions pointed toward the ruined building, others toward the sky where I'd dealt out my flaming vengeance. Antic darted among them, tossing out interjections here and there as she saw fit. As we waited for the verdict, my fingers clamped tight around Omen's.

Finally, a figure that must have been some sort of giant stepped to the fore of the crowd and raised his hand for silence. His voice carried through the lot.

"It is settled. We have witnessed that this being, whatever she is, destroyed those that threatened us. We witness that her fire has abated as the hellhound stands beside her. We will report to the Highest that he has fulfilled his duty and the danger is past."

Then, as elation welled up behind my ribs, he caught my gaze and dipped his head in a slight but unmistakable bow.

The horde vanished into the shadows in a wavering surge. I stared, half afraid to move in case my legs failed to hold me.

"It's over?" I said to Omen. "No more bounty on my head?" I lowered my voice. "No more deal hanging over yours?"

The hellhound shifter laughed. "It would appear that way. Let's wait and see if the Highest send their minions charging back after all. But I think you may just have pulled off the greatest heist of your career, thief." He offered a quiet smile that was just for me. "You stole back both our freedoms from the most powerful beings in existence."

Ruse clapped his hands, a smirk curling his lips. "And

I'd say this calls for a celebration. Come on, Miss Blaze. Wait until you see what we've done with the Everymobile now!"

"Sweet scintillating seahorses, do I even want to ask?" I shook my head with a disbelieving chuckle, pulled my best friend and my lovers close, and set off to see what the road ahead would hold.

28

Sorsha

Not quite one year later

I t was never a bad idea to blow off some steam before a heist. You wanted to go into the operation with a clear head and absolute focus. And, lucky me, I now had four sexy shadowkind to contribute to the blowing and the steaming—generally by indulging in all the fun and thrilling ways our bodies could come together.

I'd never get tired of the way Omen's breath broke when I slicked my tongue around his cock, I guarantee. The hellhound shifter's brimstone scent laced his nether regions with a sharper smoky tang that was nearly as delicious as hearing him come apart under my attentions.

More delicious still? The tingling pulses of pleasure

that shot through me with each stroke of *Thorn's* tongue over my clit, alongside Snap driving into me from behind, hitting the perfect spot of bliss every time.

Thorn lapped harder, and I gasped over Omen's erection, a quiver running through my body. The hellhound shifter growled at the loss of contact, his fingers tightening in my hair. I smiled and pressed my lips around his length again, and he thanked me with a groan and the teasing of his tail across one already stiffened nipple.

Snap dipped his head to flick his forked tongue against my spine. Thorn squeezed my ass with a scrape of his hardened knuckles that I'd discovered sparked their own bonus thrill, and at the devourer's next thrust, the final wave of ecstasy sent me soaring.

I sucked Omen down, determined to bring him with me. A groan reverberated out of him as he gushed smoky heat into my mouth. I swallowed gleefully and clutched on to him as Snap sped up. The devourer finished with a swift plunge that sent me cartwheeling over the edge all over again.

As we sagged together into a sated tangle of bodies, I glanced up at Ruse, who'd chosen to stick to watching this time. He met my questioning gaze with a smirk and a heated glint in his eyes.

"That was quite the show," he said.

I grinned back at him. "As long as you don't feel left out."

"It isn't as if I haven't gotten plenty of mine before. And I'm calling dibs on the bed tonight."

"*My* peach," Snap murmured in protest, slinging his slim arm around one of my legs.

If he could have, the devourer would have cuddled up with me every night, but as impressive as the Everymobile was, this bed was barely big enough for two bodies to sleep next to each other. When one of those bodies was Thorn's, it was barely big enough for one. My lovers had come up with some sort of schedule of fairness in which they switched off who got snuggle benefits, other than the occasional night when I wanted my space and kicked out the whole bunch of them.

Omen chuckled, his tail still tracing lazy lines over my ribs. "The next time we have an opportunity to barter for some magical renovations, we should see about having this room—and its furniture—expanded."

I wouldn't have thought *he* would ever be one to complain about missed opportunities to cozy up to me, but the hellhound shifter had proven unexpectedly cuddle-happy—possibly even to his own surprise. The nights he spent with me, he always started out on the far side of the bed, only a hand resting against my shoulder or curled around my wrist. Then I'd wake up to find myself tucked against him from head to toe, wrapped in his limbs and our matching fiery heat.

The first time it'd happened was the only time I'd swear I saw him actually blush, but the sheet-scorching sex we'd had afterward seemed to have reassured him that what his body got up to when he let it sleep wasn't so bad.

"Sounds good to me," I said, and squirmed around to

get up. Thorn grasped my elbow to help, and I leaned over to give him a quick kiss.

"Are you sure you want to charge ahead with this mission tonight?" Ruse asked. "It *is* your birthday. The creatures can survive in their cages another day."

I wagged a finger at him. "How selfish would I be to leave them to another day of torment at this collector's hands when I can celebrate just as easily tomorrow? We're here now. You can carry out whatever grand plans you've been putting together once we've taught this asshole a lesson."

"Well spoken, m'lady," Thorn said with one of his rare smiles that it still made me giddy to see on his stern face.

"Thank you." I grabbed a robe to maintain a little modesty around our RV-mates. "That doesn't mean I'm going to skip my shower. I'll be a clean cat burglar."

"A little dip into the shadows would accomplish the same thing," Omen reminded me with a teasing note in his voice.

Technically he was right. With some trial and error, we'd determined that I could meld with darkness like a full shadowkind, although I still didn't enjoy the clammy sensation that came with it, and I hadn't quite gotten the hang of jumping from one patch to another yet. Still, my answer was the same as always. "Some things are better enjoyed in a physical body—as I'm sure you know." I let my gaze trail down his naked form in all its muscular glory.

"And thank all things dark for that," Ruse said.

As I reached for the door, Snap made a soft noise in his throat. "We should still—on her real birthday—"

When I glanced back, he was shooting a meaningful glance around at the other men. Thorn had set his face into an expression that seemed designed to indicate he had no idea what the devourer was talking about, but so obviously it had the opposite effect. Ruse's smirk widened.

Omen rolled his eyes and prodded Snap in the ribs with his heel. "Let her take her shower first. There'll be time."

Time for some kind of shadowkind surprise? Intriguing. I'd better make this shower a fast one.

Of course, that was easier said than done in our current accommodations. The sylph who'd conducted our initial renovations in gratitude for getting her out of the Company's clutches had possessed an aptitude for airiness but not for plumbing, and the beings who'd attempted to pitch in since then had only partly solved the Everymobile's quirks. Any time I turned on the shower, I had a fifty-percent chance of first getting pelted with hot cocoa, sesame oil, or a rainbow of tiny gumdrops. And every now and then, even after I got the water to start, it turned into a dust shower partway through.

Today I received a gulp of coffee *and* a mouthful of gumdrops—both caught in the mug I kept on hand for such occasions, because why not make the best of it?—before the showerhead resigned itself to a spray of standard water.

I washed quickly, keeping an ear out for the faint

hissing sound that usually warned of impending dust, and then pulled on my standard burglar gear. My tastes hadn't changed in that department: all black all over, though I wasn't bothering with my hat yet. And I didn't need a scorch-knife anymore now that I could melt metal by force of will alone.

As I stepped into the hall, giving my hair one last rub of the towel, Vivi emerged from the RV's new upstairs, which was the main result of the sylph's help. The Everymobile didn't look any taller from the outside, but inside, a narrow spiral staircase beside the bathroom now led to a loft bedroom.

Vivi's eyebrows leapt up, an eager gleam coming into her eyes. "Is it time to get started already?"

I poked her in the arm playfully. "It's only just getting dark. We go by cover of night, remember?"

She bobbed on her feet in a gesture so like Antic I reminded myself I shouldn't be surprised she and the imp got along well. "Right, right. I still get so pumped up even though I'm not the one going out there!"

The destruction of the Company of Light hadn't rid the world of independent hunters and collectors. When my quartet of shadowkind and I had decided to take the Everymobile on tour as a sort of traveling Shadowkind Defense Fund, I'd known I had to invite my bestie.

It was hard to put any stake in the doubts I'd once had about whether Vivi would accept my less-than-legal hobbies after the way she'd pitched in against the Company—and all the other things she'd accepted about me. So, we'd arranged an extra bedroom for her, and she was getting the adventure she'd always dreamed of, coordinating with our various contacts, monitoring security systems, and doing reconnaissance whenever we needed someone who could pull off "normal" better than the rest of us.

She was clearly having the time of her life. I was sure it didn't hurt that she and Cori had started getting awfully chummy during his regular visits mortal-side.

Antic herself dashed past us then, giggling as she sprinted after Pickle in a game of hall tag. The little dragon appeared to have prompted it by stealing one of the jelly bracelets the imp had stolen from a tween fashion stall in a mall several cities ago. Pickle waved it at me from his jaws with a puff of smoke and dove past us into one of the kitchen cupboards.

Vivi laughed. "Always an exciting time around here."

I nudged her with my elbow. "I'll let you know when it's about to get even more exciting."

I stepped back into my bedroom to find all four of my lovers crammed along the edge of the bed, back in their clothes, with an air of anticipation that made my skin twitch. Were they nervous or just eager about whatever they were up to—or maybe a little of both?

Snap jumped up, beaming bright, apparently the ringleader of this particular venture. "We have something for you," he announced, and held out his hand to take mine.

It'd never been easy for me to deny the devourer, and I had no interest in doing so now. I reached for him, but rather than twining his fingers through mine, he gently folded them all toward my palm except my index finger. In his other hand, he produced a glinting band that he slid down my finger to the root.

The ring was delicate, so light I could barely feel its weight, rose and white gold woven together in a vine-like pattern. "It's beautiful," I said, meaning it even if I didn't totally understand what had sparked this fervor for jewelry.

Ruse had gotten up too. He took my hand from Snap and eased a ring of his own down my middle finger, equally light but this one with a pattern that looked like merging waves. I stared down at the two rings side by side, a fizzy feeling collecting in my stomach.

Before I could say anything, Thorn loomed over me. His broad fingers clasped mine less deftly but with just as much affection as the other two. The band he fit onto my ring finger shone with the same contrasting metals in an intricate spiral.

As Omen stood, the fizzing sensation welled into my chest. The hellhound shifter lifted my hand and guided a final ring over my pinkie. The strands of rose and white gold merged together like flames.

Snap touched my shoulder, leaning in to nuzzle my hair. "You told me before that humans give each other rings to show their highest form of commitment. When they want to be with only that person and no one else, always."

"Not that we haven't made our devotion to you awfully clear, Miss Blaze," Ruse added. "But our devourer here felt a concrete token was in order, and the rest of us could see his point."

Thorn rested his hand on my back and ran his thumb up and down with a stroke of warmth. "Obviously we wouldn't require that you wear them, especially when they might interfere with your endeavours. I must say it's pleasing to see them all together like this on your lovely hand, though."

I raised my eyes to meet Omen's. Maybe there wasn't any literal magic in this gesture, but it was a symbolic binding, one I could feel in the fizzing sensation that had now spread through my whole body. It'd been less than a year since the hellhound shifter had sensed the official severing of his deal with the Highest—no acknowledgment from them, just a sudden falling away of their hold that had made him jump up with a joyfully relieved cry he hadn't been able to restrain.

Less than a year since he'd won the freedom he'd lost for centuries.

"And you're ready to commit too, are you?" I said.

All it would have taken was for him to shrug it off or make some disparaging remark, and he could have shattered any meaning the ring contained. Instead, he gazed right back at me, a hint of a smile playing with his lips. "I'm afraid you're stuck with me, Disaster. Be glad I went subtle—I could have pulled out the chains again."

Any tension to the giddiness inside me broke with that joke. I knuckled his chest, unable to contain a huge smile of my own. "Hey, chains have their place. Just as long as you don't mind that you ended up with the little finger."

Omen tapped Thorn and Snap on either side of him, both of them standing half a foot taller than the shifter's well-built frame. "I think I've amply proven that smaller isn't necessarily lesser."

"Hey!" Snap said.

The wingéd let out a rumbling chuckle, and a second later we were all laughing. I closed my hand, admiring my rings shimmering next to each other and reveling in the warmth from the larger circle formed by my lovers around me.

"Thank you. You picked them well. I don't think they'll get in the way under my gloves." I tugged my lovers one by one into a kiss. "That's to hold you over until I can return the gesture, which you'd better believe I will. Here's to some good thieving tonight!"

"Scouting complete!" Gisele hollered from where she must have just emerged in the RV's main room, her melodic voice carrying through the wall. "Who's ready to take this prick down?"

As the equines and Flint shared their observations and we discussed our final strategy, I gathered all my gear. Tonight's target was a prick supreme—not just a collector but a hunter as well, keeping the rarest of his catches while selling the others. I was looking forward to sending that mansion of his up in flames. And the trinkets I pilfered would let us enjoy all our other indulgences while paying those who deserved it.

When the street was fully dark beyond the windows,

we set off with a wave good-bye and a "Ditto!" to Vivi. I slunk through the night, melding with the shadows nearly as well as my companions did.

They might be invisible, but I felt their presence all around me, their goals and their love entwined with mine like the metals on the rings they'd chosen. Tomorrow, we'd celebrate the start of the next year in my life. Tonight, we were meting out justice for those who couldn't claim it on their own.

Just call me the Robin Hood of monster emancipation. And now that I had my band of merry men, our future together would be both legendary and endless.

ABOUT THE AUTHOR

Eva Chase lives in Canada with her family. She loves stories both swoony and supernatural, and strong women and the men who appreciate them. Along with the Flirting with Monsters series, she is the author of the Cursed Studies trilogy, the Royals of Villain Academy series, the Moriarty's Men series, the Looking Glass Curse trilogy, the Their Dark Valkyrie series, the Witch's Consorts series, the Dragon Shifter's Mates series, the Demons of Fame Romance series, the Legends Reborn trilogy, and the Alpha Project Psychic Romance series.

Connect with Eva online:
www.evachase.com
eva@evachase.com

Made in the USA
Middletown, DE
03 February 2022

60342471R00201